A VINTAGE YEAR

for

INSIDER TRADING

by

ELIZABETH R. MONNET

A Vintage Year for Insider Trading
Copyright © 2015 Elizabeth R. Monnet

This is a work of fiction. The names, characters, places, incidents and dialogue are drawn from the author's imagination or are used fictitiously. Any resemblance to actual events, locales, or persons, living or dead, is entirely coincidental. The opinions expressed by the characters are also entirely fictitious and should not be construed as the opinions of the author or as providing legal advice.

Cover Design: Britton Design

Interior Layout: T&H Graphics

Author Photograph: Bill Monnet

ISBN: 978-0-9967484-0-7

Library of Congress Control Number: 2015914536

Milford Cordwent Press,
Sausalito, CA

For my husband Bill Monnet

CAST OF CHARACTERS

Wine Country

Bob Goodwin
A wine country caterer who seeks more excitement in his life than just passing around the appetizers.

Samantha Pond
A realtor who sells wine country dreams for a big price.

Peter Smith
A tasting room salesman who loves to gossip about interior design.

Juan Rodriguez
A young gardener who prefers technology to trimming shrubs.

Charlie Bartino
A wine grower with a computer chip memory for faces and numbers.

James Chistlehurst
A renowned wine expert who regularly hosts the Silicon Valley elite in wine country.

Amanda Jones
A Sonoma winery owner with a big heart and an even larger list of celebrity ex-boyfriends.

Silicon Valley

Tim Newman
A CEO of a technology company in legal hot water…and that's only the beginning.

Lucy Newman
Tim's beautiful wife who endangers her husband's career with girlfriend chat.

Jason Lee
A young innovative CTO who cannot stay away from his smartphone.

Cecil Roberts
A biotech CEO whose latest product gets thumbs down from the FDA.

Janet Parks-Brown
A CFO who gets into trouble when she buys a second home.

Tom White
A COO of a software company who feels harassed by his company's legal department.

Tony Padilla
A CMO of a smart grid company who brags about his new electric sports car.

Marc Todd and Stan Becker
Two venture capitalists who intervene to save Silicon Valley's reputation.

The Lawyers

Josh Kaplan
A prosecutor who refuses to believe that anyone in Sonoma is capable
of insider trading without outside help.

George DeRosa
A happily married plaintiffs' lawyer who cannot say "no" to a former flame.

Ann Schiller
An unemployed former federal prosecutor who persuades George DeRosa
and others to defend her aunt's friends.

Jack Murphy
A young lawyer whose earlier victory in court torpedoed his love life.

Deke Little
A lawyer with a passion for Sherlock Holmes detective stories.

Kimberly Hayward
A lawyer who joins forces with her usual courtroom adversaries.

Phil Taylor
A law partner at Horace & Fitzpatrick who comes to suspect a close friend.

The Animals

Sidney
A bossy Australian Shepherd who thinks he's smarter than the humans,
especially the lawyers.

President of the Sonoma Wildlife Council
A mountain lion who presides patiently over the other querulous Sonoma
Wildlife Council representatives, which include a crow, squirrel, deer, duck,
coyote and turkey buzzard.

Archibald, Loretta, Basil and Sebastian
San Francisco courthouse pigeons who watch and report on the latest trial
developments at the federal courthouse.

CHAPTER 1

Breakfast in Wine Country, 2010

"Man…I'm glad I don't work on Wall Street any more," thought the silver-haired man in his late 40s looking around the stark wooden interior of the VineSprings Grille in Carneros. *"Poor bastards,"* he thought. *"These winemakers and growers remind me of how hard I used to work."*

The Great Recession had cast an evil spell over Napa and Sonoma. Excess wine inventory from prior years lingered in the cellars. Grapes remained unsold, leaving vineyard owners with the heart-breaking choice of allowing their grapes to rot in the vineyards or risk their precious grapes being sold for little more than fruit juice prices. Unusual freezing temperatures in April, followed by a cool foggy summer had delayed the harvest season known locally as "crush." Everyone felt besieged.

In September, a sudden heat wave caused the chardonnay grapes destined for the region's sparkling wines to ripen quickly, heralding a fast and furious harvest. Under the intense heat, chardonnay, pinot, merlot, cabernet sauvignon and zinfandel grapes rapidly reached their optimal Brix sugar level. Following strict instructions from the winemakers, growers raced nights to harvest and deliver grapes to the wineries before the sun fried their precious harvest. After the grapes arrived and before the fierce midday heat struck, the wineries scrambled to de-stem and crush the grapes into the liquid gold that had made the area world famous.

To everyone's relief, within days after the grapes had been picked, word trickled out that the recent crop was "outstanding." Within a month, headlines proclaimed the harvest one of the best vintages in decades.

Now that the harvest season was over, the restaurant's regulars looked like they had finally been allowed a good night's rest.

Bob turned his attention to his regular breakfast buddies, who slowly assembled at his table.

Samantha Pond, an elegantly dressed, petite realtor with black hair swept up in a French twist, winked and smiled at Bob as she put down her black coffee, toasted bagels and fresh fruit. In contrast to everyone else in the restaurant, she wore chic office clothes and high stiletto heels. Even her perfume smelled exorbitant.

Peter Smith, a blond man dressed in beige designer jeans and a burgundy Keniworth Winery parka, arrived with an elegantly arranged plate of eggs, fruit, heirloom tomatoes and shiitake mushrooms. He carefully hugged Samantha across her shoulders to avoid colliding with her mascara and large hoop earrings. He high-fived Bob before he sat down.

Juan Rodriguez, a younger dark-haired man wearing blue jeans and a bright yellow parka, followed Peter. With a flourish and a grin, Juan acknowledged the others as he put down his plate overflowing with fresh flour tortillas, eggs and sausage.

An older man with the tanned face and wrinkles from years of working in the vineyards was the last to join the group. Although Charlie Bartino barely smiled as he sat down, kindness and calm crept from his tired eyes. To no one's surprise, Charlie's plate was filled with New York grilled steak, hash browns and toast. Breakfast at the VineSprings Grill was often Charlie's lunch.

As Samantha rose to give Charlie a hug, no one complained that Charlie's tanned skin under his well-worn shirt, jeans and heavy boots had the pungent aroma of a farmer straight from the vineyards, *sans* shower. Charlie's Sonoma roots were older than most of the ancient vines growing in Napa and Sonoma. In the eyes of the local residents, Charlie was wine country royalty.

After the group assembled, happily eating breakfast, Bob stopped checking the financial news and put away his iPad.

"Before you guys arrived," he addressed the group, "I was glancing at the latest from *The New York Times*. There's interesting news from the Big Apple for anyone who follows the stock market. There have been *more* arrests for insider trading."

As the rest of the group stopped eating and stared at Bob, he continued.

"Instead of doing legitimate research like our investment club, some hedgies have been getting people inside the tech companies to smuggle out *inside information*. They've traded on the information before it's released to the public."

"Ouch." said Samantha. "Isn't that a classic case of insider trading?"

"True enough," Bob nodded.

"Hey, guys, this talk is way too early in the morning for my tiny little brain," complained Peter, looking up from his cup of coffee. "How does anyone find out about this stuff in the first place?"

The group's attention returned to Bob. They knew that Bob rose early to follow the stock market. At breakfast, he seldom spoke about anything else. He thought for a moment.

"My friends, it's important to understand the way the Feds work. The regulators have everyone on Wall Street squarely in their sights. Any unusual trades on Wall Street trigger the FINRA computers to generate reports that eventually land *thump* on the SEC's desk. The FBI eventually gets involved and everyone is off to the races. Anyway…that's today's news. But who knows if the Feds' suspicions are true?"

"That's *amazing!*" Samantha was indignant. "Those hedge fund guys make billions every year. Why on earth would they risk getting caught and sent to jail on an *insider trading* rap?"

"Samantha, you're right," replied Bob. "Those guys individually make millions and billions every year. But rich people in places like New York often feel broke."

Pausing, Bob looked around the table at each member of the group.

"Do you know *why* these rich guys often feel broke?"

The faces looked back at him blankly.

Bob smiled and leaned over.

"They all suffer from a disease called "Trying To Keep Up With the Joneses," he said quietly. "These guys spend every minute of the day envying the lavish lifestyles of their wealthier friends and neighbors. They attend business conferences in places like Davos, Switzerland, and charity fundraisers in New York City alongside the super-rich, the 0.01 percent of the 1 percent. They all come away feeling as poor as church mice. Even though these guys are making millions, possibly billions, annually, they spend their enormous incomes competing with one another. It's nuts." He nodded knowingly. "I know. I used to work with those guys."

Bob paused to sip his coffee before continuing. "Ironically, one member of the Jones family, Edith Wharton, won a Pulitzer Prize writing books that damned the wealthy elite of New York City in the 1800s," he said disdainfully. "To my mind, nothing much has changed since that era. This morning, before you got here, I was thinking how glad I am that I live in Sonoma—away from all that nonsense." He paused to look around the table. "The problem is there are just way too many people involved whose every move is being monitored…"

"…by those computers that generate the reports that land *thump* on the SEC's desk," mimicked Peter, in a mocking voice. "OK, Dude, we get it!"

Bob changed the subject by asking who planned to attend the upcoming fundraiser at the renovated Newman mansion.

"Dude, *now* you're talking my language," said Peter "Raising funds to help abandoned pets left behind after a foreclosure is *such* a good cause. At the winery we're really excited about it. My boss, Jeremy, and I get to pour our *best* wines. Last weekend, I took a complete tour of the Newman's lovely home," he said excitedly. "I made the excuse that we needed to pay them a visit before the fundraiser to plan where we'll put our wine stations. Of course, while I was there, I checked out *everything*, including all the new bedrooms and bathrooms." Peter paused and looked at Samantha.

"Hon, we all love Jeremy but honest to God, he has *no taste*. He's always shocked when I suggest we renovate the winery to bring in a fresher look. If left to Jeremy, Keniworth Winery would still be a throwback to the 1970s—antlers, dead animal heads and cowboy boots. At the beginning of the tour, he made an excuse that he had to leave. Can you believe that?"

"Maybe he had to get back to his winery," said Bob pointedly. "We small business owners don't have much spare time."

"Anyway, Lucy was *such* a doll," Peter happily ignored the interruption. "Before I left, she gave me a personal tour of the mansion, the garden, *and* the separate guest cottage. She showed me the renovation plans, plus the before and after photos. She even told me where they sourced the new furniture, window treatments, bathroom fixtures *and* the kitchen appliances. I got the *full* scoop."

"I guess you really needed to know all that stuff to set up a couple of wine stations," challenged Charlie with a smile.

"Of *course*, replied Peter. "We had to work out the flow of guest traffic." When he noticed four pairs of skeptical eyes staring at him, he shrugged.

"Well…maybe I *was* being nosy, but Lucy seemed to love the fact that someone was taking an interest. While I was there, a crew from *Wine Country Interiors* arrived to take photographs. Reminded me fondly of my youth in New York," said Peter wistfully. "Lucy's hubby barely lifted his nose from his computer. I gather that he's a *real* workaholic."

"That poor bastard," said Bob. "He probably has to keep his nose to the grindstone just to pay for that renovation work."

"Anyway, guys, the place is really *cool,*" added Peter. "You'll just love it. Their interior designer did a wonderful job. I'm so jealous. Must have cost a bomb."

"It *did*…and I know precisely how big a bomb it cost," said Samantha smugly. "As you know, I sold them the house. After the closing, Lucy hired my designer friend, Betty, to do the renovation. It took nearly a year but I have to agree with Peter: it's just *amazing.* One of the best renovation jobs *ever.* Everyone who worked on the project will be at the fundraiser. Lucy is *such* a sweetheart. She insisted that we all attend as her guests to show her appreciation."

"*That's* nice," Charlie sounded weary of the entire topic. "It means you didn't have to pay for those goddamned expensive tickets."

"Darned right," replied Samantha. "Bob, you and your wife are going to be pretty busy. I hear that almost half of Sonoma is showing up just for a chance to ogle the mansion."

"Now that I no longer have to worry about the stock market, I'll be there, happy as a clam serving clams, tuna, salmon and oysters," Bob added with an angelic smile. Bob and his wife had started the catering company Not Just Olives soon after they moved to Sonoma.

"Yeah, *right!*" Peter rolled his eyes in disbelief. Bob's habit of obsessively checking the stock market while eating his breakfast was a standing joke with the group.

"I've got to be there to help my uncle with the valet parking and it *sucks*," grumbled Juan. "That's the problem with our family. Someone starts some new business and *everyone* in the family gets recruited to help out—even on weekends. Can't wait to get out of school and start working in tech. I'm so freaking tired of mowing lawns and cleaning pools for a bunch of rich people."

"*Heck!* You guys have it *real* soft," Charlie chided gently, "and *your* pay ain't so bad, young man. You do OK for yourself. At least you get a decent night's sleep once in a while. Try working for a family who owns vineyards for a change."

"Will you be there, Charlie?" asked Samantha.

"*Sure!* My bride, Diana, wouldn't miss it. I'll be in deep trouble if I don't throw on some smart clothes and take her."

Charlie chuckled. "Heck…it's the talk of the whole damn town."

CHAPTER 2

Lucy Newman Arrives in Sonoma

The next day, Lucy Newman smiled as she reached Highway 121 to Sonoma and Napa. The Sonoma countryside was always a welcome relief after the ugly, clogged Friday afternoon traffic slogging though Highway 101 in the Peninsula and Marin. The late afternoon sunlight added a peaceful golden glow to surrounding mountains and vineyards. With harvest over, the leaves on the vines were transformed into a rich array of autumn colors: dark chocolate, scarlet, rust, copper and pale yellow as the vines slowly prepared for their winter rest.

Driving through the City of Sonoma, Lucy noticed that the maple trees lining the streets also displayed soothing autumn shades. Recent rainstorms had power-washed the town, making the mansions, houses, and cottages along Second Street East look bright and freshly painted, as if they had jumped out of a child's storybook.

"*Sonoma is showing off today,*" Lucy thought to herself. As she drove into her neighborhood, several residents tending their gardens stopped, smiled and waved their gloves and gardening tools, as if to say "hello and welcome back." Lucy waved back enthusiastically. She was always impressed by how her Sonoma neighbors tended their own gardens. After leaving high-powered Palo Alto, where young moms like Lucy raced around town chasing hectic schedules, Lucy enjoyed the contrast of a more laid-back Sonoma. With her 6:00 a.m. extreme yoga instructor's strident yells still ringing in her ears, Lucy sighed with relief as she parked her SUV in the driveway.

Lucy's cell phone rang. It was her caterer, Bob Goodwin, from Not Just Olives calling to discuss last-minute catering arrangements for the upcoming fundraiser.

"OK, so how many are *now* attending? Is 80 the final number?" Bob asked.

Lucy sighed. "Yes, I think so, Bob. It seems that people in Sonoma want to invite all their friends at the last minute, so who knows?" Bob laughed and told Lucy not to worry. He reminded her that Sonoma's nickname is "*Slow*-noma" for a reason. RSVPs were always last minute. However, he warned Lucy that Sonoma was a city with a village culture. She would not wish to hurt anyone's feelings by accidentally leaving them out.

While talking to Bob, Lucy caught sight of her gardener, Juan Rodriguez, tending her beautiful shrubs and plants. She opened her door, allowing the crisp autumn air to replace the air conditioning that had battled toxic highway gasoline fumes for more than two hours. She opened the back door and her longhaired Australian sheepdog, Sidney, eagerly jumped from the SUV. Juan stopped gardening to greet his four-legged friend.

"How ya doing, buddy?" asked Juan enthusiastically.

"*G'day, mate,*" signaled Sidney with a broad canine smile. Sidney was proud of his Australian accent, which his ancestors had picked up from sheep imported from Australia. Sidney's large fluffy body wriggled with happiness as he approached Juan, who knelt to stroke Sidney behind his silky soft ears. Sidney returned the social pleasantry by carefully sniffing Juan in his gardening clothes and then licking Juan's face.

"*I'm so pleased to see you,*" whined Sidney.

The dog and human were well acquainted. When Sidney was waiting to be adopted at the local animal shelter, Juan, working as a volunteer, had trained Sidney to greet, but not jump on, the locals and visitors walking around the Sonoma Plaza.

Juan rose to his feet. He smiled and waved at Lucy as she reached into her SUV to retrieve her one-year-old daughter, Catherine. Juan was always pleased to be gardening at the Newman mansion when the slim, young blonde wife of Tim Newman arrived in Sonoma wearing high heels and short skirts that perfectly displayed her elegant long legs as she climbed in and out of her SUV.

Juan enjoyed gossiping with his friends about the Newman's' fashionable lifestyle. During the recent economic downturn, Juan's parents had been forced to lay off several employees after some supposedly wealthy clients had cancelled their services or had simply stopped paying their bills without explanation. Juan worked part-time to support his parents' landscaping and pool maintenance business, while studying computer science at Sonoma State University.

Lucy interrupted her caller. "Bob, I have to go now. Just arrived in Sonoma and there's a lot going on. Our young gardener and pool maintenance guy is here and the baby's beginning to kick up a storm."

Bob laughed. "Boy, I can *hear* her. Miss Catherine Newman has powerful lungs for someone so small. No problem. I'll check back tomorrow morning. Take care."

As Lucy unlocked the massive front door, Sidney signaled to Juan, "*Must go mate—I'm on duty,*" and abruptly turned to herd his family into their massive home. Sidney leaned over to supervise Lucy as she laid the baby in the living room cot. Catherine miraculously stopped crying as soon as she grabbed her bottle with both chubby hands. She slowly and methodically drained the contents into her tiny mouth and gurgled contentedly while her mother opened several French windows. Sidney drank noisily from his freshly replenished water bowl and lay down beside Catherine's cot with an audible sigh. He was ready for his long overdue afternoon nap.

Lucy's cell phone rang again; she glanced at the smartphone screen. It was her husband, Tim, the CEO of Meediya, a NASDAQ-listed software company in Palo Alto, famous for developing cutting-edge software to stream entertainment data to tablets and smartphones. Its applications speed left competitors in the dust.

The fortunes of Meediya and its CEO had soared, until it was caught in the crosshairs of the smartphones patent wars. When a larger software company sued, claiming that Meediya's smartphone apps infringed its earlier patents, news of the lawsuit had caused the once highflying NASDAQ stock to dip sharply downwards.

"Sweetheart, I have wonderful news! It looks like we're about to get that major pain-in-the-ass patent suit resolved," said Tim. "If this goes through, we'll be able to pay off all our debts and maybe spend more time in Sonoma."

"But, honey, why's the lawsuit being resolved *now*?" asked Lucy. "Why hasn't it happened before?"

"Well, we've had a lucky break. Everyone on Sand Hill Road thinks this patent lawsuit is *ridiculous*. Our former VC Marc Todd's been quietly working behind the scenes to get this sucker resolved in a way that's a win-win for both companies. Just got off the phone with the other side, and it turns out that they *love* our software. We're working on a strategic partnership…mutual cross-licensing agreements and more. Boy, is *this* ever a welcome change from their f-in lawyers trying to shut us down! Anyway, must go…got another call coming in. Hope to be up in Sonoma by midnight. Love you!"

After the call, Lucy put her face into in her graceful, exquisitely manicured hands. Her large blue eyes became misty with relief. Although she did not fully understand all that her husband had told her, his voice sounded excited and upbeat for the first time in months. After drying her eyes, she folded her arms and stared at the carpet.

Juan, glancing through the French windows facing the patio, became concerned that Lucy had received bad news. Although the Newmans had been late paying their invoices during the past few months, Juan had become increasingly fond of the young Newman family. When working at their mansion, Juan often played with Sidney and entertained Catherine, as if she was one of Juan's younger sisters. Juan had been glad that one of his favorite puppies from the shelter had found such a nice home. After checking on Catherine, who was sleeping like a cherub, Lucy picked up her cell phone and walked outside to her garden.

"Sally, I have to speak quietly; the baby's finally asleep," whispered Lucy. "I have *great* news. Tim and I *will* be able to go with you and Don to the upcoming de Young Gala event. We *must* go shopping so I can try on that adorable Yves Saint Laurent gown we saw in Saks," she giggled into her phone. After several minutes of girl talk, Lucy interrupted her friend. "Oh, Sally—gotta run. Must pay our wonderful gardener before he leaves."

Juan grinned to himself when Lucy paid some overdue invoices, plus a large bonus for his patience.

Things were looking up for everyone!

CHAPTER 3

A Silicon Valley Guest Disrupts Fundraiser

The weekend after Thanksgiving, Lucy and Tim Newman found themselves welcoming more than 100 guests to their Sonoma home for the fundraiser. The weather was unusually balmy for early December, allowing the guests to mingle pleasantly in the mansion, gazebo, garden and pool house.

To Sidney's dismay, before the event began he was confined in the mansion's guest quarters with baby Catherine and her sitter. Fortunately for Sidney, several guests paid them a visit, and Sidney took advantage of the open door to sneak out to the party.

Sidney loved big parties. It was his opportunity to meet-and-greet all kinds of dog-friendly people and scavenge rich pickings from the delicious food that inevitably dropped to the floor. People couldn't precariously balance everything on napkins and small plates forever. He looked around hopefully for visiting babies and toddlers. Catherine taught Sidney that tiny humans were an especially rich source of scrumptious goodies. Once their parents saw Sidney playing the role of "adorable live fluffy toy," which could be safely hugged and petted, he was allowed to lick everything up—without interference. These parents were more interested in minding their offspring than controlling Sidney's otherwise strict diet.

As Lucy greeted her guests, she carefully watched Tim. Despite his stressful workweek, Lucy was relieved that he finally seemed relaxed and happy. Catching sight of her guests in the enormous mirror over the fireplace mantel, Lucy also observed that, aside from a few hipsters from the City, she and her husband were among the youngest in the room.

Lucy also kept a close eye on her trusted lieutenants to ensure they had everything they needed to make the party a success. She watched her caterer, Bob Goodwin, handing out delicious shrimp, salmon and goat cheese canapés with the name of his business, Not Just Olives, prominently displayed on his serving dishes. Peter Smith and Jeremy Keniworth were busily pouring wine from two wine stations strategically placed in her two largest reception rooms, giving the Keniworth Winery name maximum exposure. Despite being rushed off their feet, Bob and Peter were secretly feeling relieved that *this* event hadn't been cancelled following the recent economic downturn. They gave Lucy a huge wink or a smile every time she caught their eye, which made her laugh and temporarily forget her anxiety over her first Sonoma event. Through the large window by the front door, Lucy saw Juan, her gardener, running back and forth parking cars. He gave her a friendly smile and wave when she caught his eye.

"Tim, let me introduce you to James Chistlehurst," said Phil Taylor, a tall, dark-haired corporate law partner with the prominent international firm, Horace & Fitzpatrick. "James is editor of the wine blog Chistlehurst Vintage Wines and is one of our best buddies up here in wine country. Tim, James is a valuable man worth knowing."

Tim appreciatively shook hands with a white-haired, older man whose pale blue eyes briefly glanced over Tim's shoulders at the room full of other guests. With his flowing hairstyle, navy blue sports jacket, and Etonian tie, James displayed the air of a man who had stopped by on his way to dinner at his Pall Mall gentlemen's club in London.

"James…as I mentioned driving over, Tim and I are both Stanford alumni," said Phil enthusiastically. "Tim founded Meediya, the software company developing cutting edge media apps for tablets and smartphones. Now that Tim and Lucy have moved to Sonoma, I thought it was high time that you two met."

James Chistlehurst bowed his head graciously. "Ah, Tim…welcome to wine country," said James in the soft, well-educated voice of an Englishman who had learned to mix his British accent with enough American idioms to soothe and charm his listeners. "And *thank you* for inviting me to your lovely party. I am always delighted to meet Phil's friends from the fast-paced world of technology. Although I try to keep current with my blog, we live quiet lives up here in wine country. We need up-to-the-mark young people like you, Tim, to keep us on our toes."

"James just returned from attending a prestigious wine conference in Hong Kong, where he was one of the guest speakers," gushed Phil. James sighed heavily as Phil and Tim looked on admiringly. "All in a day's work, my friends," James replied nonchalantly.

Sidney was not impressed. James had ignored him completely. "*He may be a well-dressed Brit, but he has no dog manners,*" Sidney sulked.

"Tell me more about your wine blog, James," Tim said enthusiastically. "I'm afraid that I'm a bit of a dunce when it comes to wine. Technology has been my all-consuming passion for the last few years. However, I'm hoping to learn more now that we've finally moved into our place up here."

"Well, my passion has always been the study of the finest vintage wines of Burgundy and Bordeaux, like the always popular celebrities from Chateau Laffite," replied James. "However, now that I live in this glorious modern part of the world, I also write about the great wines of Napa and Sonoma. I'm lucky enough to be a partner in a firm that specializes in arranging the purchase and proper storage of fine vintages for our clients from the top wine-producing areas of the world. This allows me to keep up with all the latest news and gossip."

James paused, leaned back on his heels and looked up into Tim's younger face. "In the new year, I would be most honored if you and Lucy would visit my Yountville cellar to taste some of our vintage wines…after I get some tiresome trips to more foreign parts out of the way."

Dreaming about the possibility of toasting his company's patent lawsuit settlement with bottles of expensive Chateau Lafite, Tim smiled broadly. As he helped himself to one of Bob Goodwin's delicious appetizers, Tim thanked James profusely, saying that he and Lucy would love to visit James' Yountville cellar. Phil then looked up and spied another friend.

"…And, James, have you met our VC buddy, Marc Todd?"

James smiled briefly and shook hands with the narrow-faced, grey-haired venture capitalist who had just walked into the party. Marc Todd responded with the caution of a man constantly hounded by eager strangers seeking millions in funding for their start-up businesses.

"Pleased to meet you, James," said Marc in a quiet, low-key voice accustomed to sizing young Stanford and other startup talent for his Sand

Hill Road venture firm.

"So, James, tell us about the latest Bordeaux vintages," said Phil. "How do they compare with prior years?"

As James began sharing the latest news from France, Bob quietly left the group to continue serving canapés to other guests. As he moved through the large reception rooms, Bob recognized most of the people in the room as either Sonoma locals or technology executives visiting their second homes in wine country. He also noticed some unfamiliar faces and guessed that these must be Tim's Silicon Valley friends visiting for the weekend.

As Bob came closer, Peter Smith, who took a keen interest in style, noticed with amusement that his breakfast buddy Bob's chef's coat, topped off with his silver hair and goatee beard, had transformed Bob into the quintessential wine country chef featured in national magazines.

"Bob looks like he was born with at least one Michelin star dangling from his cradle," Peter thought to himself. *"Who'd ever guess our Bob had once worked on Wall Street?"*

Out of the corner of his eye, Peter also noticed a young, skinny man with short spiked black hair wearing black leather jeans standing by one of the windows facing the entrance to the house. Instead of mingling, Jason Lee had his back turned to the other guests. He was glaring angrily out of the window. Eventually, he began aggressively punching his smartphone.

"Hey, Cecil man, why aren't you here? I am just *dying.*" After a short pause as he listened to his friend, Jason exploded excitedly. "*Shit* man— that's terrible! Those *bastards.* The FDA is so *fucked.*"

"Blimey! I'm outta here before I get blamed me for something," thought Sidney. He dived under Peter's wine station for cover.

Everyone in the room stopped talking to stare at Jason. With his back to the other guests, Jason remained oblivious as he continued his conversation.

An older woman, Janet Parks-Brown, an adjunct professor at the University of Santa Clara, left a group of guests and walked slowly towards Jason. She stood quietly at his side and waited patiently for his call to end.

Ending the call, Jason looked up and noticed Janet's kind eyes and dimpled cheeks smiling sympathetically. Jason, almost in tears at the sight of an understanding friend, confided to Janet that he no longer had "any appetite" for the party. Janet put her arm around him, and they walked outside.

When they reached the valet parking area, Jason looked up at the mountains bordering Sonoma Valley and said angrily, "Cecil's one of the top scientists in the country. He's onto something new that could seriously *help* people. He thought that recent clinical trials would be enough for FDA approval. Now the FDA is demanding *more clinical trials*. We all know what that means in the near term—*zero revenues*."

As they waited for Jason's car, he turned to Janet. "If Cecil's board loses confidence in him, Cecil may be forced out. If the funding runs out, his company may go down. If either happens, Cecil probably won't be allowed to continue his research because he's assigned all the IP rights to his company. Don't these shitheads at the FDA understand how much blood these guys sweat to do the research *and* deal with funding issues?"

After Jason's Porsche arrived, Jason hugged Janet in appreciation for listening to his vent. With his frustration and anger under control, Jason politely thanked Juan Rodriguez for fetching his car.

Juan, who had complained bitterly to his breakfast buddies at being asked to help his uncle with the valet parking, was pleasantly surprised to receive Jason's generous tip.

"Maybe this isn't such a bad gig after all," Juan thought.

CHAPTER 4

The Venture Capitalist Shares His Thoughts

After Jason Lee and Janet Parks-Brown left the room, Marc Todd caught sight of a loyal investor in his VC fund, Charlie Bartino, standing in front of a Keniworth wine station. Loyalty to Marc meant that Charlie wasn't a pain in the ass when the VC fund occasionally lost money—like too many individual investors. The grape growing business had taught Charlie that there were good years and bad years in everything—including technology.

Charlie was smiling at Samantha Pond as she exchanged jokes with a handsome blond man pouring wine. Two of Marc's trusted allies from the Silicon Valley, Tom White and Tony Padilla, also stood by the wine station. For many years, Marc had placed Tom and Tony inside his portfolio companies to iron out growing pains pre-IPO.

After seeing his longtime friends, Marc excused himself from James' professorial monologue on the current state of the French vintage market.

"Guys—this is fascinating but I have to say hello to one of our investors."

"Oh…by all means! We know the importance of *investors*," James said, as his eyes followed Marc's departure.

"Charlie's proud of his involvement in Marc's side fund," Phil said, replying to James' curiosity. "It's a privilege only offered to a chosen few."

"What in heaven's name is a *side fund*?" James asked chuckling.

"It's a fund for individual investors invited to occasionally participate in a VC fund, along with the institutional investors. It's hard to get in. You have to know the VC *personally*."

"Oh…*I see*," replied James knowingly. "VCs carefully select their individual investors, just as we carefully select our *wine futures* investors."

As Marc walked over to embrace Samantha and greet his other friends, he noticed with amusement that Charlie—who spent his entire working life in and around muddy vineyards—was dressed in a smart sports jacket and tie. In contrast, Tom, Tony, and Samantha, who worked in squeaky-clean offices, were dressed in the casual Silicon Valley uniform of golf shirt and khaki pants.

A large Australian Shepherd darted from behind the wine station, looked around, and immediately sat beside Samantha. A large paw touched her leg.

"*Won't you love me, feed me? I'm feeling so neglected,*" signaled Sidney looking mournful and piteous.

"Hey, that young man in the black leather jeans seemed really upset," said Charlie excitedly.

"He's Jason Lee—a former client of mine," said Samantha in a peeved voice. "I sold him a place in Glen Ellen. However I wish he hadn't been so rude. At one point, he totally disrupted the party." Her carefully coifed head shook with annoyance as she bent down to stroke Sidney. Sidney wriggled excitedly as Samantha opened her purse. Sidney knew that she always carried dog treats.

"That young man's behavior is typical of the newest generation of tech brats," concurred Tony Padilla, dropping a piece of tuna from his plate to Sidney. "Once they've run a couple of start-ups into the ground, hopefully they'll acquire some manners."

Noticing that Marc was a friend of his breakfast buddies Samantha and Charlie, Peter poured Marc a generous glass of Keniworth's best vintage wine. After thanking Peter, Marc slowly turned to his friends and pursed his lips.

"Jason's right, though. The FDA truly *sucks,*" said Marc in a smooth voice renowned in the Silicon Valley for bringing young entrepreneurs to heel during sensitive valuation negotiations. "Few VCs can afford to touch the biotech space right now…way too capital-intensive. New drugs now require at least 10 years of clinical trials before they win approval. One of my VC friends in biotech recently complained that everyone working for the FDA seemed scared shitless to approve anything. However, Jason's shop is in good shape. His apps for managing health care records don't need FDA approval."

The group nodded sagely as they listened to the venture capitalist.

"We in the telecommunications space are fortunate not to need the federal government acting as gatekeeper to our success," added Tom White in a deep, gravelly voice as he bent down to stroke Sidney and give him a cookie. "So, Marc, how's the *VC* business holding up these days?"

Marc laughed and continued in a more upbeat tone. "Things are completely *nuts*—now that the IPO window is *finally* opening up. Everyone's working on overdrive to get their companies ready for the next IPO or merger. It's a welcome change from the graveyard pessimism that rained down on Sand Hill Road when the IPO window slammed shut on us back in 2008."

He paused to eat a mouthful of appetizers. Sidney instantly vacuumed the crumbs that dropped to the ground.

"Charlie, how's the grape growing business?" Marc asked cheerfully, changing the subject.

"Well, the downturn's been real tough on many growers," replied Charlie. "Mother Nature didn't pull any punches during the recent harvest. But things are finally looking up. All the winemakers are pleased with this year's grape crop and our vintner clients are finally selling out their earlier vintages. Folks are starting to feel wealthier, I guess."

Charlie extracted a dog treat from the top pocket of his immaculate sports jacket and presented it to Sidney as some might proffer an expensive cigar to a longtime friend.

"*Wow, mate, thanks for remembering my favorite,*" signaled Sidney as he lay down to give the treat his undivided attention.

"Anyway, guys, I gotta run," said Charlie, slapping Marc on the shoulder. "My bride is giving me that 'we gotta go' look. Hey, Tom and Tony, make sure you stop by to see the *latest* tank. It's a real beauty and in great shape."

"*Sure will,*" said Tom. As a military veteran, Tom cherished the opportunity to view Charlie's and his friends' priceless collection of World War II, Korean, and Vietnam tanks; helicopters; armored cars and jeeps stored at the Bartino family's vineyards in Sonoma and Napa. After Charlie left, Marc turned to Samantha.

"So, how's the real estate market? Come to think of it, news about all the pending IPOs must also be good news for your business, right?"

Samantha's French twist nearly came loose as she vehemently nodded her head in agreement. She opened her large brown eyes wide before leaning over to speak in a husky whisper:

"It's *just amazing*. In the last two months, it seems like the market for our high-end properties woke up from a deep slumber. It's not just the new social media millionaires who feel good these days. I'm even getting inquiries from people like Janet and Joe, who've worked in Silicon Valley for *years*. They aren't quite ready to make a move just yet. But their interest speaks volumes."

The group looked over at Janet Parks-Brown. Following Jason's outburst and departure, she had quietly rejoined her husband, Joe.

"Poor Janet," said Marc shaking his head. "She's one of the Valley's nicest people—very loyal to her company. Perhaps too loyal for her own good. She's got one of the Valley's toughest jobs. Telecommunications margins are terrible. Glad we exited *that* business years ago. Janet and Joe—like the rest of us—could really use a place up here to chill. I'm happy they're working with you, Samantha.

"*Now that I've consumed Charlie's treat, I'm hungry,*" thought Sidney. "*Oh great! Here comes Bob with more goodies.*"

"So, Tony, how's your business?" asked Marc. Tony Padilla took a large appetizer from Bob before leaning over to reply.

"Don't tell everyone because, as we've observed, some people are still hurting right now," he said quietly, staring at the polished hardwood floor beneath his feet. "I've just put down a deposit on a brand new Tesla Roadster."

Tony waited while Tom lifted his head and whistled with surprise. Marc and Samantha also beamed their approval.

"Yeah. I'm really excited." Tony's grin was broad as he slipped another expensive canapé to Sidney. "Saw one parked at the Menlo Circus Club last August. Keep this under your hat, but we all got some good news at work this week, so I decided to take an afternoon off and visit some showrooms before all the rest of our sales reps start piling in. I took an *all-electric Roadster* out for a spin. Great cars! I now know why they're so popular with you VCs, Marc. But enough about me, Tom.

How's life treating you?"

Tom White folded his arms and sighed with exasperation. "Developing software for our router customers has its own share of madness," he replied. "Usage increased like crazy when smartphones first came in, but the downturn kicked our business in the teeth. Like everyone else, we're slowly starting to recover. At the end of *this* quarter, hopefully I won't have to drive up to Sonoma really late—or miss coming up here altogether—like some past quarters when we struggled to make our numbers. My wife, Leslie, is always saying that I get really cranky if I can't make it up here on the weekends."

"Hey, these appetizers are great. Can I have another one?" asked Tony. Bob smiled broadly as he proudly offered fresh crab and tomato canapés from a second plate expertly balanced on his arm.

After Bob left, with Sidney on his heels, Tom quietly murmured to the group. "Sonoma is so great…such a nice contrast to Silicon Valley. No one up here gives a damn what our stock price is doing."

CHAPTER 5

The Breakfast Group Reconvenes

The following Monday morning, Bob sat with his regular black coffee and scrambled eggs, keeping one eye on the stock market indices and the other watching for his breakfast buddies to arrive in the VineSprings Grill parking lot. Charlie was the first to arrive in an enormous farmer's pickup truck, which he parked beside Bob's vintage Jaguar.

Juan arrived shortly afterwards on his bicycle. Samantha drove up in her gleaming black Range Rover as Juan parked his bicycle. Peter was the last to arrive, in his late partner's BMW. Bob knew Peter still grieved for Shawn, the victim of a freak bicycle accident. Bob suspected that Peter's lighthearted comments in the company of his friends bravely concealed a broken heart that would take time to mend.

As the breakfast group assembled at the table, Bob stopped checking his favorite NASDAQ stocks and asked the group what they thought about the weekend's fundraiser at the Newman mansion.

Samantha was the first to speak. "Wow—it was quite a party. Bob, several of my friends commented that your food was absolutely delicious. Peter, everyone I spoke with said that your Keniworth wines were just *amazing*. Everyone stayed hours longer than expected. Lucy's such a sweetheart. She's simply thrilled that the fundraiser was such a success."

After a pause to sip her black coffee, she added, "By the way, Bob and Peter, my designer friend, Betty, may be calling you to request some catering help. She has a designer showcase coming up in May. I've put in a good word for you."

"Oh *cool*! How exciting. I love designer showcases. They're among my favorite events," replied Peter.

Samantha then turned her attention to Juan, who looked bored. She gave him a quick hug. "Juan, you did an *amazing* job with the valet parking."

"*Hey!* When are the rest of us getting *our* hugs?" Charlie demanded with a chuckle.

"Now, Charlie, Juan deserves a special hug because he got stuck doing the crummy job of parking cars while we were inside enjoying the party."

Juan smiled at Samantha and Peter chimed in. "Well, guys, everyone *must* have had a really good time because they consumed simply *gallons* of wine. One cool-looking dude threw a hissy fit over something, but he seemed the *only* guy at the party not having a good time. Does anyone know why that guy got so ticked off? Our wines weren't the problem. After he first arrived, he seemed to like our wine."

"*Hey*…who knows," said Charlie wearily. "Marc Todd said something about the FDA but I can tell you…some of those techie guys make a big deal about nothing. Last September, a winemaker forgot to tell a techie client that we were delivering grapes the same evening that his wife had planned a fancy gig in the wine cellar. After we arrived, everything had to be moved outside on the lawn. I told his wife: "Hey, lady. Call me any name you want, but *the grapes are coming in.* They all think that growing grapes is like making computers or something."

The group waited patiently while their older friend vented his frustration. "Truth is…" said Charlie, "when Mother Nature is your business partner, she doesn't cooperate like that," Charlie said vehemently. "Sometimes crush is early. Sometimes it's late. We're *all* on call…ready to pick and deliver the fruit only when the grapes are good and ready. I have to tell these guys that we don't work by anyone else's clock except *Mother Nature.* They need to get over it."

Bob sighed. "Yeah. Some of them can be murder on the catering front as well," he said, agreeing with his older pal. "Just because they've made a few bucks in technology, they can act so darn self-entitled. However, I have to say that Lucy was a sweetheart to work with. Her husband isn't bad either."

Samantha decided to speak up. "Charlie's right. I'm familiar with the young man who threw the hissy fit, Jason Lee. I sold him a home in Glen Ellen. He freaked out because Cecil Roberts didn't show."

The group stared at her dumbfounded.

"Cecil, who's also a client of mine, works in biotech. Apparently Cecil had just received some disappointing news from the FDA, which is why he was a no-show. Since Marc works on Sand Hill Road, he was sympathetic. *Personally*? I don't think bad news is any excuse for bad manners. I felt sorry for *Lucy*."

"That Jason Lee's got a really nice Porsche, though," said Juan excitedly, "and his clothes are really cool. I liked his leather jeans and matching jacket, man. He also tipped great. His business must be doing OK. Wish I was in his line of work."

Peter nodded his head in agreement. "Yeah, guys. His hair was also super cool."

"Let's *not* talk anymore about that silly young man," Samantha said with a shake of her elaborately coiffed head. "All my *other* Silicon Valley friends had a really good time. Charlie, after you left, Tom and Tony made a point of telling me how much they enjoyed themselves. Listen, guys, Tom and Tony both live in Atherton and belong to the Menlo Circus Club. That's where all the prominent VCs and Silicon Valley executives hang out. Their praise is *really* worth having."

Bob stared at Samantha above his bifocals; the rest of the group was silent. After looking up and seeing Bob's fixed gaze, Samantha also noticed that Peter was smirking at her.

"God! I'm *so* glad that I don't work in the Silicon Valley anymore," she said, responding to her friends' silent mockery. "Seeing all those guys dressed in golf shirts and khaki pants made me want to puke."

"Samantha, hon., did you take a look in the mirror before you left home?" asked Peter. "No, I'm not talking about *today*. At the party, you, too, were decked out in a golf shirt and khaki pants."

Peter paused as Samantha gulped her black coffee and then glared at him. "Of course, hon, we all thought you looked quite darling in your techie butch outfit." Everyone, including Samantha, laughed.

"I'm glad I don't have to work in Silicon Valley," Peter said, as he put his arm around Samantha to give her a hug. "From what I overhear in the tasting room, some of the people working down there can be real jerks. The lifestyle is *just awful*."

"It truly is," replied Samantha. "Everyone down in the Valley works like dogs 24/7. All my tech buddies keep telling me how they love visiting their second homes in Napa and Sonoma. It's like a sanctuary for them. I think it may even have saved some of their marriages. It's brutal working in the Valley," she added pensively. "I bet some of those guys would do almost anything to be able to retire to our peaceful wine country."

CHAPTER 6

The United States Attorney's Office, San Francisco

"You've got to be kidding me—illegal insider trading in *Napa* and *Sonoma?*"

Josh Kaplan, a young Assistant U.S. Attorney stared with amazement at his supervisor, Jane Phelps. They both looked at the speakerphone placed between them on the desk.

"We all know how you guys are doing a brilliant job of cracking down on illegal insider trading in New York," added Josh, "...but insider trading is a crime normally committed by sophisticated Wall Street types. I'm just stunned to hear that illegal insider trading might be taking place here in Napa and Sonoma."

After Josh paused, Jane raised her right hand to signal Josh to tone it down.

"In a case like this, it doesn't help to get up the nose of our colleagues in the U.S. Attorney's Office in New York," she thought to herself. *"We're going to need all the help we can get."*

After a long pause, a calm voice came from the speakerphone. "OK… Josh. I agree with you, man. It does sound unusual. However, it is one of the peculiarities of this job that one uncovers insider trading rings in the craziest of places. A few years ago, the SEC discovered a large insider trading ring involving a Russian ballroom dancer and a retired seamstress living in *Croatia*. Trust me, Josh, nowhere in the world is too remote for this type of illegal activity."

After a brief pause, the calm deep voice continued.

"FINRA and the SEC are reporting suspicious trades in technology stocks coming out of Sonoma and Napa counties. In the last three months, the SEC has identified several traders from that area who've had the *extraordinary* good luck to buy or short several Silicon Valley stocks just before a major news announcement caused the price of these stocks to skyrocket or plummet.

"This suspicious trading activity might not by itself warrant our involvement. As we all know, the SEC usually handles these cases. However, FINRA and the SEC keep seeing *the same names* on these trades and the profits from these trades are escalating. The SEC has a hunch that there may be *another* insider trading conspiracy being run out of wine country similar to the cases we're currently prosecuting in this office. The SEC has suggested that the FBI get involved. For that reason, we thought that you guys might want to take a look."

"Gus, I lived in Sonoma until I was 12 years old," Josh said, leaning towards the speakerphone. "I know the area well. Napa is a relatively small county, but Sonoma is one of our largest counties in California. Do we know *where* in Sonoma County these trades are coming from?"

"Josh, as you know, FINRA tracks all unusual stock trades that precede any news announcement, good or bad, which move the markets," replied the deep voice from the speakerphone. "Once these come up on the radar, FINRA contacts the broker-dealers for the names and addresses of all the people throughout the nation who made these trades. According to FINRA and the SEC, several trades in Sonoma County have involved one zip code: 95476. That sort of caught their eye because the zip code is hardly downtown Manhattan or even San Francisco, where one might expect to find a large volume of technology stock trades."

"Geez Louise!" exclaimed Josh as he rose from his chair to stare out the window. "*That* certainly narrows things down quite a bit," he said, turning his head towards the speakerphone. "95476 is the zip code for the *City of Sonoma* and unincorporated area adjacent to the Sonoma city limits. Everyone in Sonoma has that zip code, including my aunt and uncle, who live there."

After nodding his head while he digested this surprising information, Josh returned to the table.

"Gus…Sonoma may be a city, but in reality it's more like a small town in the middle of wine country. Are FINRA and the SEC certain that this suspicious trading activity isn't the result of some computer hacking or computer program gone crazy? We've all seen how computers can run amok, trigger crazy trades, and make some occasional big mistakes."

The voice on the other end of the speakerphone laughed and then replied, "No kidding!"

"Before you joined us, Josh," interrupted Jane, "Gus filled me in on some of the background to the spate of arrests involving East Coast hedge funds. Apparently, due to the high volatility of tech stocks, they're a favored target for insider traders. Armed with inside information, these crooks can amass huge fortunes buying or shorting these stocks days before the information hits the markets. After the recent arrests, the SEC is understandably paying very close attention to *any* unusual trading in technology stocks.

"Given the length of time it took for the FBI to penetrate the closely knit hedge fund industry, Gus recommends that we and our local FBI office here in San Francisco get involved in this latest investigation. The technology industry *and* our wine growing regions are tight–knit communities. This investigation could use some local expertise."

Josh was stunned. All he could do was silently whistle.

"Since you spent time growing up in wine country, Josh," said Jane," Gus and I both thought you'd be a good choice to handle this case." Jane nodded at Josh with an expression that signaled, *"Don't mess this up!"*

Josh ran his hand through his hair and spoke after glancing at Jane. "Sure. I can certainly help. Be glad to. I used to know the area like the back of my hand." Folding his arms, he leaned over to speak to the speakerphone. "Gus, my parents taught at the local Sonoma Valley High School for years, and I attended one of the local primary schools. Geez, guys, I may even know some of the people executing these trades. Wouldn't that be something?"

Jane handed a list to Josh.

"Gus e-mailed this before you joined us. Your first assignment is to look carefully at that list and make sure that you *don't* know any of these people." After everyone laughed, she continued, "Gus…thanks for sending this over. We greatly appreciate the confidence you and the New York office have placed in us. If you don't mind, as a courtesy, we may call you now and again to run things by you. Given your office's extensive experience in this area, there's no point in any of us recreating the wheel."

"OK then, Jane," said the voice from the speakerphone, "we'll leave it in your capable hands. Keep in touch. As the entire universe knows, we're up to our asses here in Manhattan prosecuting insider trading. However, I understand that the FBI has assigned one of their top guys to the San Francisco field office to help with this investigation. Everyone from Washington down has signaled that they want these cases handled consistently, so that no smart-ass journalist, lawyer or politician can make the argument that there's been favoritism, or that someone has been unfairly singled out, if you know what I mean. OK?"

After Jane graciously ended the call, there was a long pause.

"*Geez*…Jane, I'm blown away by the notion that an insider trading ring is operating out of Sonoma Valley and Napa Valley. From what I learned growing up, the people up there are mainly interested in one thing only: *wine,*" Josh said emphatically. "It's all about growing grapes and making fabulous wine. Unknown to many wine country tourists, there's an intense regional rivalry between Sonoma Valley and Napa Valley— rather like the Cal vs. Stanford 'Big Game.' But the rivalry here is *not* over sports—it's over *wine.* For decades, Napa and Sonoma wine country has been an artists' haven. With the arrival of Ramekins, there's now a keen interest in gourmet food. However, the one enduring theme that's always connected everyone in Sonoma Valley and Napa Valley is *wine.*

Josh paused. Jane patiently waited for him to continue.

"Knowing the attitudes of long-time wine country residents, the idea of an insider trading racket involving *technology* companies strikes me as quite extraordinary. If there were an insider trading racket involving wine or even liquor companies, it would be different. However *Silicon Valley* stocks? This is *really* hard to swallow. Although the City of Sonoma is only 45 miles north of San Francisco, it might as well be in a different country. Right now, everyone's recovering from the harvest season where no one caught any sleep. Trust me, Jane, probably nothing's on their mind except making fabulous wine from the recent harvest. The people in Sonoma couldn't give a damn about Silicon Valley companies *or* their stock prices."

"Josh, I do agree that it all sounds crazy," replied Jane. "As you know, my husband and I *love* going to Sonoma and Napa. It's one of our favorite vacation spots. It's like going to France without the language hassles and the long flights. However, Josh, you have to agree that *something's* going on up there to grab FINRA and the SEC's attention. I think we have to make sure that the right guys get nabbed, and some sweet, decent country people don't get hurt."

Josh grinned. "So you can still vacation in the wine country without someone spitting in your wine tasting glass."

Jane laughed. "That's right," she replied.

As she waited quietly while Josh mulled things over, Jane leaned back in her chair and folded her arms. "You know, Josh," she said, pursing her thin lips, "the last time I was strolling around Sonoma Plaza, I noticed several realtors advertising wine country estates as *vacation* homes. I'm beginning to wonder if these tech savvy types have bought vacation homes there and are using our lovely, peaceful wine country as a blind to hide some illegal insider trading."

Josh thought for a minute. "Well…in recent years, my aunt's complained about tech money from San Francisco and Silicon Valley buying up homes in Napa *and* Sonoma Valley," mused Josh. "Apparently they throw money around like it's going out of style. They've grabbed quite a bit of attention by outbidding the locals at the local charity wine auctions."

After a brief pause, he stared hard at Jane. "Yep," he said, "those tech guys could be in the perfect spot to learn and pass on inside information that's behind these suspiciously lucky trades."

Jane smiled and replied, "remember…those who are privy to inside information don't have to be *from* Sonoma. They only have to *use* someone living in the area to make these trades."

Josh's dark eyes looked steely. "You're right, Jane. Life's been rough for the people in wine country since the downturn. If that's what going on, that's just *unconscionable*."

CHAPTER 7

A Silicon Valley Workday Begins

The following winter, Tom White was stuck in traffic on infamous Highway 237. The rain poured down Tom's windscreen, obscuring visibility. The traffic crawled at two miles an hour. Northern California was experiencing one of its wettest storms: waves of rain and wind slammed into the West Coast from the tropical Pacific Ocean. These frequent tropical winter storms brought mudslides and floods to much of the Bay Area. Locals nicknamed them "The Pineapple Express."

Highway 237 was one of the Bay Area's busiest freeways, linking the overcrowded Highway 101 on the Peninsula with the equally overcrowded Highway 880 in the East Bay.

Highway 237 was also the main route to San Jose's busy airport. After making serious money, many Silicon Valley executives purchased private planes to fly them from the tiny San Carlos airport on the Peninsula—located close to their mansions in Atherton, Woodside, and the Los Altos Hills—to their corporate Learjet tie-downs at the San Jose airport to escape the misery of driving Highways 101, 280 and 237 during rush hour.

Highway 237 passed though Sunnyvale, the heart of old Silicon Valley. Decades ago, companies like Intel and AMD had displaced orchards and dairy farms with silicon chips, giving Silicon Valley its famous name.

Unfortunately for Tom's daily commute, his employer, Software Telecom Solutions, had established its company headquarters close to its major router clients. As he crawled along with the traffic, Tom's cell phone rang. It was his panicked boss. One of the company's largest clients and Tom's former employer, World Routers, was on the warpath over its largest customer's complaints about software bugs in a new World Network router. Tom needed to join a conference call immediately.

He dialed the conference call number. A robotic female voice announced, "Now attending: Tom White." Tom was immediately connected to what sounded like the noisy chaos of a violent bar scene instead of a corporate conference call. The noise was so unexpected and disconcerting that he momentarily forgot where he was. Rain sheets were turning Highway 237 into a car wash. Tom braked violently to avoid crushing the Porsche in front of him.

"Shit!" he unintentionally announced to the conference. Someone shouting above the general mayhem immediately greeted his virtual arrival.

"Tom, thanks for joining us on such short notice! I'm Lou Cannon, Software Telecom Solution's account manager supporting World Routers and with me at World Routers' headquarters in Sunnyvale I've got Ian Chatsworth and Anthony Kumar, World Routers' VPs of software and hardware engineering, respectively. Joining us from Atlantic-Pacific WIFI's headquarters in New Jersey we've got Heidi Warnken and Chuck Szela, who are in charge of Atlantic-Pacific's data network operations. Tom, as you know, Atlantic-Pacific's data network is built on World's routers. Embedded in these routers is *our* software. Last night, the western region data subnetwork crashed and was down for nearly four hours."

Tom began sweating, and he could feel his heart pumping hard and fast. His body had switched to survival mode. His concentration narrowed with supernatural focus to the conference call while diverting only the attention required not to obliterate the Porsche in front of him. Tom had successfully maneuvered these kinds of conference calls before, which was why Marc Todd had placed him in his current job before the company's IPO.

Tom knew that Lou, jokingly nicknamed "Loose Cannon," was an excitable but smart, experienced, and dedicated account manager. Despite his nickname, Tom knew Lou was a good man to have on a big account. Tom barely noticed the rain sheets. Very calmly Tom asked, "OK, Lou, tell me what happened."

"Tom, this is Heidi Warnken, let *me* explain what happened," interrupted a female voice firmly. "About 1:00 a.m. this morning, a problem was detected in the San Francisco central office router. Our techs, following standard procedures, ran diagnostics on the router but could find no problems. The router was taken off-line and rebooted. Everything seemed OK. But shortly after rejoining the network, the router suddenly began diverting all data traffic to other routers in the network. And then other routers in the network began diverting traffic, and very soon after that there were no operational routers and the network crashed."

Heidi continued, "Tom, this is a very important network that handles mission-critical data for Fortune 500 companies, including major financial institutions. This morning, *our* customers are very unhappy people," Heidi concluded with only slightly understated menace.

"*Not as unhappy as I am*," Tom thought, but did not say. He had been an actor in this drama many times before and knew it was vital to show sympathy, intelligence, and commitment, and to engage and control the group psychology before frustrations and fear escalated out of control. Stranded in a traffic jam in a California monsoon, he could not possibly figure out what caused the network outage. But if he could gain their confidence and a little time, he was certain that his team could solve this puzzle and make World Routers and Atlantic-Pacific WIFI happy again.

Tom decided to take charge of the conference. "OK, Heidi, thanks for the summary. But your network is built on World Routers so in the first instance we have to suspect that the problem is a router problem and…"

"Tom, this is Anthony. I'm the hardware VP at World Routers," interrupted an angry, frustrated voice. "I've been up all night with my guys dealing with this outage. It could not possibly be a hardware problem. Hardware failures are random, and this was a systemic and synchronized problem. It could only be software."

"*Yeah, I've heard that before*," thought Tom, and he knew where this conversation was going. He also knew that each participant needed to give his speech before he could bring an end to the drama. On cue, the next actor spoke.

"Tom, this is Ian Chatsworth, head of software engineering at Software Telecom Solutions. Of course, Anthony is correct that these types of problems are *usually* caused by software. And *my* engineers have been up all night running simulations in our software labs trying to recreate the problem. We can't find anything wrong in our software. But, of course, the router software includes a large element of World

Routers software, which we use under cross-license with them. World Routers software is a black box to us. We didn't write it, and we can't fully test it. We're confident there is nothing wrong with World Routers' hardware; we're confident there is nothing wrong with Software Telecom Solutions' software. The fault must be in World Routers' software. That's why I brought you in on this conference call."

The participants finished their predictable speeches and, with Tom's patient cajoling, the group promised to work together day and night to fix the problem before, in Heidi's words, "it triggers the *next* financial crisis." After the telephone conference ended, Tom barely had time to catch his breath before his car phone system instantly beeped that his personal assistant, Jen, had left him a message.

"Jen…what's up?"

"HR is bitching, *again,* that you haven't gone online yet to complete your semi-annual employee reviews. Where *are* you?"

Tom nearly cursed out loud. It was suffocating to have to waste time on such meaningless nonsense when the company faced a major meltdown crisis. But he quickly remembered that annual reviews were precious to his staff, including Jen.

Smiling grimly, Tom replied: "Jen…I'm stuck on 237. Just got off the phone with World Routers, which is doing its usual rant that the product is defective and it's entirely our fault."

"Don't worry," said Jen, "let me go online with your password and we can handle these reviews while I have you on the phone, except mine of course. For that…you're on your own, *got it?*"

Tom smiled. *"God…she's so great,"* he thought. *"I'd happily let her write her own review, if she'd allow it."*

"OK…let's start with Jeff," said Jen.

Tom sighed. "Highly competent but is still an officious prick with his reports, as I mentioned in my review six months ago. He'll never change."

"OK…I'll check the 'very good' and 'excellent' boxes for the tech stuff and add 'room for improvement' for the people-skills shit. How about Gerry?"

Tom was forced to pause while ducking more cloudbursts and kamikaze drivers.

"Gerry is one of my best engineers. He should be universally acknowledged as one of the smartest and most talented engineers on the planet…if only he would understand that all our products have to be designed so that *other* human beings can use and service them. He constantly has his head up his ass with how smart he and his team are—but they are total silos. No one wants to give his team projects that require broader teamwork because no one likes working with these guys. I have to keep reminding Gerry that it's *not* about how smart he is. It's about how good the *customer's* experience is with the product."

After expertly sanitizing this review to emphasize Gerry's technical skills, Jen asked: "How about Deborah?"

"Deborah continues to be one of my best people. She makes a concerted effort to work well with everyone, including…God help us…Gerry. Her entire team will follow her anywhere. She is tough but respected." He paused. "Christ…I shudder at the inanities she puts up with from our brilliant, but emotionally idiotic, male engineers. I guess it helps that she had brothers. When her fellow engineers give her a hard time, she uses exaggerated geek humor to make them laugh. As soon as I get to the office, I will be asking her to visit World Routers."

"I think she's already over there trying to calm things down," replied Jen.

"Thank God for that. Frankly, I wouldn't expect less."

Finally, Tom reviewed his own boss. "One back-stabbing, political, hypocritical, brown-nosing, pompous son-of-a-bitch, whose prior expertise running a smartphone application start-up made him the all-time asinine choice to replace the founders of a software company supporting the world's largest routers."

Under Jen's deft hand, this became, "Bill is an astute CEO who displays remarkable insight, hindsight, *and* foresight when working with investors, customers and colleagues alike."

After reaching his office, Tom received an urgent text message from Jen. "Legal needs U to review SEC docs on my desk. Top priority."

Tom sighed. He went over to Jen's desk and briefly glanced at the first page of a document handed to him by Jen. He saw numerous names of individuals who had purchased Software Telecom Solution shares at the end of the prior quarter. Tom contemptuously threw the document back on Jen's desk.

"Jen…take care of this, will you? Don't these lawyers have anything better to do than to keep wasting my time like this?"

It was only 8:00 a.m.

CHAPTER 8

A Private Wine Tasting in Napa Valley

A few weeks later, Tom White was in a better frame of mind as he relaxed with his longtime Silicon Valley friends, Marc Todd and Tony Padilla, at a large patio table outside James Chistlehurst's sumptuous private tasting room above Yountville. Tim and Lucy Newman, Joe and Janet Parks-Brown, and corporate lawyer, Phil Taylor, were also seated at the table. As they looked to the east and over the vineyards, they were quietly impressed by the magnificent view, which stretched across Napa Valley below to the hills above the Silverado Trail. The surrounding vineyards were beginning to show hopeful signs of an early spring. Green shoots were sprouting from the stark brown vines. From a distance, the vines looked like green braids against a brown background.

"Bud break" had begun.

The March rains had taken a brief respite for the weekend. The temperature was unseasonably warm. The group sat outside and enjoyed sunny weather for the first time since the Newman fundraiser in early December.

That morning, the Silicon Valley group had enjoyed a brief tour of James' luxurious wine cellar, which was built into the side of a mountain that had been blasted with dynamite. Some of James' guests suffered severe withdrawal symptoms while their smartphones temporarily lost their transmission signals during the tour of his cave-like wine cellar. However, once they left the cellar, the transmission returned to normal and they were able to resume texting and checking voicemails and e-mails. As the group relaxed and enjoyed the view, Jason Lee finished checking his messages and joined the group. Samantha Pond drove up the driveway in her Range Rover.

"Ah, Samantha, darling…how lovely to see you again," acknowledged

James with a courteous bow as she walked into the room. "You know everyone here, don't you?" he asked.

"Well, looking around I think I must have sold at least one house, possibly more, to almost everyone here," replied Samantha with a laugh, enthusiastically greeting everyone in the group. She gave special hugs to her high-end real estate clients, Tom, Marc and Tony.

Tom was quietly amused when Samantha gave Jason Lee one of her most dazzling smiles as she sat down on an empty seat beside the young man. *Realtors never miss a trick,"* Tom thought to himself, as he remembered Samantha's earlier criticism of Jason's angry outburst at the Newman fundraiser.

James allowed his guests time to relax as he expertly poured a delicious tasting of a vintage Chateau Lafite. He made a point of graciously addressing everyone by name as he handed a glass to each guest.

"Wow, James, this wine and the view are both *incredible,*" said Tim. "This is a truly delightful and unique spot. Tell us a little more about your wine business in France. That seems quite exotic to us here in Napa and Sonoma."

"Just a minute, Tim, and you will have my full attention," replied James in the voice of a dog trainer speaking to an overly enthusiastic puppy.

James finished pouring the French wine with great care. He then slowly sat down at the head of the table and smiled at his guests.

"To answer Tim's question, my partners and I import fine wines from around the world, not just French wine. However, I tend to provide assistance with our clients' purchases of French wine because buying the very best French wine is a particular passion of mine. Primarily, we help our clients purchase local and international *wine futures,* as opposed purchasing wine by the case."

He paused and then looked at Tim, enquiringly. "Do you know what wine *futures* are, Tim?"

After Tim shook his head negatively, James leaned back in his chair and, began speaking to the group in a professorial voice attuned to addressing conference audiences.

"By purchasing wine *in advance,* after the wine is first made but before it is bottled, my clients can *lock in* a price for what will probably turn out to be extremely expensive vintage wine once it reaches the drinking stage.

"For high-end Bordeaux wine, the drinking stage could be many years away. We are very fortunate to be able to offer our clients the most exclusive and valuable wine futures sold by the very best wineries in the world, such as the vintage Chateau Lafite that you are now tasting, as well as vintages from the famous chateau houses, such as Mouton-Rothschild, Margaux, Haut-Brion and others."

Jason asked, wide-eyed, "*Wow*—Isn't Chateau Lafite the wine that the Chinese are spending thousands to buy by the case?"

"Indeed!" James replied. "At a Sotheby's Hong Kong auction last year, a single case of vintage Lafite sold for HK $605,000. In other words, a little under than $78,000 U.S. dollars a bottle."

After the group gasped, James chuckled.

"That, my friends, is why the recent Wine Futures Conference was held in Hong Kong."

After stopping to pause for affect, James added with a knowing smile, "It is also why the *smart* money is buying wine *futures* rather than the more common method of purchasing wine by the case. Phil here is one of my longtime wine futures clients," James nodded politely at the corporate lawyer, "as are many of the guests who graced Tim and Lucy's lovely party last December," he added smugly. "A party which we will always remember so fondly," he added with a broad smile at the young couple. Then he adopted a serious tone.

"One has to know the best way to invest in wine futures, which is why our clients come to us. For example, it is possible to invest in either the first, second, or third 'tranche,' before any of the wine is bottled and released."

As the group listened attentively, James continued.

"In good years like 2005 and 2006, it proved handsomely lucrative to invest in the earlier tranches. However, ladies and gentlemen, there are never any guarantees. Wine future investments, like all investments, have risks and rewards."

After stopping to refill his guests' glasses, James again sat down.

"For example, 1997 proved an especially disappointing year for Bordeaux wine futures," he said in a somber voice. "Unfortunately, my friends, that year the wine did not mature as predicted. The result was that the bottles in the cases sold for far less than the price for the wine futures. This caused many wine future investors to actually *lose* money."

Marc Todd sighed. "This sounds all too familiar," he said shaking his head. "Investing in wine futures sounds similar to our investments in Silicon Valley startups. If one of our startups is hugely successful, we early-stage VCs make the most profit. However, if one of our startups stumbles, we are often forced to 'take a haircut' on our investments during the later rounds of VC financing or—worse—lose our entire investment."

The conversation paused as James put his elegant long nose into his tasting glass to smell the bouquet. He looked up at the group with a smile.

"Well, my friends," said James, "I am happy to report that, absent another French revolution, although wine futures investments can certainly turn sour, one is unlikely to lose one's *entire* capital investment."

All of James' guests nodded quietly at his observation. They appreciated the contrast between wine futures investments and the extremely hazardous nature of early-stage venture capital financing. Some in the room silently reminisced how they had personally benefited from both.

Jason, who had been constantly checking his smartphone after leaving the wine cellar, suddenly excused himself to take a call. He apologized profusely to the group, but said that the call was very important.

After he left to take his call, Tom White leaned over and spoke quietly to the rest of the group. "I am pleased to see that young man seems much happier than when we all met last December. I wonder how our other friend, Cecil, is doing.

"Ah…my friends," James said sadly, "I wish I had good news. After Phil told me that you are all great chums with Cecil Roberts, I invited him to join us today. Regrettably, he didn't respond to my invitation."

Phil Taylor looked around and addressed the group in a quiet, confidential voice. "Cecil must be under enormous pressure work-wise following news that his company failed…yet again…to get FDA approval for the latest product. If he's in a tight spot, he may not feel like socializing."

"Oh…the poor fellow," said James. "Unfortunately, my friends, Cecil's business sounds like the 1997 vintage for Bordeaux investors. Obviously things have not turned out as rosy as originally predicted."

Janet asked everyone to hush their conversation when she observed Jason making his way back to the group. She need not have worried. When Jason returned to the table, his mind was miles away. He had received confirmation that a patent application, which bore his name as the inventor, had been successfully registered at the U.S. Patent and Trademark Office. In his geek world, Jason was now a superstar. Taking his seat at the table, Jason's eyes shone. He even allowed himself a brief smile at his host and the other guests.

With raised eyebrows and large eyes, Samantha signaled to the rest of the group her amazement at the dramatic contrast between the sweet-faced, smiling young man who returned to the table and the scowling young man at the Newmans' fundraiser.

After James poured a second French vintage wine into new glasses, he waited while his guests tasted the older, more complex wine.

"If you want to learn about fine wine," James continued, "but don't particularly want to own a winery, wine futures can be a fun and lucrative way to do it."

Phil Taylor concurred enthusiastically. "My other investments have been lousy until recently," he said. "During the last couple of years, I've been very grateful to have James give me such good advice."

James smiled and sat back in this chair to reminisce about the past. "Phil, do you remember those wine futures that you bought in 2006? Last year, one of my partner's clients offered to buy them for double the price. Of course, after I counseled you *not* to accept the offer, you cleverly declined." They smiled at each other knowingly. James turned to the group. "Phil's wine futures are worth far more today, now that the economy has improved.

"Bordeaux wine futures have become an established international market," said James after a short pause. "New international money always chases Bordeaux wine. However new money can never wait patiently for premium wine to mature. Simply waiting two years for the wine to be bottled and another 10 years for premium Bordeaux to reach its optimum peak for drinking is not for them. That means, ladies and gentlemen, there are opportunities for the smart money, for those who are willing to invest early to make a killing off those who must have instant gratification." Everyone nodded affirmatively.

"James?" Janet Parks-Brown piped up for the first time. "I thought that it was only Americans who suffered from that problem."

"Don't you believe it!" James chuckled. "The super rich—whatever their nationality—never have any patience."

By the end of the private tasting, everyone present was in a happy, lighthearted mood. James even kidded Samantha when he saw her and Jason whispering quietly together after the other guests left the table.

"Samantha, *darling*, Jason's *far* too young for you to snuggle up with," James teased.

"James…you are *incorrigible*," replied Samantha with a laugh while the young man blushed. "I was merely asking Jason about our friend, Cecil."

Those who felt optimistic about the future eagerly signed up for the next available wine futures. Others less sure about their companies' immediate future prospects still felt that their time had been well spent. Everyone left thinking that they had learned something valuable.

CHAPTER 9

Wine Tasting in Sonoma Valley

A week later, as Peter Smith poured wine at Keniworth Winery in Kenwood, he quoted acid balance, fruit flavors, barrel origin, and yeast selection just enough to dazzle—but not bore—his visitors. While they tasted the wine, Peter also made small talk by enthusiastically asking his visitors about their hometowns. Many replied that they were visiting from Europe or the East Coast. Some were visiting wine country from other parts of the Bay Area.

Shrieks of "*Hey*, what are *you* guys doing here?" filled the tasting room, when Tom White walked in with his wife, Leslie, and spotted Joe and Janet Parks-Brown.

"Leslie, it's so great to see you," said Janet. "It's been *ages*."

"Tom, how come you're not hard at work, buddy, maximizing shareholder value?" Joe jokingly asked his friend as the two couples moved to the end of the bar away from the other visitors.

"As everyone here knows, I usually work 24/7, even on weekends here in Sonoma," Tom replied with a groan. "However, this weekend we're celebrating our anniversary. Leslie has been traveling like crazy the last several months. She insisted that we take time off to relax and enjoy our favorite wineries and restaurants."

Janet and her husband both chanted: "Cool!"

"Yep," said Leslie proudly, "I practically had to drag him away from his computer at gunpoint."

Joe put his arm around Janet. "If Janet's company's stock *continues* to go up, we're thinking about buying a weekend place up here ourselves," he said with a beaming smile. "Yesterday, we had lunch with Samantha Pond, who gave us the lowdown on the local property market. She's offered to show us properties, once we're ready to make a move."

Suddenly the door flew open and Sidney rushed into one of his favorite tasting rooms, followed closely by Tim. Like other Sonoma Valley wineries, Keniworth Winery welcomed dogs. Once a year, Keniworth hosted a dog appreciation day where owners could bring their dogs to mingle freely off leash.

"Hi, Sidney," a chorus greeted the large sheepdog, as he made the rounds to shake paws with everyone in the tasting room.

"Hi, guys," said Tim, greeting his friends. "Lucy sent me over to pick up our wine shipment. Don't mind Sidney. He's just been groomed and is very clean."

"*I'm always clean,*" thought Sidney, giving his human a withering look.

"Want to taste anything while you're here?" Peter asked.

"Sure, I'll have *one* quick tasting while I pick up our shipment," replied Tim.

"You're in luck. I'm about to pour one of our best pinots for Tom and Leslie, who are celebrating their anniversary," said Peter. Leslie gave Peter a big smile of appreciation. As the group tasted the beautifully clear red wine Peter carefully poured into their tasting glasses, they murmured with pleasure. While Tim ignored him, Sidney happily sneaked behind the bar to extract a dog treat from Peter.

"Yeah, that 2006 vintage pinot is drinking *really* well right now," replied Peter, as he bent down to pet Sidney and give him a dog treat. Looking up he added in a quiet whisper, "We keep it tucked away for our wine club members."

"I know it's heresy to say this," said Janet, "but I prefer some of *these* wines to the fancy French wines that James Chistlehurst poured for us last weekend." Peter smiled at Janet. Since her glass was empty, he poured her a second generous tasting of the most expensive wine in his tasting room.

"You guys were at James Chistlehurst's place last weekend?" Leslie asked. "Tom was able to go, but unfortunately I was off traveling *again*. How was it?"

"Lucy and I had a *great* time," replied Tim enthusiastically. "We even signed up to purchase some wine futures."

"*I wanted to join the party…but I was left at home,*" Sidney's green–blue eyes complained mournfully to Peter.

"We had a great time, too," added Janet. "However, those wine futures prices are a little daunting for our pocketbook right now. Maybe in a year or two, we might be able to do something. It certainly sounds like you could make a killing if you get in on the ground floor."

Tom nodded in agreement. "Leslie and I first met James through my longtime Stanford buddy, Phil Taylor, who's now a partner at Horace & Fitzpatrick. Since buying our second home up here in Sonoma, James frequently invites us to his very special wine tastings. Last year, we finally bought some of his recommended futures purely as an investment. However, I agree with you, Janet. When it comes to *drinking* wine, I prefer to engage in 'inventory depletion' of our wines here in Sonoma. Maybe I don't have a sophisticated palate or something, but I think, for the price, these wines are pretty unbeatable."

Peter rewarded Tom with another generous tasting of the vintage 2008 Pinot Noir.

"I couldn't agree with you more," replied Janet. "As a CFO who's always looking for ways to cut expenses, I think this wine is great at any price."

"By the way, are you and Joe members of the Keniworth Wine Club?" Leslie asked. Janet and Joe both shook their heads negatively.

"Tim and Lucy are members; we joined last year," said Tom. "They have some fun events here and the wine discounts are really good. Peter always remembers what we like. He takes the trouble to call ahead and see if we want to substitute the varietals that we're not keen on for the ones that we really like—great personal service. You guys *should* join. We could attend the events together."

Janet turned to her husband.

"Tom's right. We *should* think about joining," said Janet emphatically. "It's a heck of a lot cheaper than buying those wine futures. We learned today that Keniworth sells out its entire production from its tasting room, so we can't buy these lovely boutique wines anywhere else."

"Yes. But sweetheart, how do we take delivery of the packages when we both work late? We're just *never* home. It's easier for Tom and Leslie. They drive by this winery most weekends. I'm not certain we should sign up until we get our own place up here."

From the other side of the bar, Peter interrupted. "Don't worry, guys," he commiserated. "Here's the trick. You can always have the wine sent to your office. That way, someone can sign for the packages. As long as they're over 21, it doesn't have to be *you.* If you like our pinot, it's on sale to our wine club members today at a 30 percent discount. It's a great deal—but it's very popular and it won't last long."

Tim signed for and picked up his wine shipment from Peter. "Gotta go," he said. "Lucy and Catherine are waiting for us."

Hearing the familiar words, "Gotta go," Sidney immediately left Peter and bounded towards the door. As Tim and Sidney were leaving, a man in his 30s with thinning dark blond hair and the exhausted expression of an ER physician, walked into the tasting room. He looked around and then approached Peter.

"Is Jeremy in today?" he quietly asked Peter.

"Good to see you, Cecil," replied Peter. "Sorry; Jeremy doesn't work on weekends. He's usually here Monday to Friday working in the office, if you want to come by then."

Janet Parks-Brown approached the young man.

"Hey, Cecil, we missed you at James Chistlehurst's tasting event last weekend," Janet said enthusiastically.

"Yeah…all the usual gang from the Silicon Valley was there," added Tom. "We were sorry you couldn't make it."

"Sorry I wasn't *asked,*" scowled Cecil.

Janet and Tom looked surprised but recovered quickly. "Anyway, it's *great* to see you," said Janet trying to sound cheerful and friendly. "How are things?"

"Oh…OK…could be worse," Cecil replied grudgingly. After he saw the concern in Janet's eyes he added, "Thanks for asking," in a more pleasant voice. "And how are things with the rest of you guys?" Cecil asked as he turned to the rest of the group.

"Oh…OK…could be worse," replied Tom wearily, which provoked a smile from Cecil.

"Tom, you always were the eternal optimist," he kidded his friend. "However, I saw Tim with a big smile on his face. Life's evidently treating him well. Business must be improving for *some* people."

After a nervous pause, Peter broke the silence.

"Want to taste some pinot?" Peter asked Cecil politely.

"Now, this man is a *real* optimist," replied Cecil with a chuckle. "Peter, man…do you think I'm likely to buy your wine when I'm trying to sell my own?" asked Cecil cynically. "Anyway, I have to rush, so, if you can just give me Jeremy's phone number, I will call him this week."

"Sure," said Peter.

After Cecil left, Peter returned to his tasting room guests. "Whew, I'm glad that's over," Peter said, blowing out his cheeks. "I have a sneaky feeling that Cecil wants to speak with Jeremy about Keniworth purchasing grapes from Cecil's vineyard. Cecil's vineyard has some very fine quality grapes and he's a great winemaker. But…no tasting room license. Problem is, Jeremy likes to grow his own grapes and make his own wine. I don't think Cecil's going to have much luck with Jeremy.

"But…guys," he added after a pause, "*I'm* not going to be the one to give Cecil the bad news, if you know what I mean."

"That's why the owner gets paid the big bucks," said Tom, smiling grimly. As the tasting ended, the two couples left the winery.

"That's unfortunate for Cecil," said Tom to Janet. "I've read someplace there's *still* a surplus of wine right now due to the downturn. This is a tough time to be selling very fine quality wine. Everyone's cutting back. It's funny that Cecil didn't reply to James' invitation…he *was* invited."

"It doesn't surprise me," replied Janet. "Lots of people don't check their e-mail unless forced to at work. It's *all* social media nowadays. If Cecil's under serious pressure, perhaps the *last* thing he'd do is check e-mail."

A couple of hours later, Peter and the rest of the tasting room staff were rushed off their feet. Buses, cars and wine country limousines— many carrying corporate groups—kept them busy all afternoon. By the end of the day, a large quantity of cases had been pulled from the cellar and sold.

When Peter joined his friends for dinner in Glen Ellen, he happily reported that it had been a great day for the Keniworth Winery. Many of the visitors had joined the wine club, including Janet and Joe.

CHAPTER 10

The United States Attorney's Office, San Francisco

Several weeks later, in the United States Attorney's Office in San Francisco, Josh Kaplan and his boss, Jane Phelps, discussed a recent insider trading conviction handed down by a jury in a Manhattan courtroom.

"Wow…our Manhattan office is getting some great results on those insider trading cases," remarked Jane, "and it looks like they're continuing their major crackdown on the hedge funds. I wish them luck. Talking about insider trading, any news about that suspected insider trading ring operating out of wine country?"

Josh smiled at her. "Well, while you've have been away in southern California these past few weeks, there were some interesting developments on that front. As you know, our agents are carefully monitoring the group of wine country traders who keep making suspiciously lucky trades on Silicon Valley stocks, and any Silicon Valley insider with access to the information behind these lucky trades. Jane, you were right about something: our agents have learned that several Silicon Valley insiders own second homes in Sonoma Valley and Napa Valley. However, the FBI hasn't uncovered anything that you and I would view as the 'smoking gun.'"

Jane blinked. She knew from experience working with Josh that he was holding something back.

"Go on. I'm all ears," she said.

"Well," Josh said excitedly, "several weeks ago, our agents interviewed one wine country trader at his home. They confronted him about a particularly lucky bet that he'd made a few months ago. The suspect was caught so off guard that he *admitted* to the agents that he had made this lucrative trade after overhearing a tip."

"Wow, that *is* interesting," replied Jane.

"Yeah!" Josh agreed. "After further questioning, this suspect told our agents that he had taken to day-trading to make some extra money because his business was going through a really rough patch. He also told our agents that he didn't realize he'd broken the law." Josh paused to let the news sink in.

Jane nodded. "With all that wine flowing, wine country might be the prefect place for people to spill the beans about all kinds of inside information they're supposed to keep confidential. There's nothing like a few glasses of wine to loosen tongues, especially if they think that no one in Sonoma is interested in tech gossip. It was only a few weeks ago that you thought that yourself."

"*True!*" replied Josh. "But, during the interview, this guy…out of the blue…came up with a *very* clever theory of how an insider trading ring might be operating in wine country."

Josh paused briefly to collect his thoughts.

"Jane…what *if*, when the wine is flowing freely, an insider *pretends* to negligently blurt out inside information about their company in a manner that allows his or her co-conspirator to overhear the information and then trade on it? This would look quite innocent, wouldn't it?"

Jane raised her eyebrows and whistled. "Are you sure this suspect's name is not Professor Moriarty?"

"Yes, I know," agreed Josh. "This suspect surprised our agents by coming up with the scenario without any prompting. He's a sharp guy and quite a piece of work."

"Maybe he's just trying to win favor with our FBI agents," replied Jane. "Having the FBI arrive on the doorstep will intimidate almost everyone but the career criminal, who almost expects the FBI to knock on the door at some point in his or her career. By the way, Josh, can we take it that you still don't know any of the people in Sonoma making the trades?"

Josh grinned. "Nope. My family's hands are clean. From what I hear, none of their friends are getting rich by dabbling in technology stocks, either." He winked at Jane, as she smiled. "You know, Jane," he said in a more serious tone, "after talking with our agents, I've been thinking about all the wonderful people I knew in wine country during my childhood. If the tech guys are using wine country residents to conceal illegal trading, they're going to get these local people into some very serious trouble. Some people have no conscience!"

There was a pause, while Jane silently congratulated herself on choosing the right prosecutor for the case.

"Anyway," continued Josh, "getting back to the investigation: a few days later, our agents returned and asked this guy to review lists of traders and insiders. He readily agreed and carefully studied these lists. Guess what? Out of hundreds of names on the lists, he identified some of the *same cast of characters* from wine country and Silicon Valley that our agents are carefully monitoring. Apparently, this guy knows a couple of the suspected Silicon Valley insiders quite well.

"After picking out the names, he told our agents that, during the last six months, he knew of at least one occasion where the Silicon Valley insiders came into contact with the wine country residents making the suspicious trades. He also agreed to wear a wire and help gather evidence. Needless to say, after that interview, we took his deposition right away—before he changed his mind. The FBI already has one tape recording of the tech guys talking with this guy and one of the traders. There's a fancy wine auction coming up where this guy expects to run into more of these characters."

As Josh Kaplan ran his hand through his hair he added, "Yes, Jane. I think we finally have a breakthrough."

CHAPTER 11

The Wine Auction

A month later, several hundred attendees slowly made their way to reserved tables at the huge Sonoma Valley of the Moon Wine Auction.

This year, the theme was the famous TV program "Bonanza" with the banner on the stage proclaiming: "Let's make this a *Bonanza* for charity."

The event drew the cream of Sonoma society, and attendees included the biggest names in the Sonoma Valley wine industry. Although not as famous as some of its Napa County counterparts, the Sonoma Valley of the Moon Wine Auction attracted a generous crowd. Even during the recent recession, the auction had raised more than $500,000 for local causes in one afternoon.

Since the event was widely publicized throughout the Bay Area, it also attracted many from outside wine country who liked to mingle with the local wine community and participate, if only briefly, in the romance of the "wine country lifestyle."

Every table in the auction room was generously supplied with excellent wines and hors d'oeuvres. During the afternoon auction, many different courses of imaginative *nouvelle cuisine* would be bought to each table, and wine generously resupplied. The organizers had long ago learned that a happy auction was a generous auction.

As the crowd poured in, Charlie Bartino spotted and waved at his breakfast buddy Samantha Pond as she made her way to a table reserved in her name. Samantha's newest clients, Joe and Janet Parks-Brown, were already seated as her guests.

Samantha was happy she could finally relax. That weekend, she had shown Janet and Joe several properties for sale in Napa Valley and Sonoma Valley after the stock at Janet's company reached a price where Janet and Joe felt comfortable buying a wine country property. Some of the listings they saw had extensive wine-producing facilities. Others were "lock and leave" homes, designed to allow busy people to relax on weekends. Samantha was relieved that Janet and Joe had been realistic about what they could afford. By the end of the second day, her clients made an offer on a pretty Sonoma cottage. Their offer was accepted.

At one point that weekend, Samantha had discreetly taken them to view the wine producing estate owned by Cecil Roberts. Prior to the visit, Cecil had been anxious that it not become public knowledge that his estate was on the market. Samantha appreciated Cecil's concern about secrecy. She understood how gossip about the health and well-being of a CEO of any publically listed Silicon Valley company could instantly damage the company's stock. Samantha also understood how hard it was to keep a secret in Sonoma Valley. The prior week, Samantha had carefully coached Cecil on how to remove his personal belongings, so that his identity as the seller would remain a secret—except to his closest friends.

When Samantha finally reached her table, she greeted Joe and Janet Parks-Brown, Marc Todd, Tony Padilla, and Tom and Leslie White. All had received Samantha's help when buying their own slice of wine country heaven. She liked to show her appreciation by inviting clients to attend the annual wine auction in Sonoma as her guests. The auction was always one of the preeminent events on Sonoma Valley's annual social calendar. Before her arrival, the group discussed Janet and Joe's successful offer for the cottage. As Samantha took her seat, Marc Todd congratulated her on finding an ideal home for the couple.

"Hey, cowgirl, ready to hoedown and join me in some square dancin'?" Samantha looked up to see Peter Smith, dressed in elaborate cowboy attire, grinning down at her. Samantha threw back her head and laughed. The two couples enthusiastically greeted their friend from the Keniworth tasting room.

"Guys, do you know how Texans describe someone who's all talk and no cash?" Peter asked. "*Big* hat—*no* cattle. I'm afraid that sort of describes all of us from Keniworth Winery. All cowboys...*no* cattle. Not even one horse in the whole crowd. Just a bunch of frou-frou dogs," he added with a grin. The group laughed, and Peter continued. "But we'll make up for it with our stirring rendition of 'Home on the Range.' We've even managed to rig up a couple of deer and antelope costumes for Jeremy's kids. Samantha, hon, wait'll you see Juan in his cowboy outfit. He looks *real* cute."

James Chistlehurst was the last guest to arrive at Samantha's table. After mingling with other friends and clients at other tables, he threw his normally haughty British reserve to the wind and cheerfully greeted everyone as if they were lifelong friends. Although James was notoriously condescending about Sonoma wines in his blog, he deigned to honor this wine country event with his VIP presence so he could mingle with his wine futures clients.

With several people looking on curiously as he sat down, James carefully surveyed the bottles on the table. After taking his time to look for something interesting, he finally selected a Sonoma Valley Cinsault. He poured some into a tasting glass from his own tasting room and examined the color. He smelled and finally tasted the wine. His surprise was evident. Looking up at the other guests, he remarked, "*Pas mal!* In fact, not bad at all."

Cecil Roberts came over to hug Samantha and greet her guests. Everyone seemed in a good mood that afternoon. After complimenting Peter on his cowboy outfit, Cecil approached James, putting his hand on his shoulder to get his attention. Cecil struggled make his voice heard over the din in the auction room as a loudspeaker urged the guests to take their seats.

"James, man, how come you haven't returned my calls?" Cecil yelled.

James politely put down his wine glass and rose to greet Cecil. After he shook Cecil's hand, James signaled to Cecil that they should go outside so they could hear each other. After they left the auction room, James looked around to make sure their conversation wasn't overheard.

"My apologies, my dear friend," James added with a flourish. "I have been traveling overseas far too much lately. How *stupid* of my personal assistant not to give me your messages."

"I called because a while back, you suggested that I talk to you about your business selling my wine as wine futures. Are you still interested?"

James stared at Cecil blankly for a few moments. "Ah…my friend, *now* I remember receiving your message," he said. "I wanted to wait until I returned to the Bay Area before calling you back." He looked down at the path they were walking. "Cecil, my pal," he said, "we'd love to eventually handle your wine. Unfortunately, we are not taking on any new vineyard clients at the moment due to the downturn. In a few months, I will be visiting Hong Kong, Singapore and China. That might be an *excellent* time for me to see if I can find some buyers for your wine futures."

"What about those Silicon Valley guys who are supposedly friends of mine sitting at your table. From what I hear, they're acting like they're *loaded*," said Cecil. "Didn't you invite them over to your place back in March?"

James became annoyed. Cecil was pressuring him, almost pumping him for information. James swiftly decided that his best course of action was to ignore Cecil's remark.

"Let's not spoil a lovely afternoon with business talk," said James jovially with a smile that concealed his disdain. "Shall we return to our friends?"

Cecil walked away dolefully before they reached the auction room. James returned to Samantha's table and sat down. He rolled his eyes at the rest of Samantha's guests.

"Dear me! How inappropriate. This is not the time to discuss business. Doesn't Cecil understand that this event is about *giving*?"

CHAPTER 12

Glamour in Sonoma

Bob Goodwin was also in a good mood that afternoon. Bob and his catering staff had worked tirelessly to provide wine and appetizers to auction patrons as they arrived on the terrace outside the auction room. After the crowd began to move inside, Bob knew that the auction food and wine would, blessedly, not be his concern. As the guest of a celebrity from the fashion industry, Bob could sit back and enjoy the fine wine and food donated by many of the Sonoma Valley wineries and restaurants.

"Bob, darling!" His host, Amanda Jones, greeted him with her rich, husky British voice as he arrived at the table. "Do you know my friends George and Jackie DeRosa from San Francisco? They're staying with me as my guests for the weekend."

Bob looked appreciatively at the beautiful older woman who had invited him to join her table. Despite living in the laid-back world of Sonoma wine country, Amanda Jones unabashedly maintained the glamour of her past as one of Britain's top supermodels. In contrast to the casually dressed locals and Silicon Valley visitors, Amanda wore a beaded pearl and silver gown, which sparkled and reflected light every time she moved a well-toned muscle. Her long, wavy silver-blond hair was swept high above her head, allowing a few carefully chosen tresses to cascade down her elegant bare back and shoulders.

Bob acknowledged George DeRosa, one of San Francisco's famous class action trial lawyers and a name regularly boldfaced in San Francisco society columns. When he stood up to shake Bob's hand, George towered over the small group gathered at Amanda's table.

"Amanda, honey, you've forgotten that Bob always travels to our home in Pacific Heights to help us with all our political fundraisers," said George in a deep, sonorous voice as he stroked his seaman's beard. "We wouldn't make a move without him. Isn't that right, Jackie?" George's petite wife, Jackie, nodded in agreement. After many years of happily married life, she left most of the talking to her loquacious husband.

Bob shook hands with Amanda's other guests, including Amanda's friend, Lady Roberta Romakoff, a tall slender brunette, who had stunned the wine country crowd by wearing an enormous purple fascinator hat rarely seen beyond the presence of British royalty. Her husband, Dmitri Romakoff, a Russian oligarch, had decided on a whim to bring their mega yacht to the Bay Area after hearing that San Francisco would be hosting the America's Cup. Although Lady Roberta was originally from Newport, Rhode Island, she had acquired an English title and accent from her fleeting marriage to her first husband, an English lord. Two husbands later, Lady Roberta insisted on being addressed as Lady Roberta against the British etiquette rule that only those born into the aristocracy use their title with their first name. Blithely ignoring her British critics, she had endeared herself to Amanda by confiding, "frankly, *darling*, I don't give a horse's arse what they think."

Also seated at the table was Amanda's niece, Ann Schiller, a serious looking, slim young lawyer with long, ash blond hair.

"Bob, did you know that darling George was one the earliest investors in my winery—bless him!" Amanda gushed, flashing her large blue eyes at the group.

George laughed. " Yep, I was one of your investors, along with your more famous friends from the glamorous world of fashion, movies, and rock and roll."

Amanda partially closed her blue eyes and continued in a stage whisper: "Listen, my darlings…when a girl gets too old for modeling, she has to reinvent herself. After I gave it up, I moved to Sonoma and bought an ancient winery that had been neglected for donkeys' years. Honestly, I didn't have a bloody clue what I let myself in for. I would have been totally lost without my darling Charlie Bartino and his family's help. Charlie went out of his way to introduce me to a top-notch, brilliant winemaker. In the early days, Charlie even sent in some of his crew to help tend my vines. Such a sweetheart!"

The group smiled and waved at Charlie Bartino, who was making his way through the crowd to join his table at the other end of the room. At his wife's insistence, Charlie had put on a shirt and tie, light brown suede jacket, and new cowboy boots. Charlie waved back at the group.

"I *will* admit," said Amanda, "that, if placed under cross examination by our esteemed counselor, when I decided to buy the winery, many of my former flames from the entertainment industry *did* invest with me… and boy, it really helped! When articles about the winery began appearing in the business press, journalists expressed absolute amazement that my winery turned out to be a half-decent investment. Of course, they all think models are bubbleheads." Everyone laughed as George added, "More fool *him or her.*"

"Anyway," Amanda continued, "…the key to my winery's success was that rock stars and movie stars love their wine, just like everyone else. Wine tasters adore the idea of possibly rubbing shoulders with a few celebrities. It's the perfect combo." Looking around, Amanda then added in a hushed, conspiratorial voice: "Of course, darlings, the trick is to combine celebrities and their 'public' in a manner that does not unduly burden or embarrass anyone."

"Amanda, you are incorrigible!" boomed George. "Of all the people in the business world, you supermodels must be among the most savvy. One cannot open a magazine without seeing one of you starting yet another lucrative sideline."

"But, George," said Ann Schiller, calmly and quietly," I bet most fashion models don't stay up all night fretting about the grape harvest. I'm sure most don't get their hands dirty trimming vines in the vineyards, like Aunt Amanda. Since staying with her in Sonoma, I have been truly amazed at her hands-on dedication to winemaking."

Ann put her arm around her aunt and continued. "I certainly worked hard at the U.S. Attorney's Office and later at Hampton & Elliot. But I never realized how hard it is to grow grapes and make wine until I came to stay here in Sonoma. From a distance, it all looks so easy and glamorous. Up close, it's anything but…"

Everyone looked at Ann, noting that she had the same facial structure and body build as Amanda. Ann's formal black dress and quiet, button-down demeanor, however, were stark contrasts to Amanda's celebrity glamour.

"Oh, Ann, you are such a darling," replied Amanda. "Just give up the law completely and come into the wine business with me."

The group smiled sadly at Ann. Everyone knew that she was staying with her aunt in Sonoma after the venerable San Francisco corporate firm, Hampton & Elliot, had collapsed a few weeks earlier. Although corporate partners like Phil Taylor were quickly recruited to join other law firms, Ann Schiller, along with dozens of other associates, had suddenly found themselves unemployed during the worst recession in 50 years.

During her stay with her aunt in Sonoma, Ann was surprised to discover that she missed her former life fighting cases in federal court. *"In this idyllic part of the world, it all seems so far away,"* she thought nostalgically. *"I feel like an alien visiting from a different planet."*

As the auction patrons took their seats, Charlie Bartino reached his table in another corner of the room. He was looking forward to entertaining his family and senior employees, all of whom had worked long, hard hours during the prior fall and winter months. Charlie also used the wine auction as an opportunity to mingle with his vintner customers and catch up on wine industry gossip.

As the bidding began, Charlie watched familiar hands raise their paddles as each auction item was called. Many were personal friends and long-time customers.

Charlie also focused on the visitors. As he looked around the room, he saw some new faces.

Over the next five hours, Charlie's wife, Diana, an enthusiastic Sonoma Valley volunteer, collected the names of successful bidders. Some of them came from Charlie and Diana's closest friends; others from deep-pocketed strangers. All had a great time bidding on the excellent wine and event packages donated by Sonoma Valley vintners to support local nonprofits.

As his wife focused on the successful bidders, Charlie paid special attention to those who dropped out from the final bidding. He mentally compared their bids with bids made during prior years. He also separated in his mind those who were bidding seriously from those who were only making a big pretense at bidding. Like all wine growers, Charlie had a keen memory for people and numbers.

Charlie was nobody's fool.

CHAPTER 13

The Breakfast Group Compares Notes

Two days later, as they ate breakfast at VineSprings, Bob Goodwin, Samantha Pond, Charlie Bartino, Peter Smith and Juan Rodriguez compared notes about the weekend's festivities, culminating in the wine auction.

"Guys, all of us at the winery were rushed off our feet *all weekend*. I guess the Great Recession has must be over for some people," complained Peter. "Even when the wine auction was in full swing, my colleagues back at the winery reported steady traffic. They actually had to throw people out when it was time to close up shop."

Bob looked skeptically at Peter. "Don't complain, my friend. Just remember what Samantha told us about working in Silicon Valley. In a recession, the only status symbol that counts is a *job*. Nothing else matters."

"Yeah…and during the boom times, the only status symbol that counts is *a good night's sleep*. Nothing else matters," added Samantha with a smile.

"OK, OK, I'll stop whining. To be honest, things weren't quite *that* bad," admitted Peter grudgingly. "I guess that's why most of us live here. Did everyone have a good time at the auction? Our Wild West skit seemed to go down well."

"We all had a ball," agreed Samantha. "Peter, you and your Keniworth guys were *amazing*. I especially loved seeing the kids dancing around the stage as deer and antelope. We all laughed *hysterically*. One of the funniest performances all afternoon. Peter and Juan, you *both* looked adorable in cowboy gear. You should wear western style clothing more often."

As Juan and Peter smiled at the compliment, Samantha turned her large brown eyes towards Bob.

"Bob, I forgot to tell you…everyone thought your delicious nibbles at the pre-auction reception were also *amazing*."

"Everyone seemed in good spirits," replied Bob with satisfaction. "Everyone sitting at our table also seemed to enjoy themselves."

"Oh…and we all saw you fraternizing with our local glitterati," said Peter mockingly. "The lovely Amanda Jones is holding up well against the forces of gravity. Looks like *she's* had some expensive work done recently," he said with a smirk.

"Don't be mean about my girlfriend," complained Samantha.

"Oh, *hon*…I was just joking," laughed Peter. "Amanda's also a pal of mine. I'm always over at her place volunteering when she has fundraisers. They're a kick in the pants."

Recovering her good humor, Samantha smiled at Peter. Suddenly remembering the fundraising at the auction, she leaned over to speak to Charlie. "I was entertaining clients all afternoon, so I wasn't able to compare this year's bidding with prior years. The auction room was jammed. We could hardly *move* to visit the restrooms, so I guess they must have made some money this year. What was the final result? Did people pay more or less for this year's auction items?"

"*Hey*—the bidding sure was *fierce*," he replied. "According to Diana, it was a sellout crowd, so we're also hoping that this year's auction made more money than last year. I noticed plenty of new folks at this year's event. My friends think that we may have attracted some of the big money from the recent social media IPOs. I also tracked some large bidders who attended during the dot-com boom, but who didn't attend during the worst of the recession. Sadly, I noticed that some of the old regulars weren't there. Either that, or they weren't bidding like they used to."

Bob turned his attention to Samantha.

"Changing the subject just a little, any new big fish biting for wine country real estate?" Samantha smiled and shook her head.

"Bob, you know I can't discuss my clients' specific needs, even to help our investment club. However, we *are* expecting some very large transactions over the next few months, as the latest IPO money makes its way over the Golden Gate Bridge, up 101, and into the neighborhood. It's only a matter of time."

"Yeah!" said Juan, speaking for the first time, "and, once that happens, my family will be among the first to feel it. The phone will start ringing like crazy with people wanting new landscaping and pools. Wow, we'll be *so* happy. Things have been tough since the downturn. I've had to put off attending school full-time. With the money I've saved over the past few months, I'm looking forward to going back, once my folks have enough business to hire more help. Yep," he said after a pause, "when things start ticking again, my folks will be among the first to feel it."

CHAPTER 14

The United States Attorney's Office, San Francisco

Josh Kaplan was also feeling optimistic as he updated his boss, Jane, with the latest developments regarding the insider trading investigation in Napa and Sonoma.

"You'll recall that the FBI managed to get a suspect to wear a wire to monitor the suspected Silicon Valley insiders. Well, the good news is we've obtained some impressive evidence that these Silicon Valley insiders come into regular contact with the wine country traders making those fabulously lucky trades."

"Ah ha," remarked Jane.

"We've also corroborated these regular contacts from other witnesses. These other witnesses are all squeaky clean—meaning that none of them are involved in any trading activity picked up by FINRA and the SEC.

"What's really amazing," he said excitedly, "is that at least one Silicon Valley insider may have deliberately 'withheld information'—in other words he flat out *lied* about knowing *any* of the wine country traders. However we have evidence from several sources that the insider knows at least two wine country traders—one quite well. The wine country traders have made huge profits from trading the shares of this guy's company for the last three quarters, just after the official quarter ending. Jane, that's *three quarters in a row.*"

"Do we have any wire or other evidence that these Silicon Valley insiders *intentionally* transmitted inside information about their tech companies to the Sonoma people executing the stock trades?"

Josh shook his head negatively.

"It's only circumstantial at this point. However, our FBI agents think that with the insider trading arrests and convictions in New York grabbing national headlines, it's unlikely that these smart Silicon Valley guys will speak too loudly in front of anyone who's not part of the conspiracy… including our guy who's been wearing the wire. They're also probably too smart to transmit damaging information over their cell phones or the Internet."

"So…are you planning to have the original wise-ass—who came up with the theory that Silicon Valley guys are deliberately dropping tips to other wine country traders—testify before the Grand Jury?" Jane asked.

"Yes, but our agents remain a little cautious about him. He seems overly enthusiastic about helping us nail the Silicon Valley insiders. It's almost as if he bears a grudge against them. From the get-go, he's been almost *too* eager to help."

"Ah, that's *not* good," said Jane. "Jurors at trial can smell a witness with a grudge miles away. This undermines witness credibility in the eyes of the jury at trial, even if, at the Grand Jury stage, everyone believes the witness. Trouble is, it's almost impossible to find a witness that doesn't have some type of agenda, even if it's just saving his own skin."

"*Agreed*," replied Josh. "Since we're not certain about this guy's agenda, we plan to move slowly before taking action against the insiders. None of us want a case involving some high profile Silicon Valley executives blowing up in our faces."

"True enough!" replied Jane.

"We plan to indict the traders," said Josh, "but, in the indictment, refer to the Silicon Valley guys anonymously as the source of the information. The indictment will allege that the information was *misappropriated* from these insiders. Hopefully when one or more of the traders comes clean about what's been going on, we'll have enough evidence to proceed against the Silicon Valley insiders." Josh paused long enough to allow Jane to absorb this approach.

"Jane, there's *another* problem. Our agents are concerned that word about the investigation might leak out in the near future," he said cautiously. "Although everyone's been cautioned to keep the FBI investigation confidential, our agents believe that it's only a matter of time before someone goofs up and unwittingly lets something slip.

"For this reason, we plan to seek indictments from the Grand Jury against the Sonoma traders as soon as possible, so we catch them by surprise. This will decrease the likelihood of a fatal leak, and increase the likelihood one of them will roll and agree to testify in return for a more lenient sentence.

"Frankly, I share our agents' concern," he said with exasperation in his voice. "In Sonoma, nothing remains a secret for long."

CHAPTER 15

The Sonoma Plaza

A few weeks later, a motorcycle made its way up the wide, straight, four-lane road known as Broadway, leading into the City of Sonoma.

The motorcyclist knew he was close to the Plaza once the stone facade of Sonoma's historic City Hall came into view. As the four-way intersection at Broadway and Napa streets slowed the traffic, he saw the people of Sonoma milling around the fresh fruit, vegetable, and flower stands erected around the lawn in front of City Hall. Many were picnicking in the balmy evening sunshine.

Sonoma's Tuesday night farmers market was in full swing.

The motorcyclist parked in front of one of the town's liveliest Sonoma Plaza bars, a popular destination for Bay Area motorcyclists. As he dismounted and took off his helmet, two female patrons sitting on the bench outside the bar observed a handsome freckled face with blue eyes and a full head of red hair emerge from underneath the helmet.

To the disappointment of these female patrons, the motorcyclist did not walk into the bar. Instead he followed the crowds into the Plaza. After he spotted a tall, slim blond woman inspecting jars of honey in one of the stalls, he tapped her on the shoulder.

"Ann! I was hoping to see you here."

Ann Schiller turned around and immediately hugged him. "Jack! It's great to see you. What are you doing in Sonoma? Hunting for fresh flowers, fruit and vegetables 45 miles north of San Francisco?"

Jack Murphy looked down at his motorcycle helmet. "Well, no, actually." One of my personal injury cases just settled. Thought I'd drive north out of the fog and look for some warmer weather.

As he looked up at her, he smiled and added sheepishly, "To be honest, I was also hoping to see you. I understand everybody in Sonoma goes to this Tuesday farmers market, so I figured there might be a chance I'd see you this evening."

Later, as they sipped a cool Sauvignon Blanc in the back patio of the Orchard Café, Ann and Jack looked at each other shyly, as only former lovers can.

Ann spoke first. "Jack, your timing is brilliant. I adore this area, especially staying with my aunt in her vineyard. It's been a *wonderful* break. But now I'm homesick for the City. God help me! I even miss litigation." They both laughed. "But tell me, Jack, what have you been up to? Fighting the good fight against large, nefarious corporations and their evil lawyers on behalf of your 'victim' clients?"

He grinned. "Every second of the day, except that I would hate to fight with this particular formerly evil litigator, now that she's plying me with such great wine!"

Ann laughed and then added pensively, "It looks like my days defending large corporations may be over. You know, I really loved those guys at Hampton & Elliot. It's not their fault things fell apart. It's an extremely tight market for associates since the downturn. Too many of us looking for too few jobs."

Jack, who had been hesitant to raise the subject, used this as an invitation. "What exactly happened, Ann? Hampton & Elliot was a *huge* firm. One of the largest and most famous in the City. I was really surprised when it crashed and went out of business. I heard rumors, but nothing very clear."

Ann paused and looked down. "Frankly, it was quite a shock for all of us, Jack. The firm was more than 80 years old!" After a sip of wine, Ann continued. "Hampton & Elliot's corporate practice took a nosedive after the 2008 financial crisis kicked in. There wasn't enough litigation to keep many of us busy. Several partners—personal friends—have since told me that that the firm had a large revolving line of credit with its bank. Finally, after a few key partners left, the bank got spooked and refused to extend it. One Friday afternoon, the firm simply couldn't make payroll and we were all suddenly laid off. Many of the partners have joined other firms but many associates, like yours truly, found themselves suddenly unemployed."

Jack sighed. "I am so sorry to hear that."

Ann laughed and leaned over and gave Jack a kiss. "Jack, I'm sorry that I didn't respond to your calls and e-mails. I just had to get away and think for a while. Clear my head. I didn't want to be a burden to my friends, even one that I love as much as you."

Jack smiled. This was working out just as he had hoped. Ann continued. "I haven't been totally idle. To keep up my MCLE credits, I took a course on wine law offered by a firm in Santa Rosa. It focused on many of the complex wine licensing regulations that really bug the industry up here. I've used the course to help my aunt and her friends understand how and why the federal government will make life extremely difficult for wine sellers if they don't pay attention to these regulations. While I've been up here, I've learned that the legal restrictions for making and selling wine to the public can be daunting."

Jack, although not terribly interested in these regulations after a long drive from the City, displayed his famous boyish charm. "Tell me more."

"Well, for one thing, I learned that after alcohol was legalized in the 1930s the wine laws and regulations were designed to keep the Mob away from the wine business. These laws make a lot of sense when you understand the history. But now, in the twenty-first century, the tough restrictions drive everyone up here *crazy*." Ann laughed. "I've been trying to explain to my aunt and others why the government, in its infinite wisdom, makes it difficult if not impossible to do something simple, like opening a public tasting room."

She took another sip of wine and added, "By the way, Jack, whenever you see signs stating 'By Appointment Only,' it sounds exclusive and forbidding. It's not. It probably means they haven't got a tasting room license…yet. Most of the wineries up here love visits from people who call ahead to make an appointment. They often spoil them. It's one of the best deals in wine country."

Jack smiled. "I'll remember that."

Ann looked down at her glass. "My aunt has been wonderful. She's given me the space to think about my next move without feeling pressured. I moved out of my flat in the City and moved my stuff into storage. I've been using one of her studios. The last several months in Sonoma have been fabulous. I have been *spoiled*."

"Well, after what you've been through, it's well deserved. I'd like to meet your aunt. She sounds great."

Ann looked up. "Speak of the devil…here she is now."

Amanda arrived at their small table burdened with sunflowers and other farmers market produce. She smiled at the handsome, red-haired biker.

"How do you do, young man?"

"Aunt Amanda, this is Jack Murphy, a lawyer friend of mine from the City. Would you like some help?"

"No, darling, except I need to pick your legal brains."

"What's up?"

"Several people in Sonoma have just been arrested this afternoon and they're *all* good friends of mine. According to the press reports, they have one thing in common: they know someone who works in Silicon Valley and owns a second home in wine country."

Ann stared at her aunt. "You have *got* to be kidding! Last time I looked, it wasn't illegal to own a second home up here or know someone who does. What's going on?"

Amanda looked at Ann and Jack in turn. "You're not going to believe this but the charges have something to do with…*insider trading?*" After glancing around the outside patio area, Amanda continued in a hushed voice. "We can't talk about it here. This town is such a rumor mill. Can you both come to the winery now? My priest and good friend, Father Graham and I have someone for you to meet. Afterwards, I'll make dinner for everyone—my spaghetti and meatballs with a fresh heirloom tomato salad. I can use all these goodies I just picked up."

As Ann walked Jack to his motorbike, she said quietly: "I don't have anywhere to hang my shingle out right now. I can only listen to what Father Graham has to say. Would your office handle an insider trading case?"

"Ann, you know our firm handles mostly civil contingency fee cases. However, a couple of us have defended criminal cases in the past. If we can't assist, we'll probably know someone who can. Besides, after a long drive, I could kill for some spaghetti and meatballs!"

As they all entered Amanda's home, Ann and Jack saw a priest and a young man rise from their seats. The priest was the first to speak.

"Ann, Juan Rodriguez and his family are my parishioners. Juan also tends your aunt's garden. Today, Juan came to me seeking advice. However, once I heard his story, I knew that he should consult a lawyer right away."

Ann invited Juan and Father Graham into a separate room and closed the door. Father Graham continued.

"Juan doesn't think he's done anything wrong but he's desperately worried. He's heard that four of his friends who meet regularly at the VineSprings Grille have just been arrested. He's scared to death that, at any moment, he, too, might be arrested and charged with illegal insider trading."

CHAPTER 16

One Main Street Bar and Grill, San Francisco

At lunch in San Francisco, George DeRosa leaned on one of the elegant arms of a restaurant chair and focused his famous courtroom gaze on his longtime friend and high school classmate, Phil Taylor.

"*Thank God* for the young people of today," George exclaimed, leaning back in his chair to allow his dish of salmon and asparagus risotto to be served around his huge frame. Phil Taylor sighed inwardly. He knew he was in for a lengthy George-style monologue.

"Their protests here and abroad using Twitter show a return to the Free Speech Movement days, when young people fought for social justice. They've shown how this new social media can be used for something other than the usual narcissistic 'look at me' nonsense."

"*George is such a ham,*" Phil thought with a smile, as he listened patiently. "*Even at lunch, George is mentally on his feet addressing an imaginary jury. He never leaves the courtroom.*"

Although George lived in a Pacific Heights mansion twice the size of his own home in Menlo Park, Phil knew how George loved to talk as if he was still a radical student attending UC Berkeley School of Law. Phil knew better than to argue with his excitable, loquacious friend at lunch. After attending Stanford Law School and pursuing a corporate law practice in Palo Alto, Phil had learned to be the consummate diplomat who always thought twice before saying nothing.

After graciously allowing George to hold forth, Phil thought it was time to raise the subject uppermost on his mind, and the reason why he'd invited George to join him for lunch that day.

"Speaking of free speech, am I now allowed to contact Ann Schiller? Is Ann working yet? If not, I'd like to offer to help her out, if I can. Now that the economy's improved, I've managed to help some of the other laid off associates from Hampton & Elliot."

"*Ah!*" replied George. "Well…as we both know, she's staying with her aunt, Amanda Jones. Amanda used to be a flame of mine during one of my many single phases before I met Jackie. After we stopped dating, Amanda and I kept in touch as friends. We talk constantly about grapes because my family's in the grape growing business. As you may know, I am also one of her investors—along with most of Amanda's former pop star boyfriends."

"How does Jackie like that?"

"Jackie *adores* her. Amanda has always been a big favorite with all my wives. Amanda often comes across as a hippy dippy girl…whenever that's in fashion. Don't be fooled! She is very smart about money and relationships."

George took another bite of his salmon and asparagus risotto and continued. "Whenever one of Amanda's many romances ends, she always makes a point of remaining the best of friends with former flames, and later she befriends their spouses. That's what happened with Jackie and me. Jackie even invited Amanda to our wedding.

"Now that her winery is famous, Amanda invites all her former boyfriends to perform there. They can still bash out the old rock and roll songs, even though some of the musicians are getting rather long in the tooth!"

"Aren't we all?" Phil finally interjected. "But, George, you haven't answered my question."

"I'm getting to it!" George snapped.

"As I told you back in April, Amanda wants Ann to take time out from practicing law to 'recharge her batteries,' as the British say." George leaned over and spoke in a stage whisper that could clearly be heard by patrons sitting at nearby tables. "Last year, Ann was devastated when your old firm went under. As we all know, she gave up a promising career with the Feds to join you guys, only to find herself another casualty of the financial crisis. After your old firm collapsed, she was out of a job. Understandably, Amanda, as her closest relation here, persuaded Ann to take a serious breather before starting the interview process all over again."

George leaned back and continued in a quieter voice. "Amanda may have wisely surmised that Ann's former relationship with one of the young stars of our San Francisco Trial Lawyers Association, Jack Murphy, might not sit well with the large corporate law firms in *this* town—for example, your current firm, Horace & Fitzpatrick?"

Phil nodded affirmatively. "Well, Amanda is one sharp cookie. She may be right." He paused and looked a little shamefaced. "Just between us, George, even though we were all delighted when Ann joined us from the U.S. Attorney's Office in San Francisco, some of my Hampton & Elliot litigation partners were seriously spooked when her boyfriend, Jack Murphy, won a $100 million verdict against one of our clients. You have to understand, George, at that time, Jack Murphy and his pals seemed to be on the other side of every lawsuit that Hampton & Elliot's litigation department was defending."

As Phil paused to drink a sip of water, George chuckled. "Good for Jack!"

Phil continued. "I'm sorry to say that I suspect some of my former litigation partners gave Ann a hard time about her romance with Jack. A couple of them may have bypassed her when it came to new case assignments and such. Since I was the firm's managing partner, they trooped into my office to complain about Ann's relationship with Jack. However, I refused to say anything to her. I always trusted the cool, calm, and collected Ann Schiller not to do anything stupidly indiscreet or unprofessional."

George smiled at his friend. "Phil, I know you're a decent guy, even if you *do* work on the wrong side of the bar. Thanks for sticking up for Amanda's niece. You were absolutely right to trust Ann professionally. However, just between us, I have always found Ann to be far too serious. Amanda's a riot. Loads of fun. Sometimes it's hard to believe that Ann is Amanda's niece. There again, a lot of young lawyers are too serious these days. In my day, we could always have a damn good laugh with opposing counsel after leaving the courthouse, especially if the judge was in a bad mood and had torn strips from both our hides. These days, the young lawyers take themselves so seriously that they can barely look at each other after a hearing or a deposition. They take whatever happens so *personally.* Whenever I walk out of a deposition or court hearing these days, I want to give these younger lawyers the following advice: 'Just take your head out of your ass, and *never* make the mistake of falling in love with your client or your client's case!'"

Phil smiled. "Well, you will be pleased to know, George, that we corporate lawyers *never* have that problem. We may have our heads up our asses on occasion, but we never fall in love with our clients. We know far too much about them."

Both men smiled. George added seriously, "I'm sure it must have been really rough for you when your former firm went down."

Phil looked at his plate and continued. "George, Hampton & Elliot going out of business was very sad for a lot of people. We all loved the firm. Paying off the firm's debts was costly for the partners. I nearly had to sell all my valuable Chateau Lafite wine futures."

"Oh, no! Not your Chateau Lafite wine futures! The very thought makes me want to weep." Phil noticed gratefully that, to his surprise, George wasn't kidding. Instead, George looked very compassionate.

"Yeah, I *know*," replied Phil. "Fortunately, our wine guru, James Chistlehurst, talked me out of it. A few days after I approached James about selling my most valuable futures, a big merger deal came in, which saved the day."

"Well—as large corporate law firms go—I have to say that Hampton & Elliot was probably one of the more decent ones—if that's saying anything!" said George. "Hold that thought; my phone's ringing. Only a couple of people have this number, so it's important."

George leaned over to answer the phone. "Hi there!" He paused and looked at Phil. "Well, well, *well*! Ann, what a coincidence. I'm having lunch with Phil Taylor, one of your former colleagues," he winked at Phil. As he continued to listen to Ann Schiller, George stopped smiling and looked down at the table. His expression became unusually grave. George continued to listen several more seconds before he replied. "Counselor, I'm in a public restaurant right now. Can I call you back from my office? OK…15 minutes."

After ending the call, George looked at Phil. "That was Ann. Jackie gave her my phone number. Ann needs to speak with us separately—but urgently."

Both lawyers raised their eyebrows.

CHAPTER 17

George DeRosa's Office, San Francisco

"Damn your aunt, Ann!" George thundered. "We both know that she won't give me a moment's peace if I don't defend our caterer friend, Bob Goodwin."

Ann did not reply. Instead, she waited patiently for George to calm down. A day after calling George and Phil about the arrests in Sonoma, she had traveled to San Francisco to meet with them in person.

After a few moments, George continued in a milder tone.

"Problem number one: it's been a while since I handled a criminal case in federal court. There's not enough money in that line of work for us starving plaintiffs' lawyers," he said, giving Ann a wink.

"George, I can bring you up to speed with the Federal Rules of Criminal Procedure law and the law of insider trading," Ann said in a soft, but firm voice. "Aunt Amanda asked me to assemble a team of top-notch trial attorneys to stand up for these little guys in Sonoma so they get a fair shake," she added while George quietly stroked his beard. "You know she thinks highly of you. She wants *you* on the team."

"Honestly, my friend, this also sounds like a *very* complicated insider trading case to me," George said, leaning back in his chair and looking out the window of his red brick Jackson Square office at other Gold Rush era buildings recently renovated by wealth from the latest technology boom.

"Another problem," George said as he turned to face Ann, "I know for a fact that Bob really fancies himself as some clever-ass stock picker. It's not difficult to imagine Bob trying to beat the markets with some trading gimmick that may be illegal."

"According to my aunt's gardener, Juan Rodriguez, the Feds have got it all wrong!" Ann said, ignoring George's groans. "Although Juan's investment group met regularly—for breakfast—at a place called the VineSprings Grill, the group *wasn't* trading on *inside* information, as the

Feds allege in the indictment."

"Are you *sure*?" George asked skeptically. "How do we know? I've known clients to lie through their teeth when confronted by the Feds in full battle gear. Besides, if Juan's the charming gardener I met at your aunt's home one time, he's very young. He probably doesn't have a clue on what would be considered illegal inside information, or whether they *were* trading on inside information."

"True!" Ann continued patiently. "We'll all eventually find out whether Bob, Juan, and the others are lying…or are merely clueless …or whether the Feds are jumping to the wrong conclusion."

After a long pause, she added thoughtfully, "My hunch is that the Feds suspect Juan and his friends were in cahoots with the insiders anonymously mentioned in the indictment—but they don't have enough to charge everyone. By charging the stock traders first, the Feds expect *someone* will roll and help them nail everyone else. It's their standard MO."

"It's their standard MO because it *works*," George replied gloomily.

Ann persisted. "If Juan and his friends were in cahoots with the insiders, you'd expect some of the profits to go back to the insiders. However, Juan says that the only money that changed hands between the Silicon Valley guys and the Sonoma defendants was for legitimate goods and services, such as landscaping, catering, and wine shipments."

George looked hard at Ann.

"Is that *enough*?" he asked with one eyebrow raised. "Can we win a dismissal if the bank account deposits, etc., are clean?"

"Ah…so you *do* know something about this area of the law, George."

George smiled smugly. "I may be a bit long in the tooth but I can still hit the law books on occasion. After your call yesterday afternoon, I was sufficiently intrigued to research the latest developments."

"I've also spent time in the law library researching the law of insider trading," said Ann. "We didn't have any insider trading cases when I was working at the U.S. Attorney's Office here. Insider trading cases are normally handled by the U.S. Attorney's Office in Manhattan. I was surprised to learn that our local U.S. Attorney's Office is handling this case. I can only guess they've decided to bring the case here in the

Northern District because all of the defendants are here, or they want to send a message that insider trading is *not* just a Wall Street crime.

"Anyway, I digress," said Ann after a pause. "To answer your question, for an insider trading rap to stick, money does *not* necessarily have to change hands. In a case like *this*—where the defendants allegedly *stole* the information from the insiders—the Feds can still prosecute if the traders were *under a legal duty of trust and confidence* with the source of the information."

"Ann, you got me and the jury snoring already. This doesn't sounds like my type of case at all."

She ignored George's protests. "George, the defense will have to convince the jury that *no one stole inside information from anyone.*"

"I don't like the fuzziness of it," George grumbled. "From my admittedly brief research, the law of insider trading looks like a *Frankenstein monster.* It's a labyrinth of case law stitched together with various SEC rules and regs, all derived from section 10(b) of the 1934 Securities and Exchange Act. The appellate courts have to keep weighing in on who's breaking the law—and who isn't—because there's no clear statutory guidance on what constitutes illegal insider trading. It's an unnatural beast."

Ann nodded enthusiastically. "George, you're absolutely right. The law on insider trading is extremely complicated. The facts in this case are also highly unusual. Anyone who defends these Sonoma defendants will be in for a big fight. *That's* the challenge."

George leaned forward. "Have you found any helpful—or even unhelpful—case law that applies to *this* case?"

"There's little case law on point regarding the type of situation I think we have here," Ann replied. "Most of the reported cases involve situations where employees, lawyers or other professionals stole and then illegally traded on the information before the information was made public."

"Oh, *great!* I just love a Supremes fight," said George sarcastically. "Ten years from now, we'll finally get the answer on how the law should be applied in *this* case. Anyway, Ann, why don't you contact the bigwig, white collar defense lawyers who specialize in this type of crime? After your work for the DOJ, you must know all their names by heart."

"I made a few calls to the usual suspects," Ann replied. "Many are already representing the alleged insiders, Tim Newman, Tom White and others who work in Silicon Valley *and* have second homes in wine country. Although none have been indicted, they have been anonymously fingered in the indictment as the *source* of the information. According to the gossip swirling around Sonoma, the Silicon Valley guys have been placed on paid leave. Their companies probably don't want anyone sticking around who's suspected of spilling inside information, however innocently."

George roared with exasperation. "Oh…I get it! The White Collar Federal Defense Bar gets to represent the Silicon Valley mega millionaires who can afford armies of lawyers. We get to defend your aunt's mow-and-blow guy who hasn't a flowerpot to piss in, and my caterer, who's going to have to sell a load of appetizers the size of Mount Tamalpais to pay my fees. Great!"

After a pause, George added, "By the way, is Boy Wonder involved? He also has a criminal defense background."

Ann laughed at George's nickname for Jack Murphy—the result of Jack's $100 million verdict at his first civil jury trial.

"Well, as a matter of fact, I *am* trying to persuade Jack to defend the tasting room guy, Peter Smith."

George smiled without saying a word. He was amused to see Ann blush when her former boyfriend's name was mentioned. After a pause, George recalled his earlier conversation with Phil Taylor.

"What about Horace & Fitzpatrick. Is the firm involved?"

"After yesterday's call, Phil's arranged for me to meet with their *pro bono* committee. I'm hoping to work from their firm to defend the gardener, Juan. Apparently they've just hired a former assistant U.S. attorney from the U.S. Attorney's Office in Miami, Tracy Sanchez, to set up a white collar crime practice. When I was with the U.S. Attorney's Office here in San Francisco, Tracy had a reputation of being one of the Miami office's top prosecutors. It might be a great opportunity to work with her on this case."

George was a little disappointed that Ann wanted to work with yet another large corporate law firm—his usual adversary in court. However, George remembered Ann's aunt once telling him how the collapse of

Hampton & Elliot had nearly broken Ann's heart.

"*Maybe lawyers, like Ann, are not cut out for the rollercoaster life of the plaintiff's bar,*" George sadly thought to himself. "*Some lawyers need the security of a steady income.*"

Thinking about the lack of steady income from contingency fee work, George frowned.

"Ann, I still don't know how any of us are going to recoup our costs—let alone fees. What's wrong with these Sonoma defendants using the Fed's Public Defender's Office?"

"George—you're missing the point. Sonoma is a very tight-knit community. Aunt Amanda really *cares* about the Sonoma people who've been caught up in this mess. She's fond of Juan and his entire family. Bob's not just her caterer. She's learned through the Sonoma grapevine that Bob's used his Wall Street smarts to coach other lawyers how to challenge sloppy paperwork behind those subprime loans that have caused so much grief."

"Good for Bob! As a former Wall Street lawyer, he'd know where *those* bodies are buried."

"Charlie became a good friend after giving my aunt invaluable advice about setting up her winery. Don't you remember her singing Charlie's praises at the recent wine auction?"

George slowly nodded.

"Peter Smith also has a really good heart. When he's not working in the Keniworth Winery tasting room, he volunteers at fundraisers to help wine country non-profit groups. Samantha Pond is also a close girlfriend. She frequently sends my aunt referrals for weddings and other private events, which proved a godsend during the downturn."

Ann paused to let George absorb her words.

"George, as I said earlier, Aunt Amanda thinks highly of you. She wants *you* on the defense team. Besides, these Sonoma defendants *do* have resources. Some of their recent trades have done extremely well—which is part of the problem."

"Yeah, and we won't see a cent of it." George replied grimly. "The Feds will try to impound the lot!"

Ann's cell phone then rang. She answered, and after listening a few moments, put her caller on hold. "George, it's Aunt Amanda. She wants to set up a defense fund in aid of the 'Sonoma Five,' as she calls them. She plans to hold a series of rock concerts at her winery. She doesn't want anyone to feel bullied into pleading guilty if they're innocent, just because they can't afford the legal fees."

George sighed deeply. "Well…OK, OK! Tell your aunt I'll take a look at Bob Goodwin's defense just to keep her happy."

After Ann left, George spent a few moments thinking about their conversation. He finally chuckled. Although he'd kept his options open in front of Ann, George was warming up to the idea of defending Bob.

To defend the *caterer*—of all people—in an *insider trading* case appealed to George's image of himself as a modern day Robin Hood lawyer, fighting for the underdog against the powerful.

As one of the top trial lawyers in the country, George DeRosa was not going to be left out of *this* fight—not in *his* town!

CHAPTER 18

Jack Murphy Visits Deke Little

"Mr. Little? Jack Murphy is in the lobby and wondered if you might be able to spare him a few moments of your time."

The lawyer smiled, revealing deep facial crevices.

Deke Little punched a button on his phone. "I knew that he'd finally cave after he read our lead counsel brief in the pharma class action. Show him *in*."

When Jack Murphy was shown into Deke Little's office, he found the older man smirking with contempt.

"So you've finally come to admit that I've got the better argument to be lead counsel?" The older lawyer barked at Jack.

"Not exactly," replied Jack.

The smirk disappeared. "Well, then…get the hell put of my office and stop wasting my time, damn you!"

Jack waited a few moments, rubbed his chin, and sat in one of the client chairs positioned in front of the massive desk in the middle of a huge, sumptuously furnished office.

Deke Little rose and came from behind his enormous desk. "Didn't you hear what I said? I'm *busy*," he yelled in Jack's ear.

Jack looked up and smiled sweetly, without saying a word.

Deke laughed at the younger man's insolent charm, "OK, Jack, our wonder child of the San Francisco Trials Lawyers Association…so what the heck *are* you here for?"

Jack waited patiently until the older lawyer sat down in his chair and put his feet on his desk, displaying expensive Italian leather soles. He put his hands behind his head, revealing enormous gold cufflinks on both wrists. Deke's piercing grey eyes, grey crew cut, and square jaw contrasted sharply with the soft cut of his European suit.

Jack looked down at his own casual shoes and spoke quietly. "A very good friend of yours is in serious trouble and needs *your* help."

"Who?"

"Charlie Bartino."

The Italian shoe leather and gold cufflinks abruptly disappeared from sight. Deke Little sat upright in his chair.

"I'd die for that guy," said Deke, remembering how Charlie had sent him valuable referrals that paid the rent when he first opened his contingency fee practice. "Charlie's the salt of the earth. What the hell's going on?"

"He and others have got themselves arrested on an insider trading rap."

"OK, Jack. I can take a joke like the next guy but *enough is enough*! I need to get back to work."

Jack rose from his chair and handed Deke copies of recent articles published in the Sonoma County newspapers. Jack sat down and waited patiently while the other lawyer read the articles at least twice. The lawyer then glanced at Jack. Jack was the first to speak.

"I just happened to be in Sonoma when this thing blew. A relative of a close friend of mine sent me to talk with Charlie's family to try to calm them down. However, the first thing they wanted to know was whether I knew *you*. Deke…Charlie wants *you* to represent him in this case. He and his family think that you're the best trial lawyer in the world."

"Shit man, this is no longer my bag."

"Mine either…but I've agreed to represent the tasting room guy."

"Why?"

"Ann got me involved."

Deke looked at Jack and thought to himself, "*No man's a dumber shit than this guy when he's in love with that woman.*"

He paused. "Jack…listen to me. When her high-class corporate lawyer friends didn't approve of you, Ann threw you over. We saw your pretty face in bars all over this City looking like a sick puppy for *months*. Don't you remember? Do you really want to go back to *that*? What's wrong with all the other gorgeous dames in this town?"

"Deke…it wasn't like that. Ann and I had a quarrel when she felt that I was putting my career first, after some of the partners in her firm were giving her the harsh, silent treatment over my line of work. We decided to break up and give each other some space for a while. Then her firm collapsed, and she disappeared to Sonoma. This case is my opportunity to win her back."

"Yeah, until she joins another smart firm and throws you over *again*."

"I'm going to have to take that chance," said Jack firmly. "Besides you've just said that you would die for Charlie…but you won't take his case."

The two lawyers glared at each other. Deke was the first to smile.

"OK, hot shot. I'll contact Charlie to see how I can help."

CHAPTER 19

Ann Schiller Recruits Kimberly Hayward

A few weeks later, Ann was having drinks with Kimberly Hayward, an old friend from Hampton & Elliot who had set up her own litigation firm following Hampton & Elliot's demise.

"So how do you like being your own boss, Kimberly?" Ann asked her friend and former colleague.

The 35-year-old auburn-haired lawyer, who exuded confidence both in and out of the courtroom, smiled at Ann. "After dealing with the politics of a large law firm, I just *love* it. It's a breath of fresh air. My husband recently commented how much more fun I am to be around these days, now that I don't have to worry about pleasing my partners at Hampton & Elliot." She paused to take a sip of wine. "As the head of my own firm, I'm always anxious about where the next piece of business is coming from. But I was *really* lucky that many of my clients followed me to my new firm. One general counsel told me that he figured out that I was the lawyer handling his corporation's work, not the big-name partner. After Hampton & Elliot collapsed, he was happy to continue to work with me. After I bagged that large corporate client, I convinced some of the others to follow me. I'm really enjoying the freedom and lifestyle."

Ann was not surprised to hear that her friend and former colleague was now successful. "Anxiety about having enough work…that's not unusual in our profession," added Ann. "Inside the big law firms, everyone is under enormous pressure to bill enough hours to keep the firm's management committee happy."

"Precisely," agreed Kimberly. "The best part is that by keeping my overhead low, I can make more money, but bill less. The only people who care about my billable hours are my husband, my bank manager, and me. It's just great."

She smiled at her friend. "But that's enough about me, Ann. How's wine country treating you?"

"Well…I'm handling a new white collar crime case out of Phil Taylor's new firm, Horace & Fitzpatrick."

Kimberly stared in surprise. "No kidding!"

"Did you hear about the insider trading arrests in Sonoma?"

"I vaguely recall something about that."

"I'm representing one of the Sonoma defendants, Juan Rodriguez, a young man who works for his family's landscape and pool maintenance business."

"Wow, that's radical. Why did Horace & Fitzpatrick decide to take this on? Is it *pro bono*?"

"It started out that way because they've recruited Tracy Sanchez out of the Miami U.S. Attorney's Office to head up a new white collar crime department. But my aunt Amanda, who was at one time a famous fashion model, is helping pay the legal fees. She's sponsoring several rock-and-roll fundraisers for the Sonoma defendants at her winery. So far, the events have attracted a large amount of financial support, even from outside the state."

As Kimberly quietly listened, Ann continued. "Kimberly, we need your help. One of the defendants, Samantha Pond, a wine country realtor, is unhappy with her current lawyer. She was initially represented at the time of her arrest by one of her lawyer friends who was also a real estate client. However, when she had dinner with my aunt and me last week, she mentioned that her own lawyer seems almost *embarrassed* to be involved with the case. Apparently Samantha's lawyer only took it on as a personal favor. His law firm is not cut out to handle a fight like this. Criminal law matters, even white collar crime cases like this, are not their gig. Samantha asked me to recommend someone else. I don't want to recommend anyone who doesn't have the right background. She's been through enough already."

Ann paused and added, "Samantha Pond is one of the more wealthy defendants from Sonoma. I think she has the resources to pay you— otherwise I wouldn't ask you to get involved. So far, the defense lawyers in the case have successfully fought back the Fed's attempts to freeze all the defendants' assets. The judge has ruled that the defendants are entitled to pay their lawyers using assets that were acquired by activities unrelated to the allegedly illegal stock trades. Would you be willing to take a look at Samantha's case?"

Kimberly smiled. However, before answering Ann's question, Kimberly had a couple of her own.

"So...apart from our friend Phil's new firm, who else is involved?"

"George DeRosa, my aunt's good friend. He's defending the caterer, Bob Goodwin."

"*George DeRosa?* And who else?"

Ann blushed, but looked her friend squarely in the eye said: "Jack Murphy. He's defending the tasting room sales guy, Peter Smith."

Pretending to ignore the name that Kimberly knew had caused Ann so much heartache in the past, Kimberly asked patiently, "The *tasting room guy?* And who else?"

"Deke Little. He's defending the grower, Charlie Bartino."

Kimberly raised her eyebrows. In her view, Ann had just identified three buccaneer plaintiff's lawyers who were consistent thorns in the side of Kimberly's corporate clients.

"You know, Ann, during my career, I have sat across the conference table in numerous depositions taken by counselors DeRosa, Murphy, and Little, where the civil allegations might involve criminal wrongdoing. In every deposition, I've had to watch them like a hawk to make sure that none of them puts a noose around the necks of my gullible clients. Obviously, they aren't *trying* to put anyone in jail. They're just out to make money for themselves and their greedy clients. However, these lawyers can be *clueless* about the criminal law implications of their clients' fanciful allegations.

"If a criminal rap sticks *and* there's a finding that my client acted outside the scope of his or her employment, these lawyers can kiss goodbye to any available insurance. If my clients work for a large corporation with deep pockets, these lawyers may think this isn't a problem. However, these companies will also argue that, because the criminal act was outside the scope of employment, they needn't pay a dime either. That leaves personal funds, which are *never* enough. Sometimes I can't help but wonder what these idiot lawyers are thinking! There have been times when I could have killed those lawyers *and* their clients!"

After both women laughed, Kimberly thought for a moment and added, "I have to say that a case involving a wine country caterer, tasting room guy, gardener, grape grower, and realtor does sound intriguing."

It did not take Kimberly long to make up her mind. She was damned if she'd allow the Feds to throw a friend of Ann's in jail without a big fight. She was concerned that some clueless civil litigator was not advising Samantha correctly.

"Ann, you caught me at a good time," said Kimberly finally. "I just settled a Foreign Corrupt Practices Act case by convincing our 'friends' over at the DOJ that my client was personally unaware of any of the wrongdoing. I'd be happy to meet your realtor friend, after I've conducted a conflicts check to make sure that I don't have prior connections with the other defendants." She smiled at her friend.

"Besides, I'd love to have a good excuse to visit the beautiful wine country."

CHAPTER 20

Defense Counsel Meet in Lillian Johnson's Office

Everyone sitting in the elegant red brick Jackson Square conference room was quiet. On strict instructions from Ann Schiller and Kimberly Hayward, even George DeRosa was quiet.

Since she knew many of the lawyers in the room, Kimberly began the discussion.

"As everyone knows, we're all here under a joint defense agreement so that we can speak openly. My client, Samantha Pond, has told me that none of the trades about which she was aware resulted from her receiving inside information. My colleagues representing the other Sonoma defendants are being told the same story. We have all performed extensive due diligence on our own clients and have not uncovered any 'smoking gun' that might be evidence of an insider trading conspiracy between your clients and ours. We are here to propose that we all pursue a strategy that hopefully clears not just our clients, but also your clients."

On the other side of the table, the lawyers representing the Silicon Valley executives named anonymously in the indictment looked at Kimberly with expressions of deep skepticism.

As planned beforehand, Ann then spoke. "We all know that our clients, the Sonoma defendants, must explain what they did and why," Ann said. "However, if our clients go down, the odds are high that your clients won't be far behind."

She paused to look at the lawyers sitting on the opposite side of the conference room table. None of them moved a muscle.

"We all know how the Fed works," Ann said, her eyes darting from one lawyer to the next. "They nail the little fish first before going after the big fish. In this case, *our* clients are the little fish and *your* clients are the big fish.

"We're here today to argue that your clients' interests might be best served if they were to take proactive steps and tell the truth to the jury at our clients' trial, instead of waiting for the Feds to make the first move. With the help of your clients, we think we have a good chance of convincing the jury that *our* clients' trades were *not* the result of an insider trading conspiracy. That's got to be in *everyone's* interest."

The lawyers for the Silicon Valley executives all looked at each other as if someone had suggested they catch the next bus to Mars. Finally one lawyer spoke.

"Counselor, we certainly respect your overtures," said Hugh Jamison, Tom White's lawyer. "However, you have to concede that whatever the outcome of this case, the Sonoma defendants managed to get our clients into this awful mess. It's a very tall proposition to suggest that it's in *our* clients interests for any of them take the enormous risk of waiving their fifth amendment rights before any criminal charges are brought against them, even if you and the other defense counsel think these may be imminent."

"You and your clients all have a right to be skeptical about the situation," said Ann in a quiet, calm voice. "If my client had been placed in this situation, I would be deeply skeptical, too. However, as things stand, although your clients are not currently charged with any criminal wrongdoing, at trial Josh Kaplan will do a great job of draping the cloak of suspicion over everyone…our clients *and* yours."

Ann looked down and sighed.

"I've worked with Kaplan in the local U.S. Attorney's Office here in San Francisco," she said. "For those of you who have worked in other U.S. Attorney's Offices, Kaplan had the reputation of being the bleeding heart of our local office. He stood up for what he thought was right, even when it was not always smart, career-wise.

"Getting Kaplan to take on a case that he doesn't immediately buy into can be tough," she added. "He's very conscious of how the power of the federal government can ruin people's lives and how this power should be used sparingly. He really beats up his own side to make sure that the Feds are doing the right thing. Some FBI agents joke that they dread him being assigned to one of their cases. However, once he gets behind a case, he also has the reputation of being a formidable opponent."

She paused to let the other former federal prosecutors in the room quietly mull over the image of Josh Kaplan as an idealistic prosecutor. Many in the room silently recognized themselves at an earlier point in their careers before government politics or other pressures dampened their youthful hopes and aspirations.

Phil Taylor decided it was time to speak up. "Guys, you probably know that many of your clients are dear friends of mine, so obviously, in your eyes, I'm biased," he said to the lawyers representing the Silicon Valley executives. "However, I would bet my life that *your* clients are all telling you the truth. I've also heard—secondhand—what some of your clients are going through. Recently, things have been grim for them. Even if the Feds don't bring criminal charges against your clients, some may never fully recover from the damning innuendo that they leaked inside information or even engaged in insider trading. Despite all the iconoclastic talk about 'destructive technology,' Silicon Valley is a pretty straitlaced place. At some point, these people have to be allowed to tell their side of the story, for the sake of their future careers."

"I guess that none of you have any doubts about *your* clients' innocence, right?" Tim Newman's lawyer, Lillian Johnson, a handsome woman with black hair pulled into a Victorian knot, raised one eyebrow. Her question was greeted with laughter, but it helped break the ice.

George's eyes twinkled. "I'm as confident as any lawyer can be," he replied.

"Ditto," replied Jack.

Deke added, "But, as I tell my evidence students, none of us were there when the butler did it."

Lillian decided it was time to end the meeting. "We really appreciate you and the other defendants' counsel attending this meeting," she said in a kind voice. "This case is obviously hard on everyone, including my client, Tim, who's been placed on leave like the other Silicon Valley folks represented here today. It might be helpful ultimately for counsel to work together to bring a successful conclusion for everyone. However, I hope that you'll understand that Tim, Tom White, and the other Silicon Valley executives are under an enormous amount of pressure. Not only have their companies placed them on leave, but, as we know, they also face the serious possibility that they, too, might be indicted. I agree with my fellow counsel that for the immediate future, the contribution of these Silicon Valley executives will have to be strictly limited for their own protection."

After the attorneys for the Sonoma defendants escaped to George's favorite North Beach lunch spot, he exploded. "Kimberly and Ann, no offense to you brilliant lady lawyers, but God save us from the Federal Bar. Except for the lovely Lillian Johnson, who seems rather a doll, those defense lawyers strike me as a bunch of pompous…!" He didn't have to finish the sentence.

Everyone laughed. It felt good.

Ann laughed also, but secretly she was not in complete agreement with George. She'd noticed that Lillian Johnson had appeared warmer and more responsive than the other white collar defense lawyers. She thought they might have made some inroads.

Horace & Fitzpatrick's new partner and Ann's new colleague, Tracy Sanchez, a petite, middle-aged woman with sparkling eyes and short, blond hair, arrived. She had not been present at the earlier meeting.

"My, my, you all look so gloomy!" said Tracy after introductions. "You're putting me off lunch and I'm *starving*."

After she quickly ordered her lunch, the group updated Tracy on the morning meeting. She listened attentively to each lawyer's description of the skeptical reception they'd received from the lawyers representing the Silicon Valley executives. When they finished, she smiled at the group.

"My friends, I doubt that the Feds would have proceeded this far unless our wonderful FBI agents have dug up more than just a few suspicious stock trades." Tracy spoke quietly, preventing others in the restaurant from overhearing. "Mark my words: *someone's* agreed, or is close to agreeing, to plead guilty. *Someone's* cooperating with the Feds. Counsel for the Silicon Valley guys probably have their suspicions about *all* our clients, however much we love them. Frankly, I don't blame those lawyers for being cautious. They can't trust any of us because they can't trust our clients."

She paused as her main course arrived. She picked up her fork and looked at the group in turn.

"So…which of our clients is the snake in the grass?" Tracy asked with a cynical smile.

CHAPTER 21

A Sheepdog Appears Before the Sonoma Wildlife Council

Tim and Lucy Newman's Australian Shepherd sheepdog, Sidney, had decided to take matters into his own paws.

While he watched the wild animals begin to gather in a grove near Mountain Cemetery in Sonoma, he thought miserably about the emptiness of his Sonoma home. His attention abruptly switched to the present when a huge mountain lion stealthily descended from a nearby tree and gave a low-key roar to the assembled wild animals.

The Sonoma Wildlife Council meeting was now in session.

"We understand that a domestic animal wishes to address our council," said the mountain lion majestically. *"Mr. Sidney Newman, please come forward and state your business."*

Sidney moved to an empty space within the circle of wild animals either standing in tall grass, ready to make a quick move if the lion threatened them, or perched aloft in the surrounding trees.

"G'day, Mr. President, and members of the Wildlife Council of the great City of Sonoma," Sidney said. *"As a proud descendent of the Australian Shepherd breed, I know how to take care of my humans, but I need your help. I need your permission to enter the Sonoma Overlook Trail for at least 24 hours."*

"Dogs are not allowed on the Overlook Trail," retorted the black crow representative in a raucous voice from a nearby tree.

"We all know that," replied the mountain lion impatiently. *"That's why Sidney Newman is here to seek our special permission."*

"Sidney Newman can't be trusted, Sidney Newman can't be trusted," sang the grey squirrel representative, showing off his handsome tail as he darted in circles around a nearby tree, *"He's always chasing us squirrels up trees,"* chattered the squirrel accusingly during the brief moment he stayed still.

"Maybe he's keeping you out of harm's way," said the deer representative,

blinking her lovely brown eyes at the group. *"The traffic—people on foot and in cars—is getting worse around the Plaza. Recently, my two fawns and I were nearly knocked down just outside Readers' Books,"* she said breathily.

"Quack! I couldn't agree more," said the handsome white duck, representing the duck pond community inside the Plaza. *"It's just impossible to cross the street around the Plaza these days."*

Sidney thought that the deer and the duck must be complete dingbats for walking into busy traffic around the Sonoma Plaza. He always kept his human family on a tight leash when they walked around the Plaza. However, looking at the kind faces of the deer and the duck, he thought that perhaps, like most sheepdogs, he was being a bit too judgmental. Meanwhile, the group started to gossip about recent changes in downtown Sonoma.

"So whaddya think of Union Bank leaving a water bowl outside its front door?" the squirrel asked, jumping from tree to tree. The squirrel was proud of his reputation as the main instigator of gossip among Sonoma's wildlife.

"I think water bowls around the Plaza attract far too many domestic dogs… like Sidney," replied the crow with a condescending sniff.

"You crows think you own Sonoma," said the mother deer shaking her head in exasperation.

"Quack, quack, I kinda like the water bowls," replied the duck. *"It keeps the dogs, cats, and other animals away from our duck pond."*

"Quiet," roared the mountain lion, *"we don't have all night. Sidney, tell us why you need access to Overlook Trail, and we might look more favorably on your application."*

"Mr. President and members of the Sonoma Wildlife Council," Sidney paused dramatically, *"as many of you know, I am the guardian of three humans: Lucy and Tim Newman and their baby daughter, Catherine. Lucy and Tim are not allowed to see any of their friends at the moment, and it's making all of us miserable."*

"Why aren't your humans allowed to see their friends?" The lion was perplexed.

"Tim's not allowed to go to work, and Tim's lawyer, Lillian Johnson, won't let Tim or Lucy speak to anyone. It's some kind of people controversy. Apparently,

Tim knows other humans who have recently been arrested."

"Has Tim been arrested?" asked the lion sharply.

"No…*that's just it,*" replied Sidney vehemently.

The wild animals stared at the sheepdog blankly. The lion was the first to speak.

"*Are you telling us that your human, Tim, is not allowed to work or see his friends merely because he knows some of the people who have been arrested?*" The lion, though wise, was often bewildered by human action.

"*Yeah, mate. Isn't it the darnedest thing you've ever heard? Apparently there's been some illegal activity going on in Sonoma and they think my Tim is guilty by association. But, Mr. President, I give you my word. Even if Tim knows some of the people who have been arrested, he's completely innocent. My Tim would never do anything illegal.*"

"*Family members of criminals always think the criminals are innocent,*" retorted the crow haughtily, preening a wing feather.

"*OK, Sidney, so perhaps your human is innocent,*" said the lion, ignoring the crow whose caustic remarks frequently got on his nerves. "*You still haven't explained why you need access to our Overlook Trail.*"

"*Mr. President, let me explain. We sheepdogs protect sheep by herding them together. We position ourselves between the sheep and any predator who might harm them. However, it's sometimes difficult to protect humans in this way. They escape too easily.*

"*Recently, an elderly blind dog in Palo Alto went missing, and the entire community organized a search party. My doggie pals and I were all involved. We eventually found the poor bugger unharmed in a clearing walking around in circles because he couldn't find his way out. This rescue gave me an idea how I might be able to herd Tim and his friends together, despite their lawyers' advice to stay apart. If I also go missing—and I'm briefly sighted on the trail—Tim and his friends are bound to organize a search party to look for me. A search party will give Tim a chance to talk to his friends. Maybe, just maybe, they'll discover new information that will clear everyone.*"

"*Humans, especially those in law enforcement, can be very stupid at times,*" remarked the mountain lion disdainfully. "*I wish humans would stop blaming us for their mistakes. We wild animals struggle daily to find food and water, yet humans try to shoot us every time we eat someone's pet dog, cat, or chicken they've left outside."*

The coyote representative let out a piercing jagged howl to signal vehement agreement with the mountain lion.

"Once they've shot us, they don't even leave our carcasses for other wildlife to eat," added the lion indignantly. *"Don't they understand how hungry we are out here?"*

The turkey buzzard representative flapped her large wings in agreement with the lion. The lion had identified her major complaint with the entire human race, namely burying juicy carcasses that would otherwise have been her family's dinner.

The rest of the animals waited patiently. They thought it unwise to interrupt the lion, especially when he was thinking about his next meal. The lion sighed deeply and looked at the domestic sheepdog.

"Okay, Sidney, I can see some merit in supporting your plan to disappear for a few hours. Maybe the humans will leave us alone for a bit. Are you willing to abide by our wildlife council's rules that you are only on Overlook Trail for a maximum of 24 hours and that you refrain from chasing any of us during that time?"

"Yes, sir," replied Sidney respectfully. He had no intention of chasing any mountain lions.

"Okay, let's wrap this up." The lion turned to the circle of wild animals. *"As your president, I propose that we allow Sidney to visit Overlook Trail for 24 hours, provided he follows all our council rules. All in favor nod your heads."*

All the wild animals nodded in agreement. They wanted the meeting to end before the lion became any hungrier. At council meetings they were all colleagues, but caution was wise when it came to meals.

"Well, Sidney, you have our council's decision," pronounced the lion. *"However, **you are hereby warned**, if you mess this up and disobey any council rules—such as chasing any wildlife, or staying on Overlook Trail longer than 24 hours—I will exact the maximum penalty. You could become my family's next dinner. Understand?"* the lion added with a deep roar.

"Yes, sir," replied Sidney with trepidation.

Ann Schiller Meets With Lillian Johnson

Meanwhile, Ann made an appointment for a private meeting with Lillian Johnson. As she waited in Lillian's reception room, she had mixed feelings about this meeting. She pretended to read a copy of *The Recorder*, a local legal newspaper.

At long last, Ann felt optimistic about her professional career. Over a glass of wine the previous evening, Tracy Sanchez had confided that, once Juan Hernandez's trial was over, she hoped that Ann would be offered a permanent position with the firm. Feeling grateful, Ann had asked politely whether Tracy wanted a role at Juan's trial.

"No, Ann," Tracy replied with a laugh. "You're more than capable of representing Juan on your own. Juan, and your aunt wouldn't want it any other way. Just let me know if I can help from the sidelines. I'm available any time day or night as a sounding board."

For personal reasons, Ann was apprehensive about her meeting with Lillian.

Ann and her aunt had persuaded George, Jack and Kimberly to enter the fray on behalf of the Sonoma defendants. Jack then persuaded Deke Little to join the defense team. To everyone's surprise, all five lawyers were getting along well. Now, Ann was about to embark on an attempt to win favorable treatment for her own client, Juan, which she couldn't share with any of these other defense lawyers—not even Jack.

She and Jack had put their romantic relationship on hold until after the case was resolved. She now planned to suggest to Lillian that their clients jointly cooperate with the Feds. If Ann's strategy was successful, she would suddenly be on the opposite side from Jack, George, Kimberly and Deke. Knowing the enormous fear that the DOJ case was causing Juan and his family, Ann knew she had no choice but to explore this approach to try to end her client's pain.

"Being a lawyer is lonely at times," she thought.

Lillian Johnson, wearing her long, black hair down around her shoulders, warmly greeted Ann in the lobby. She escorted her to a small, informal conference room: a contrast to the larger, more formal room where the defense counsel meeting had taken place. They sat and Lillian apologized for the brusque nature of the prior meeting with the other Silicon Valley defense lawyers.

"Ann, they suspect that one or more of the Sonoma defendants is close to pleading guilty and will cooperate with the Feds to nail *their* clients," said Lillian, echoing Tracy. "Frankly, I share their concerns. We should all be concerned that anyone cooperating with the Feds will twist, exaggerate, or flat out *lie* about the activities of everyone else on the planet to get themselves a favorable deal. Unfortunately, this behavior is not uncommon."

Ann thought for a moment before replying. "Given the huge sentencing discrepancies between cooperating with the Feds and fighting a case like this through trial, we *all* have to consider the possibility of getting our clients to enter some kind of deal. There's nothing unusual about that."

Ann explained her strategy: she would approach Josh Kaplan to discuss a lenient deal for Juan Rodriguez as the 'lesser wrongdoer.' Juan would testify that he'd not learned inside information from Lillian's client, Tim Newman. Tim would support Juan's account. If Juan and Tim agreed to cooperate with the Feds and testify about what they knew, Juan would be treated leniently and the cloud of suspicion hanging over Tim's career would be removed.

Lillian listened attentively but after a long pause, shook her head.

"Counselor, after listening to my client, Tim, say over and over that he *never* divulged inside information to *anyone*, I've also given considerable thought to approaching the Feds. I would like nothing more than to get my client a deal so that he can return to work. However, I see two major stumbling blocks."

Ann waited for the other lawyer to continue.

"Correct me if I'm wrong, but typically the Feds—like you when you were with the U.S. Attorney's Office—are in the business of nailing the *bad guys* in such a way that it makes an example of everyone involved. In a case like this, the criminal indictment acts as a deterrent to all the *other* bad guys out there who might contemplate setting up their own insider trading conspiracy. The federal agencies, especially the DOJ, have a keen nose for criminal behavior and usually assume the worst motives when judging anyone's behavior. Once the DOJ has taken the trouble to seek a criminal indictment, it rarely offers a deal where a suspect claims that he or she was clueless. This may be a powerful defense argument at trial, but not at the plea bargaining stage."

As Lillian spoke, Ann reluctantly recognized her younger, more self-righteous self when she had been a U.S. federal prosecutor. Now that she was on the defense side representing Juan, everything seemed much more nuanced and complex.

"As we both know," continued Lillian, "the indictment is short on details about *how* the alleged inside information changed hands. Unfortunately, there's one aspect that *isn't* vague. It's crystal clear from the indictment that the Sonoma defendants made *huge* profits from trades involving Silicon Valley companies like Tim's."

Both women smiled grimly.

"Because of those *huge* profits," said Lillian, "my worst fear is that the jury will agree with the Feds that Tim *must* have given inside information to Juan. Looking at it from the Feds' standpoint, *how else* could the Sonoma traders have known to invest in these companies at just the right time to make those extremely lucky trades?"

Ann nodded as Lillian described an all-too-likely worst-case scenario.

"As I see it, for Juan to seek a favorable plea bargain and get my client exonerated, we'd need to make one of two arguments. First, we'd have to prove that our clients' noses are completely clean—that no inside information was divulged. However, we've *no proof* that our clients are innocent. For example, we can't *prove* that Tim didn't give Juan inside information about the pending litigation settlement that caused Tim's company stock to skyrocket unexpectedly."

Ann pursed her lips as she listened to the seasoned defense lawyer.

"As we know only too well," continued Lillian, in a pleasantly musical voice, "the only *other* way to get a favorable plea bargain is for a defendant to plead guilty and be willing to offer some serious dirt on the other defendants."

The pleasant musical voice stopped. Lillian's voice hardened. Her almond eyes looked stern.

"Ann, after listening to *my* client, I don't think your client's got enough dirt."

"Ah…you mean that my client isn't guilty *enough*. I get it!" said Ann with a smile. "Maybe I've just been away from criminal cases too long. At Hampton & Elliot, I only handled civil matters," she added sadly.

"Bottom line," said Lillian, "I just don't see Kaplan offering a deal acceptable to *either* of our clients. The good news," said Lillian, trying to sound upbeat, "to our knowledge, the Feds haven't hit a home run…*yet*. However, I've been in this business long enough to know that it's still early."

Lillian's phone rang and she excused herself. When she returned to the small conference room, an anxious look had replaced her normally calm expression.

"Ann, I've just received some distressing news from Sonoma. On top of all their other troubles, Tim and Lucy's Aussie Shepherd, Sidney has disappeared. He's been missing *for more than 48 hours*."

CHAPTER 23

Deke Little Meets With Josh Kaplan

Ann wasn't the only defense lawyer hoping for a favorable plea bargain for her client. The same morning that Ann met with Lillian Johnson, Deke Little hoped he might win a favorable plea bargain for his client, Charlie Bartino.

Deke pondered Charlie's defense as he traveled to meet Josh Kaplan. *"Charlie did tell the other defendants about the bidding from a public wine auction, true! But bids at public auctions weren't confidential inside information."*

As Deke's chauffeur dropped him off near the Federal Building, Deke thought about the Feds' possible counter-argument. *"Charlie put up most of the capital for the trades—true! However, Charlie lacked the sophistication to understand the illegal nature of these trades."* Deke remembered Justice Ruth Bader Ginsburg's ruling that lack of knowledge could be a valid defense in criminal misappropriation insider trading cases.

As Deke arrived at the Philip Burton Federal Building and walked though security, he noted how the enormous skyscraper differed from the human scale state courthouses in which a younger Deke Little had honed his trial lawyer skills. The elegant Art Deco courthouses of Alameda and Contra Costa counties, the stunningly handsome Frank Lloyd Wright Marin Civic Center, and the former location of the San Francisco County Court in San Francisco's majestic City Hall nostalgically crept into his memory. *"The architects of this monstrosity must have hated beauty,"* he thought grimly, as he marched through the lobby.

At the beginning of his meeting with Josh Kaplan, Deke summed up the young prosecutor as earnest, but naïve. He quickly changed his opinion.

Deke began the meeting arguing that, at most, Charlie may have provided the capital for the trades and information about bidding at a *public* wine auction. However, he argued that, if his client's activities were illegal, others had duped his salt-of-the-earth farmer client into making investments in stocks for which he was ill-suited.

Josh Kaplan didn't smile. "I appreciate you sharing with me that your client contributed the lion's share of capital behind the defendants' lucky trades. However, has your client told you that he's also invested in several venture capital funds organized by a venture capital firm on Sand Hill Road?"

"*Shit! Why didn't he tell me*," thought Deke.

"Maybe my client decided to diversify some capital away from the wine industry. Is that a crime, counselor?"

"No…not by itself. However this type of investment is normally made by very *sophisticated* investors."

The next few words took Deke's breath away.

"*Coincidently*, this venture capital firm was instrumental in placing two guys in senior executive positions with the *same* companies traded by your client and the other defendants," Josh said firmly. "We know that these senior executives had access to information that would have helped your client and his friends make their very lucky stock trades. The Silicon Valley is famous for innovation. Your client's investments in this VC firm's funds might be a very *innovative* way to reward someone for insider trading tips."

After a long pause, Josh spoke again. "Your client needs to proffer a more complete account of his actions, including *everything he knows* about the VC firm, the insiders and the defendants."

On that note the meeting ended. As Deke waited for the descending elevator, he pondered the implications of what he had just learned.

"*If the Feds are right, what a racket!*"

He began to worry about his client's honesty.

"*Charlie's always a straight shooter. How come he never told me he was investing in a Sand Hill Road VC firm with close ties to the suspected insiders?*"

As Deke sat in the back of his chauffeured car, he remembered that his client had faced difficult times during the downturn. He worried that Charlie got himself caught up in an illegal insider trading conspiracy to help the family's grape growing business.

As his driver maneuvered downtown, Deke also observed how Silicon

Valley money had recently poured into San Francisco. As an old-time San Franciscan, he was *not* impressed. Too many huge cranes heralded new skyscraper construction—the very type of construction he loathed.

Deke's thoughts returned to his conference with Josh Kaplan. If the Feds already had the goods on the insiders and the VC firm, they'd have requested more indictments by now.

"The Feds need Charlie's cooperation before seeking these indictments."

Maybe Charlie *could* get a sweet deal by helping the Feds nail those Silicon Valley slime balls who had dragged Charlie and his friends into this mess.

CHAPTER 24

The Search Party Assembles

"My family has owned Aussies," said Lillian, looking at Lucy's tear-streaked face. "I can't believe that Sidney *disappeared* like this. It's most uncharacteristic of the breed."

All of Tim and Lucy's friends who could leave work were assembled in the Newmans' living room in Sonoma.

"Where was he last seen?" asked Tom White.

"On the first day he went missing, some of my friends reported seeing him on the Overlook Trail," replied Juan, who looked distraught.

"Dude, we've looked *everywhere*," added Peter Smith, raising his hands in despair. "We've had the whole community searching. I can't imagine why we haven't been able to find the big guy yet."

"Sidney was behaving strangely when he was spotted," added Juan. "My friends reported that he kept stopping to look over his shoulder."

"A friend of Charlie's and mine is a military helicopter enthusiast who stores his decommissioned helicopters with Charlie," Tom said. "He's agreed to lend us one for an air reconnaissance. I propose that Charlie, Tony and I go pick up the helicopter. Ann, why don't you take Juan, Jack and Peter to the top of the Overlook Trail with the others and wait for us. Try to position yourselves somewhere where we can see you easily from the air. Kimberly and Samantha, please visit the Police Station for any other developments. Lucy, I suggest you stay here with Lillian so we can use the house as our communications HQ. Line up Sidney's vet to be on standby…just in case. Also, give us any of Sidney's medical supplies."

"I'll get you Sidney's first aid kit. We put it together in case of an emergency evacuation," said Lucy, pleased she could help. As she handed Tom a case with a large red cross and dog paw emblem on it, everyone struggled to hold back tears. "His microchip information is in there, too."

"Good job," replied Tom, smiling at her.

The mountain lion was silently waiting. *"Can't believe the humans can't find him,"* he thought despondently, *"and they're supposed to be the smart species."*

He and the other members of the Sonoma Wildlife Council had kept watch ever since the turkey buzzard representative had reported that Sidney, injured by a long nail stuck in his paw, had accidentally fallen over the edge of a precipice at the top of Overlook Trail and rolled down onto a grassy ledge several feet below. Sidney managed to stay alive by licking dew from the grass, then eating it for nourishment. At times he blanked out, only to awaken and see the same birds flying overhead.

"Don't worry Sidney! We're all rooting for you! Keep your hopes up," they chirped.

Suddenly the wild animals heard a deep roar. A black apparition with a whirling blade and no wings came into view. Hearing a loud, threatening noise, the mountain lion made a quick retreat to a nearby tree, which camouflaged his large head and body. The other wild animals ran or flew for cover. They watched from afar as another group of humans arrived at the trailhead.

"And about time!" The mountain lion thought. *"Guess they couldn't do it without the machine."*

Hearing the huge engine overheard, Sidney also felt hopeful. *"A big engine might mean big help is on its way,"* he whimpered.

"I see him," yelled Tony excitedly as he flew the helicopter across the top of Overlook Trail. "Look over there. He must have fallen over the edge. He's stuck half way down the hillside. Hold on, guys, I'm going in closer."

The helicopter turned and hovered over the hillside. A few moments later, a tall man with long legs was gently lowered on a long steel rope from the helicopter. He landed expertly on the grassy ledge where Sidney was lying. Sidney lifted his head and tried to move.

"You poor bastard," said Tom looking at the dog's paw with a large rusty nail protruding from it. "I'm taking that out right now."

Tom held Sidney's paw, poured disinfectant over the nail and wound and pulled the nail out gently. He knew he was taking a risk but calculated that moving the dog from the steep hillside with a long nail still protruding from his paw might be a larger risk. After the nail was removed, Sidney licked the man's arm. Tom took a small, collapsible water bowl and bottle out of his jacket pocket and filled the bowl with water. He scooped his hand into the water bowl and poured small drops of water on Sidney's mouth and behind his ears. He held the bowl to Sidney's mouth, and was relieved to see how the cool water quickly revived the animal. After taking many licks, Sidney leaned against the tall man.

Satisfied that Sidney was not suffering serious dehydration, Tom poured more disinfectant on Sidney's paw where the nail had been extracted and expertly bandaged the dog's paw.

"Don't worry, fella…we'll get you out of here real soon," said Tom to the dog.

He bent down to grasp the 70-pound dog and hold him in his arms. Tom placed a large strap around himself and the dog. He then signaled to the helicopter to pull him up.

A large group cheered as they saw Tom and Sidney slowly pulled up to the helicopter. Tears came into many eyes watching the large sheepdog with a bandaged paw being held by the tall slim man. Sidney lay tense in Tom's arms as they were slowly pulled to safety. He was afraid to move a single canine muscle. When they reached the helicopter, Charlie pulled Tom and Sidney into the cabin and immediately slammed and latched the door.

"We'll see you back at the Newmans," yelled Tony into his headset at the rest of the search party below, turning the helicopter towards the City of Sonoma. "Wow, this is just like the old days," he said to Charlie and Tom.

The search party on the ground raced down Overlook Trail to spread the good news to the rest of Sonoma. A deer and squirrel followed them closely.

"Sidney's been saved, Sidney's been saved," sang the squirrel after he reached the Plaza—rather an exhausting hike, especially during the daytime. He leapt from tree to tree, showing off to his friends and the other Plaza animals as he broadcast the latest news.

"*Hurrah…Sidney's finally saved,*" quacked the Plaza duck noisily to his friends as he splashed around in the Duck Pond.

"*Darling Sidney is OK,*" reported the deer to her family and friends, who were all waiting for her in the creek below Fourth Street East.

"*Darn…there goes another decent meal,*" sighed the turkey buzzard to the mountain lion after they were left in quiet stillness.

CHAPTER 25

Big Decisions

"Don't make me go to the vet's office," pleaded Sidney with his mournful eyes as Lucy held and stroked him. *"I want to stay home."*

"Doctor, after you gave him that shot and rebandaged his paw, I think that Sidney just needs some food and rest," said Lucy. "He'll do much better if he can stay in his own home. Lillian and I will take turns watching him tonight. Lillian's family has owned several Aussies. I think you can trust us to watch him carefully."

"OK, I know when I'm defeated," said the kindly vet, knowing it was hopeless to separate Sidney from Lucy now. "Call me if he shows any change in behavior or breathing. I'll come right over."

Sidney felt weak and exhausted but happy to be back in his own home. He could also smell that many humans had visited his human parents since he had disappeared. He was content in discovering that he had finally brought everyone together. However, he realized that the effort had nearly cost him his life.

"Wow…you are much prettier than I expected," thought Sidney, looking at Lillian Johnson gently massaging his legs and paws. *"Guess I better leave the lawyering to you from now on."*

"This is a good time to chat without our lawyers getting in the way," said Tom to his friend over a glass of beer that evening. "Tony…as I see it, we've got to do the right thing for our buddy Charlie and his Sonoma friends. My lawyer keeps advising me not to talk with anyone. He doesn't want me to testify until my own indictment and trial. *Great*…but by then it may be too late."

"Same here," Tony replied excitedly. "I'm getting the identical piece of advice from my lawyer. It's amazing how they all think alike. Must learn this stuff at law school."

"Plenty of pressure's already been put on a lot of good people," Tom said grimly, "and pressure can cause some to buckle."

"People make stuff up when they're scared," acknowledged Tony. "Plenty of lies will be told about *us* at this trial. I can just *feel* it—whether we testify or not. If we testify, at least we'll get our side of the story out there," Tony said.

"I expect the lawyers will make mincemeat out of us," Tom replied less enthusiastically, "but it can't be as bad as being in battle during wartime. We wouldn't leave our guys wounded on the battlefield then. We can't let Charlie down now."

Tony concurred. "We've been in tighter spots in the past. Let's not let our lawyers frighten us away from doing the right thing by Charlie."

They clinked their glasses in agreement.

"I don't need some goddamn *rat* of a lawyer telling me to *rat* on my friends."

Charlie stood in his living room and glared at Deke Little.

"OK. Fire me right now so that we can go outside and fight this out," Deke said as he glared back at his client.

"Gentlemen, will you kindly remember that you are in *my* living room—not some saloon—and kindly *sit down*."

After Diana Bartino had restored sanity to her home, she spoke again quietly.

"Deke, we know that you have Charlie's best interests at heart. However we hired you to defend him—not provide aid and assistance to the enemy. That's how it's looking to us right now."

"Diana, I know how you and Charlie hate the idea of doing any deal that might put Charlie on opposite sides with his friends. However, the Feds suspect some kind of set-up by the suspected insiders. They think Charlie might have been duped by some of his friends into participating in an insider trading conspiracy, which wouldn't be such a friendly act on their part." After a pause, Deke looked down at the floor and said, "Charlie's investments in the VC fund look highly suspicious to the Feds."

"None of their goddamned business!" Charlie interrupted indignantly.

"Hon, let Deke finish," replied his wife as she put her hand on his arm. "We might as well hear the worst before this trial starts."

After she listened to Deke's recital of his meeting with Josh Kaplan, she sighed.

"Deke…I don't think that you'll ever persuade Charlie to snitch on his friends. It would be against our family's principles. He'll also want to protect the people in our Sonoma community. Our community has its fair share of quarrels for sure. Sparks really fly over issues like building hotels and moving the hospital. But this community comes together when things get *really* tough. I can't see Charlie going against his people. It's not in his nature."

She looked at her husband, who looked lovingly back at her.

"Babe, you took the words right out of my mouth and made them a whole lot better," he said, smiling at her. "Don't know what I'd do without you."

Deke knew he was beaten. He looked resigned as Charlie walked him to his car.

"Deke…thanks for coming up to Sonoma. I'm damned sorry I said those mean things to you earlier. You can slug me anytime you want and I won't hit back."

Deke laughed. "The California State Bar might have something to say about that, my friend" he grinned. "They'd haul my ass over the coals."

When Charlie returned to his wife, she looked up at him.

"Charlie…I hope and pray that the Feds are wrong and that no one has taken advantage of your loyal and trusting heart."

CHAPTER 26

The United States Attorney's Office, San Francisco

On the eve of trial, Josh and Jane felt besieged by recent press articles lambasting their office for bringing insider trading indictments against people from Sonoma, instead of the Silicon Valley insiders cited anonymously in the indictment.

"Why haven't the rich and powerful—the 1 percent—been charged?" It was a common theme in the press. "Why is the government *again* only going after the *little* guys?"

Jane dialed and waited for Gus Holmes to answer. After the preliminary introductions, Jane began the conference call.

"Gus, as we all know, the press is clamoring for the heads of the Silicon Valley guys who we believe were the source of the inside information. Let's recap for everyone's benefit why no indictments have been brought to date against these insiders, so we're all on the same page. Josh, why don't you give Gus a quick overview of where we stand."

"Gus," said Josh folding his arms and leaning over the speakerphone, "we have solid evidence that the Sonoma defendants made huge profits trading in the tech stocks of companies where these insiders worked as senior executives. From interviews with the General Counsel of these companies, we know these executives had access to the inside information that we suspect was used to make the trades.

"We also have evidence that the defendants developed close personal and business ties with these insiders while these insiders were visiting their second homes in wine country. Taken together, this circumstantial evidence leads to the inevitable conclusion that the Sonoma defendants must have learned the scoop from these insiders to make their spectacular trades. OK…it's circumstantial, but jurors are capable of using common sense. They will convict where the circumstances are blindingly obvious, as we have here. At present, we're still proceeding under the theory that the Sonoma defendants *stole* the information from the insiders. Interestingly, the press has jumped to the same conclusion we have: that the insiders were in cahoots with the defendants. Hence the reason why they're clamoring for more indictments."

"Any evidence of kickbacks between the defendants and the insiders?" asked Gus.

"Good question, Gus. Some of the defendants have business relationships with the insiders, so there's a history of payments going back and forth. However, we haven't found any *suspicious* transfers between the Sonoma defendants and the Silicon Valley insiders or their families…with one important exception. Our agents have uncovered that one Sonoma defendant, Charlie Bartino, invested in a venture capital fund with very close ties to the insiders. Coincidentally, this defendant put up most of the capital for the trades. However, without more, this connection by itself is too nebulous to charge the venture capital firm with money laundering insider trading profits for the insiders."

"You bet!" said Gus. "The VCs are the darling of the press and the politicians for helping our country crawl out of the Great Recession. No one will want to see any of them indicted without rock solid evidence."

"There's another snag," replied Josh. "Our agents have a hunch that one of our cooperating witnesses bears a grudge against the insiders who work in Silicon Valley. With all this in mind, we decided to go slowly in proceeding against these insiders until we get more corroborative evidence. Let's hope that one of them's stupid enough to take the stand so that the truth will finally come out at trial."

"How's the case coming against the Sonoma guys?" asked Gus. "Anyone roll yet?"

Josh spoke. "Unfortunately, Gus, the short answer is 'no.' A former *Vogue* model, Amanda Jones, has managed to raise more than *half a million dollars* by hosting several rock concerts at her winery to aid the Sonoma defendants' defense. To say that this case has not followed the usual pattern is an understatement."

"*Wow*," said Gus, "that's a *very* large sum of money. What are your thoughts on this?"

"I don't know, Gus," Josh answered. "Seems crazy to us. However, the only thing we have on Amanda Jones is that she personally knows the Sonoma defendants and has taken an interest in helping with defense costs. However, if we move against her, we have another celebrity insider trading case on our hands. In this case, we don't even have a stock trade by Ms. Jones to hang our hat on."

"Oh, great!" replied Gus. "Members of the press will really love *that* development. The public hates their favorite celebrities being dragged through the mud. Let's not forget that it's the public we're trying to protect. I'd go real slow proceeding against Ms. Jones."

"I'm with you there, Gus," said Josh. "Our undercover guys reported that her rock concerts in aid of the 'Sonoma Five,' as she calls them, were all squeaky clean. Only one guy was busted for dope, and he was one of *our* undercover guys. He had a great time spending the night in Sonoma County drunk tank!"

Everyone laughed, then sighed with exasperation. After a pause Gus spoke.

"Well, good luck, guys. And keep us posted. Be interesting to see what the jury makes of this case, not to mention how the judge in your neck of the woods views the law on insider trading."

"Yep…this is going to be an interesting case to take to trial," said Josh.

On the other side of town Ann, Jack, George, Deke and Kimberly were feeling equally wary.

Despite hopeful phone calls with Lillian Johnson and the other Silicon Valley executives' lawyers, they were still skeptical that the Silicon Valley executives would testify in support of their clients' version of the facts at trial. These witnesses could easily change their minds and decide at the very last minute to invoke their constitutional right to remain silent.

Even if *everyone* agreed to testify, how would this testimony come across to a jury? *Would the jury believe their clients?*

On the eve of trial, all the lawyers felt they were sailing into a dense cloud of coastal fog.

CHAPTER 27

The Prosecution's Opening Statement

A tall man, soberly dressed in a dark brown suit, walked to the lectern. After putting down his papers, Josh Kaplan turned to face the jury. As he looked up, his striking dark eyes and intense expression matched his sober attire. Before he even opened his mouth, Josh Kaplan had the courtroom's complete attention.

"Tall, dark, and handsome…and he's on the other *side,"* thought Peter. *"Just my luck."*

"Members of the jury, as the judge explained during *voir dire*, my name is Josh Kaplan and I represent the people of the United States of America," said Josh. "The People of the United States of America, to whom I will refer as the People during this trial, have brought these proceedings against five defendants: Robert Goodwin, Juan Rodriguez, Samantha Pond, Peter Smith and Charles Bartino.

"During this trial, you will hear evidence that these defendants, all residents of the county of Sonoma, met periodically at the VineSprings Grill in Carneros. You will hear evidence that, during the course of a year, the defendants used capital advanced by defendant Charles Bartino to purchase shares in technology companies located in the geographical area from San Francisco to San Jose. As many of you probably already know, this geographical area is also known as the Silicon Valley.

"Members of the jury, you will also hear evidence that, almost immediately after the defendants purchased these shares, the price per share of all these technology companies made *very substantial gains*," he said emphatically. "After purchasing these shares, the defendants split the profits."

Josh Kaplan paused briefly to give the jury time to absorb the information.

"You will hear evidence that several Silicon Valley executives, working at the same technology companies in which the defendants invested, frequently traveled to the Napa and Sonoma areas to visit their second homes. The evidence will further show that these Silicon Valley executives had either a business relationship or some other contact with at least one of the defendants.

"For example, you will hear evidence that the defendants purchased 20,000 shares of an entertainment software company, Meediya, whose stock had previously plummeted due to patent infringement litigation brought against it by a much larger company. You will also hear evidence that the CEO of Meediya, Tim Newman, owned a second home in Sonoma at the time that this trade was made. You will also hear evidence that Mr. Newman and his wife, Lucy, knew several of the defendants. Shortly after the defendants purchased this stock, the stock of this entertainment software company suddenly skyrocketed 40 percent on news that the patent litigation, which had previously depressed this company's stock price, had settled and that the parties to the lawsuit had entered into a strategic partnership agreement. By purchasing these shares just before this public announcement, the defendants made a profit of more than *$310,000.*"

Hearing this number, several jurors' eyes opened wide. Someone in the back of the courtroom whistled before being admonished by the judge.

The defendants and their team of lawyers inwardly cringed. They knew that the magnitude of investment profits would be a dark moment in the trial.

One consolation for the defense: the judge had ruled in pretrial motions that Charlie's VC investments could *not* be mentioned in the prosecution's opening statement. She had ruled that such potentially prejudicial evidence was irrelevant in a misappropriation case—where the charges involved *stealing* inside information. Such evidence would only be allowed if Charlie's lawyer later argued that his client was an unsophisticated investor.

"You will hear evidence that, on *three separate occasions*, the defendants purchased shares in Software Telecom Solutions, a telecommunications software company, shortly before that company released its better-than-expected quarterly earnings. You will also hear evidence that another part-time wine country resident, Mr. Thomas White, the chief operations officer for Software Telecom Solutions, had contact with one or more of the defendants during this period. As a result of purchasing Software Telecom Solutions shares, the defendants made a profit of more than *$456,000."*

As Josh Kaplan paused to take a sip of water, many in the courtroom stared at the defendants. The prosecution had now cited profits in excess of three quarters of a million dollars.

"You will also hear evidence that the defendants purchased shares of In-Grid, a Redwood City company creating smart-grid technology for countries worldwide, shortly before that company's stock rose on favorable news it had better-than-expected sales results. You will hear evidence that Mr. Tony Padilla, the marketing vice president of InGrid, also came into contact with one or more of the defendants during the period that the defendants were investing in InGrid. The evidence will further show that, as a result of the purchase of the InGrid shares, the defendants made an additional profit of over *$245,000.*

"The evidence will also show that the defendants purchased shares in a company where another part-time wine country resident, Mr. Jason Lee, worked as chief technology officer, shortly before this company announced that it had successfully registered a U.S. patent for an invention developed by Mr. Lee and his team. You will hear evidence that Mr. Jason Lee also came into contact with one or more of the defendants during the period that the defendants invested in his employer's company. As a result of the purchase of these shares, the defendants made a profit of more than *$166,000.*

"Finally, you will hear evidence that the defendants purchased shares in a telecommunications company where Ms. Janet Parks-Brown, another frequent visitor to wine country is employed, shortly before *that* company released better-than-expected quarterly earnings. You will hear evidence that Ms. Janet Parks-Brown came into contact with one or more of the defendants during the period that the defendants invested in her employer's company. As a result of the purchase of *those* shares, the defendants made a profit of more than *$124,000."*

Josh Kaplan paused to take a sip of water.

"Members of the jury, the evidence will show that these stock trades—earning profits in excess of $1,300,000—all occurred between December 2010 and September 2011."

$1,300,000? Wow!

The courtroom was spellbound.

Josh Kaplan described the witnesses he planned to call to testify at the trial. At the end of his opening statement, he politely thanked the jury for their time.

CHAPTER 28

The FBI Agent Testifies

After a brief intermission, in which the defense informed the Honorable Camilla Baker that they were deferring their opening statements, Josh Kaplan called FBI Agent, Herb Nelson, to the witness stand. The jurors saw a dark-haired man with a buzz cut, wide face, and square build take the stand. As he swore to tell the truth, the whole truth, and nothing but the truth, his voice conveyed, "I'm a no-nonsense guy."

Following careful questioning, Herb Nelson told the jury that he was based in New York but had been temporarily assigned to the Economic Crimes Unit of the FBI's San Francisco field office. With the aid of bank statements, he testified how the FBI had traced funds from a personal bank account in the name of defendant Charlie Bartino to a brokerage account in the name of the five defendants. With the aid of stock trading records, he testified in detail how the FBI tracked stocks trades made by this brokerage account over a one-year period. Using additional bank statements, Agent Nelson testified in detail how the FBI had tracked the proceeds from the stock trades into individual bank accounts of each of the five defendants.

Using NAZDAQ stock price charts showing the rise in share price of each of the companies traded, he testified how the FBI calculated the gross profits made from each trade. Once all of the trading records, bank accounts and stock charts had been admitted into evidence, they provided conclusive proof of the profits cited in the prosecution's opening statement.

After Josh Kaplan finished his questions, George DeRosa rose to cross-examine the FBI agent. George's enormous frame, bushy eyebrows and seaman's beard provided a visual contrast to the clean cut, intense young prosecutor who had, up to then, dominated the courtroom.

"Agent Nelson," George said in his baritone voice, "you testified that my client Mr. Robert Goodwin and the other defendants made a series of successful stock trades. Mr. Goodwin and the other defendants made all these stock trades in their own names, isn't that correct?"

"That's my understanding, from my review of the records," replied the agent.

"…And you also testified that a portion of the proceeds from these successful trades went into a bank account in my client's name, did you not?" He asked, with a gracious smile.

"That is my understanding from my review of the records."

"Agent Nelson, to your knowledge, Mr. Goodwin never attempted to disguise his participation in these trades, isn't that correct?"

"I don't know what you mean by the word *disguise* in this context," the agent replied.

After an objection from the prosecution, George bowed his head and smiled graciously at the judge. "Allow me to rephrase the question," he said. "My client Bob Goodwin's name was on the brokerage account that placed the order to buy the shares that were the subject of your testimony earlier this morning, isn't that correct?"

"Yes."

"Mr. Goodwin did not use *anyone else's* name instead of his own; isn't that correct?"

"Not to my knowledge."

"And my client's name was on one of the personal bank accounts that received proceeds from the stock trades were transferred. Isn't that correct?"

"Mr. Goodwin's name was on one of the five bank accounts that received the proceeds, as I have previously testified," the agent replied patiently. Only a brief blink signaled that the defense lawyer might be trying the agent's patience.

"Agent Nelson, you work for the Criminal Fraud Division of the FBI, isn't that correct?"

"Yes."

"And, please remind me and the jury, how many years have you worked in that particular division?"

The agent smiled wearily and replied: "Twelve years."

"And working in that division, it's fair to say that you have investigated *many* instances of securities fraud involving alleged insider trading, isn't that correct?"

"Yes."

"And in the course of investigating these cases, you and the FBI have uncovered instances where suspects have used their friends and relatives to *hide* their involvement in certain financial transactions, have you not?" asked George, fully confident of the answer. Early on, Ann and Tracy had briefed the rest of the defense team on Agent Nelson's background.

"I have seen instances where that occurred, yes."

"Isn't it fair to say that, in *most* insider trading cases, someone usually makes an effort to hide their involvement?"

"If they are *insiders*, usually yes," said the agent with a smile.

"When you say *insiders*, you mean people working inside a company who have access to inside information before this information is released to the public, do you not?

"Yes, that's correct."

"…And it's your testimony today that insiders who engage in illegal insider trading *usually* try to conceal their involvement in the stock trades, isn't that correct?"

"Correct."

"…And this concealment can take the form of *using others*, such as friends, family or shell corporate entities to conceal their involvement in the trades?"

"That's often the case, yes."

"However, in *this* case, *none* of defendants, including my client, worked for the companies they traded, isn't that correct?"

"Yes, that's correct."

"Therefore none of the defendants were *insiders* for the purpose of this discussion, isn't that correct?"

"That's true," conceded the agent.

"In the course of your investigation of insider trading, you and the FBI have also uncovered instances where the person *making the trade* tried to conceal *his or her* identities, have you not?"

"On some occasions, yes."

"…And in those instances, the traders sometimes used a corporate entity to make the trades or receive the profits, isn't that so?"

"Some did, certainly," replied the agent.

"But on those occasions, you and your FBI team managed to uncover the true identity of these traders, is that not so?" asked George with a bow to the witness.

"Yes, that is true," smiled Agent Nelson. Many in the courtroom, including the jury, smiled appreciatively at the calm, confident witness.

"However, in *this* case, you and your FBI team *quickly* identified my client as one of the traders, isn't that so?" asked George. A tougher tone had crept into in his voice.

"We identified Mr. Goodwin as one of the traders," said the agent, looking at the jury.

"…And it's fair to say that you were able to *easily* identify my client as one of the traders because my client Mr. Goodwin's name was on the brokerage account that made *every single stock trade*, isn't that correct?"

"Yes, your client's name was on the brokerage account that made *every single stock trade*," the agent agreed emphatically.

The jury avidly watched the courtroom edge into swordplay.

"There's no evidence that my client, Bob Goodwin, attempted to *hide* his identity by, for example, setting up a corporate entity to make the trades, isn't that correct?"

"We did not find a corporate entity involved."

"…And, you found no evidence that my client used a third party intermediary, such as friend or family member, to make the trades, isn't that correct?"

"That is correct."

"And you found no evidence that my client, Bob Goodwin, used a corporate entity to *receive* these profits, isn't that correct?" asked George increasing the pace of his delivery.

"We found no corporate entity involved, that is correct," replied the agent calmly.

"And you found no evidence that my client, Bob Goodwin, used the bank account of a family member or friend to *receive* these profits, isn't that correct?"

"We found no third party bank account involved, that is correct,"

"…And the same is true of the other four defendants. Isn't it fair to say that you were able to *easily* identify the other four defendants as the traders because their names also appeared on the brokerage account that made the stock trades, isn't that correct?"

"That is correct," replied the agent.

"…And you were able to *easily* trace the profits made by the other four defendants because, shortly after these trades were made, these profits went *immediately* into personal bank accounts of each of these other defendants, isn't that correct?"

"That is also correct."

"I have no further questions for this witness as this time," George said to the jury with a gracious smile.

CHAPTER 29

The Prosecution Calls Henrico Rodriguez

The following day, Juan's father, Henrico Rodriguez, was called to the stand.

"Mr. Rodriguez, you are the father of Juan Rodriguez, are you not?" asked Josh Kaplan.

"Yes, sir," answered the witness nervously.

"…And you and your wife own a pool and landscape maintenance business, isn't that so?"

"Yes, sir," he replied meekly. He hated being in the intimidating, vast courtroom. However, as he looked over at the defense table, he took pride in seeing that his son seemed to be holding up well under the pressure.

"And one of your customers is a couple, Lucy and Tim Newman, who own a home in Sonoma, isn't that so?"

"Yes, sir."

"And your son works for your business, isn't that so?"

"Yes, sir, when he is not studying hard," Henrico managed to add proudly.

"And part of your son's duties for the family business includes cleaning the pool and tending the landscaping at the home of Tim and Lucy Newman, isn't that so?"

"Yes, sir."

"Did Juan Rodriguez have a work schedule?"

"Yes, sir, we *all* do," the witness replied.

"What was his schedule for cleaning the pool and tending the garden at the home of Mr. and Mrs. Newman?"

"Well, sir, I have bought those records that you requested me to bring in the legal document. Do you want to see them now?"

"By the legal document, you mean the subpoena, don't you?"

The witness looked blankly at the prosecutor.

"Have you brought some documents with you today?"

Henrico Rodriguez bent down and took several documents from a briefcase. "I don't know what it's called, but these are the papers here," he said nervously as he held up a court document.

"And did you bring your work schedule showing the dates when your son worked at the home of Mr. and Mrs. Newman?"

"Yes, sir, it's all here."

"And did you bring copies of the invoices that showed the bills sent to Mr. and Mrs. Newman for your business services?"

"Yes, sir."

"And, according to the invoices, did your company provide services at the home of Mr. and Mrs. Newman on November 24, 2010?"

"Yes, sir."

"Did anyone else from your company work at the home of Mr. and Mrs. Newman?"

"No, sir."

"So your son worked at the home of Mr. and Mrs. Newman on that day, isn't that so?"

"I think so, yes, sir."

Josh Kaplan finished his examination, and Ann Schiller rose to question the witness. Many in the courtroom were impressed with her blonde good looks, slim frame, and serious demeanor.

"This lovely lawyer, who looks like an angel, is my son's savior," Henrico thought to himself. *"I must do my very best to help her."*

"Mr. Rodriguez, I represent your son, Juan Rodriguez, in this federal criminal proceeding brought against him," said Ann. Her sweet, calm voice filled the courtroom. Her words reminded Henrico that his beloved son was facing very serious criminal charges. The witness nodded politely, but tears welled in his eyes. Although he fought hard to maintain his composure and his dignity, he felt thoroughly humiliated when tears began slowly falling down his cheeks.

"I am so sorry," he said, his voice choking. "I am so embarrassed but…this is hard on me and my family."

The Honorable Camilla Baker asked the witness sympathetically if he would like to take a short break. Without waiting for an answer, she immediately called for an adjournment.

During the break, Deke Little leaned over his client, Charlie Bartino, to speak with George and Kimberly.

"For the first time, Kaplan's fucked up," he whispered. "The jury now feels enormous sympathy with this charming older man who has done nothing wrong."

George sagely nodded agreement.

"The FBI must have grabbed all the business records including invoices, time sheets, pay slips—the whole nine yards," replied Kimberly firmly. "For crying out loud, someone in charge of maintaining these records, such as the bookkeeper, could have authenticated those records without dragging the father into testifying against his own son."

Their clients—Charlie, Samantha and Bob—all looked at each other. They began to feel relieved that the prosecution seemed to have *finally* slipped up. Ten minutes later, in a hushed courtroom, Henrico Rodriguez again took the witness stand.

"Mr. Rodriguez, you are here today as a result of a demand by the prosecution to appear to testify, isn't that correct?"

"Yes, counselor," he said calmly.

"And you have been requested to produce business records, isn't that so?"

"Yes, counselor."

"Did my client, Juan Rodriguez, ever tell you that he invested in the stock market?"

"Yes…he was *always* talking about it."

"Can you remember when he told first told you that he was investing in the stock market?"

"I seem to remember it was sometime in 2010. The economy was *lousy*. He told us that he had made lots of money in the stock market and could help us out financially if we needed the help. He's very generous that way."

"Did he help you financially?"

"No…my wife and I wouldn't let him. We told him to keep the money for his education."

"Did he ever tell you *how* he was investing in the stock market? Was he using a stock broker, for instance?"

"He told us that he had joined an investment club that was putting up capital to invest in technology stocks. He's very eager to work in technology after he graduates. He was proud of the fact that this investment club asked him to advise them on the technology part of the business before this investment club purchased any shares."

"Did he ever seem shy or secretive about the activities of this club or its investments?"

"Not at all! He was very excited about this group. He was always bragging about how clever everyone was." Henrico Rodriguez then shook his head. "Sometimes he just wouldn't shut up about it."

"Did he ever tell you how the group decided to invest in any particular company?"

"He said things like the company's doing real well…stuff like that. But, to be honest, I didn't really listen. My wife and I were too busy managing our own business to pay much attention."

CHAPTER 30

The Prosecution Calls Jeremy Keniworth

After Henrico Rodriguez stepped down, the prosecution called Jeremy Keniworth to the stand. The jury observed the tall, lanky grey-haired man, dressed in a brown parka with the Keniworth Winery name and logo emblazoned on it, blue jeans and cowboy boots take the stand.

"Mr. Keniworth, you are the owner of Keniworth Winery in Kenwood, California, are you not?" asked Josh Kaplan.

"Yes, sir," replied the witness in a soft Texan accent.

"And do you recognize any of the defendants sitting at the defense table?"

"Sure do," replied the witness with a country and western lilt in his voice. "Pete's one of my employees," said Jeremy, looking at Peter Smith. "Juan has also helped us out occasionally with some of our charity events," he said, nodding his head at Juan Rodriguez. "I also know Bob," said the witness after a pause, looking firmly at Bob Goodwin.

"And, by Bob, do you mean Robert Goodwin?"

"Oh, yeah…sorry," said the witness, nodding his head nervously, "I meant Robert Goodwin. He and his wife have done some catering at some of our special events," he explained, turning to the jury and nodding his head nervously.

"Do you know any of the others?"

"Oh, yes! I know Mr. Charlie Bartino. His folks are prominent growers in our wine country. I've also met this real nice gal, Samantha Pond, a couple of times."

"Do you know a couple by the name of Lucy and Tim Newman?"

"Sure do."

"And how do you know this couple?"

"They were kind enough to hire us to pour our wine at a fancy big gig at their home."

"And…when was this fancy big gig?"

"I think it was sometime in December 2010."

"Did you visit the Newman home before this event?"

"Yes, sir. Pete and I visited the home one time before the event."

"And what was the purpose of your visit?

"We needed to figure out where to put our wine stations."

"Did you both drive together?"

"Nope. We drove separately. I was coming from another meeting."

"Did you leave together?"

"Nope. I seem to recall that Pete stayed behind after I left."

"Why did he stay behind?"

"Oh…he stayed behind to kinda butter up the customer."

"Do you know what they discussed?"

"I didn't stay long, but I could tell that the lady of the house wanted to show off her place."

"Do you know how long he stayed at the Newman home after you left?"

"I seem to recall that it was about an hour," said Jeremy casually.

"Did any of the five defendants all attend the 'big gig,' as you called it, at the Newman home?"

"Well, let me see now. Pete helped me pour our wine. I saw Bob passing around his food and Juan was there parking cars," he said and then looked down at the floor, as if concentrating on the question. "Wait a minute, now," he said looking up. "Don't hold me to it, but I seem to remember Samantha Pond and Charlie Bartino were also there. Most of the town of Sonoma was there, come to think of it," he chuckled.

"Did you see any Keniworth Wine Club members at the event?"

"Lucy and Tim are wine club members. Tom White and his better half were there. It was truly great to see them. The Parks-Brown might have been there. They later joined our wine club at the suggestion of Tom and his wife."

"Do you recall seeing Mr. White talking to any of the five defendants?"

"Yeah. I saw Tom White standing in front of Pete's wine station at one point talking to Samantha and a couple of other guys. Nothing illegal in that, is there?" he asked challengingly.

"Did you recognize the two other guys?"

"No, sir, I did not."

After Josh finished his questions, Jack Murphy rose. The jury listened attentively as the red-haired lawyer tilted his head slightly to one side and slowly began to question the witness. During Jack Murphy's gentle cross-examination, people in the courtroom began to relax.

"Mr. Keniworth, I represent your employee, Peter Smith, in this proceeding," said Jack Murphy slowly and patiently. "How did you first meet my client?"

"We used to date—way back when," said Jeremy proudly to the jury. "Pete and I broke up some time ago, but we always remained friends. *Yes, sir*," he said emphatically with a nod.

"When did my client start working at your winery?"

"When I bought the winery a few years ago, I asked some of my San Francisco friends, including Pete, to come and work for me on weekends. When Pete and his partner, Shawn, moved to Sonoma in 2005, Pete came and worked for me full time."

"And does Shawn still live in Sonoma?" Jack asked gently.

"No, sir. Shawn, died in a bicycle accident a couple of years ago now," said the witness sadly.

"Does your winery have a tasting room?"

"*Yes, sir*," replied the witness, more upbeat now.

"And have you made any changes to the tasting room since you bought the winery?"

"Oh, yes. We remodeled it from top to bottom."

"Who handled the remodeling of your tasting room?"

"Well, as a matter of fact, Pete handled most of it. He's nuts about that stuff and we just let him run with it."

"To your knowledge, has my client ever worked as an interior designer?"

"Yep. I think he worked as an interior designer at one point, but I don't know all the details."

"Did anyone at the winery ever joke about my client's interest in interior design?"

"Yep. We are always kidding Pete," he said with a broad grin. "When he isn't working, Pete's always out shopping for something for his home.

He remodels his home about once a year, even though it always looks perfectly fine to me."

"Now, in answering the prosecution's questions, you mentioned seeing a couple of the defendants talking in front of my client's wine station at the event at the Newmans' home. Do you recall that testimony?"

"Yes, sir."

"Were you able to hear any of their conversation?"

"*No, sir.* I was working clean across the room."

"Has my client been fired or placed on a leave of absence since his arrest in this matter?"

"*No, sir.* We've had to give him time off to attend this trial. However, as far as we are concerned, Pete Smith is still very much part of our Keniworth Winery family," he replied defiantly.

As he left the witness stand, Jeremy looked over at the defense table, where his friend and employee, Peter Smith was seated. In a sad voice, Jeremy whispered under his breath, "Take care, you guys," before leaving the courtroom.

For the remainder of the day, Josh Kaplan called other witnesses to testify that the five Sonoma defendants either worked for, or had otherwise come into contact with, the Silicon Valley executives mentioned in the prosecution's opening statement. These contacts took place at two wine country events: a fundraiser at the Newman home and the Sonoma Valley of the Moon Wine Auction.

Finally, before the case adjourned for the day, Josh Kaplan informed the court that on the following day, the prosecution would be calling James Chistlehurst to the witness stand.

When the defense lawyers first saw James Chistlehurst listed in the prosecution's pretrial witness list, they assumed that James would be yet another witness called to merely corroborate other prosecution evidence. However, each defense lawyer soon learned to his or her dismay that James Chistlehurst had also been investigated for insider trading. He had made a large profit by shorting Cecil Roberts' company stock days before the stock plummeted on news that the FDA was demanding more clinical trials for its latest product. As a result of this investigation, James Chistlehurst had entered into a settlement with the Securities and Exchange Commission to disgorge all profits from this trade. More alarmingly, Chistlehurst had agreed to wear a wire to help the FBI implicate their clients.

The defense lawyers all feared that they were about to meet the criminal defense lawyer's worst enemy: the witness who either distorts the truth or lies to save his own skin.

CHAPTER 31

James Chistlehurst Testifies

"All rise! The court is now in session," shouted the bailiff.

James Chistlehurst was dressed immaculately as he took the stand. He recited the oath with sleepy eyes and an English drawl.

After the usual preliminaries, during which the witness was introduced as the editor of the wine blog Chistlehurst Vintage Wines and a wine futures consultant, Josh Kaplan, turned to the witness.

"Did you ever attend an event at the home of Timothy and Lucy Newman in the City of Sonoma?"

"Oh, yes. It was a most *lavish* fundraiser. My pal, Phil Taylor, invited me and we drove over together from Yountville."

"Can you recall the date?"

"Not exactly, but I remember that it was sometime in December 2010. I *particularly* remember the month because I just returned from Hong Kong. As we drove over from Yountville to Sonoma, I was feeling relieved that I was not rushing to catch yet another plane."

"At that event, did you learn anything that caused you to trade some shares of stock?"

"Yes…at that fundraiser I learned some information that caused me to immediately short a biotech stock. *Very naughty* of me, but I simply had no idea I had done anything wrong."

"Please explain to the jury what do you mean by *short* a biotech stock."

"My broker allows me to borrow a stock, which I immediately sell. Later I have to buy the same stock in order return the stock I borrowed earlier. If the stock price goes down in the interim, I make a profit."

"So, by shorting the stock, you were betting that the stock price would go down, is that correct?"

"Yes, that's correct."

"Why did you think that this particular biotech company stock price would go down?"

"At this lavish fundraiser, I heard a young man, Jason Lee, speaking loudly on his cellphone with someone called Cecil. During this conversation, Mr. Lee made an extremely rude comment about the FDA, which shocked everyone in the room. I had a hunch that he was speaking with my friend, Cecil Roberts, who works for a biotech company. I knew that disappointing news from the FDA was likely to sink Cecil's company stock price—so I shorted it"

"Did the stock price later decline?"

Oh, *yes*…the stock price sank quite dramatically."

"Did you make a profit from shorting that stock at that time?"

"Indeed. Quite a handsome profit."

"Did you later enter into a settlement agreement with a federal agency regarding the profit you received from shorting that stock?"

"I am very happy to say that when your wonderful FBI agents approached me and explained that I *might* have done something wrong, I *immediately* tried to put things right."

"Which federal agency did you enter the settlement agreement with?"

"I believe in this country it's called the Securities and Exchange Commission, or the SEC for short"

"And what were the terms of this settlement agreement?"

"I disgorged *all* of the profits that I made on this trade. You see, once I realized that I might have done something naughty, I was frightfully keen to clear up any misunderstanding."

"Do you know some of the people in this courtroom today?"

"My dear chap, how kind of you to ask. After we spent countless delightful hours in each other's company, it must come as no surprise that I feel I have come to know even *you* rather well."

Maintaining his composure with a tired smile, Josh Kaplan replied, "Other than myself," he then paused and looked squarely at the witness, "do you know anyone *else* sitting in this courtroom today?"

"I have had the immense pleasure of knowing Miss Samantha Pond, who is sitting at the defense table over there." James acknowledged

Samantha with a flourish of his right hand. "George DeRosa is also a friend and client of mine."

"*Former friend*," George thought angrily. However, conscious of the jury's presence, he carefully refrained from expressing anything other than a mild curiosity in the testimony.

"Mr. Robert Goodwin's catering company, Not Just Olives, has helped me with events at my Yountville establishment."

"*Not after you nickeled-and-dimed me on my invoices*," Bob Goodwin thought angrily to himself.

"Returning to the fundraiser that you attended at the home of Lucy and Tim Newman in December 2010, did you meet any executives who work in Silicon Valley at that event?"

"My dear chap…the place was simply crawling with techie types. Our host, Tim Newman, works at a company called Meediya in Palo Alto, so he invited several people from Silicon Valley."

"Did you meet anyone from the Silicon Valley at this event?" Josh Kaplan persisted.

"When we first arrived, Phil introduced me to my host, Tim Newman, and a venture capitalist who works on Sand Hill Road, Marc Todd. My wine futures clients, Tom White and Tony Padilla, were also there. Oh yes…and that young man Jason Lee, who was so frightfully rude about the FDA, works in Silicon Valley. Mr. Lee thankfully left rather suddenly. I think we were all relieved!"

"Were any of the five defendants sitting at the defense table at this event?"

"Samantha Pond was there as a guest. I also remember seeing Bob Goodwin handing around *hors d'oeuvres*. The young man with the blond hair was also pouring wine. The young man with dark hair was parking cars. I think that the older gentleman, Mr. Charlie Bartino, was also a guest."

"At any time during this event, did you observe any of the five defendants speaking with any of the people who work in the Silicon Valley?"

"Well, let me see now. I *do* recall the venture capitalist, Marc Todd, breaking up a conversation with Tim Newman, Phil and myself to walk over and speak to defendant Charlie Bartino," James said, adding an ominous tone to his voice.

"Where were they standing?"

"Right in front of a wine station where that young man with the blond hair was pouring wine," James said pointedly.

"Did you observe any *other* interaction between any of the defendants and the Silicon Valley executives that you previously mentioned?"

"After Mr. Bartino left, I observed Mr. Goodwin leaning over and listening intently to a conversation between Tony, Tom, Samantha and the VC fellow Marc Todd while Mr. Goodwin was passing around the *hors d'oeuvres*. At the time I thought to myself, 'isn't that odd?'"

Bob Goodwin could hardly contain himself. "*The bastard!*" he thought angrily. "*He's deliberately putting my head in the noose to please the Feds.*"

As he listened to James' testimony, Bob's nostrils flared and his breathing became heavy. Later that evening, George joked that Bob looked like a warhorse ready to take off at a full gallop and crash through the enemy lines. After a hard stare from George, Bob simmered down.

Over the objections of the defense lawyers, the judge instructed the jury to disregard the witness' last comment. She also instructed the witness to testify only as to what he saw, and *not* express his opinion about what he observed.

"Oh I'm *frightfully* sorry, Your Ladyship, I mean Your Honor. In England, we address senior judges like you by the title of 'Lord' and 'Lady,'" James added unctuously .

"Did you observe any *other* contact between the defendants and anyone from Silicon Valley at this event?"

"Not at *that* event, no," said James meaningfully.

"Did you observe any contact at any *other* event?"

"Oh, yes *indeed*."

"And when was that?"

"In March 2011, I hosted a private wine tasting event at *my* establishment in Yountville. I'd originally planned to invite Lucy and Tim Newman and my pal, Phil Taylor. However, after the FBI contacted me, I included Samantha, the venture capitalist chap Marc Todd, and my clients, Tom White and Tony Padilla. At Samantha's request, I included Joe and

Janet Parks-Brown. She explained that they might be prospective clients. I even invited that rude young man, Jason Lee, because he was a friend of the Newmans. I tried to get Mr. Goodwin to cater the event but he was too busy."

"Did the FBI agents ask you to invite all these people?"

"Well no...*not exactly*. However, during their first visit, the FBI agents scared the life out of me by hinting that I might be in cahoots with another group of traders from Sonoma. I felt I had to go out of my way to convince them otherwise. During their second visit, I was shown scores of names and asked to identify those I knew. I picked out Samantha, Bob Goodwin, Charles Bartino and the Silicon Valley chaps who were either clients of mine or I'd met at the fundraiser. To convince the FBI that I *wasn't* in cahoots with these people—even though I knew them—I suggested that I help the FBI's investigation by inviting everyone to a wine tasting. At that point, the FBI agent suggested that I wear a device to record everyone's conversations. Most exciting! Just like in the movies."

After being admonished by the judge to "simply answer the question and not editorialize or comment," Josh Kaplan continued.

"During the private wine tasting event at your establishment in Yountville, what did you observe?"

"On *that* occasion, all the Silicon Valley chaps seemed *very* chummy. They also seemed very tight with Samantha."

"Did you observe anything else?"

"Samantha watched Jason Lee like a hawk. She could hardly take her eyes off him. This rather surprised me because she's a realtor and Jason Lee already owned a home in Glen Ellen. At one point I even caught them *whispering* together. I remember joking at the time that the young man was far too young for her."

Hearing this testimony, Samantha suddenly had difficulty breathing. She feared that she was going to have a heart attack. It was as if a dagger had been thrust in her back between her shoulder blades. *"How could James act like this?"* she wondered to herself. *"I always thought he was a really good friend?"*

Although her lawyer had warned her to expect lies and distortions emanating from the witness stand, this testimony from a close friend took her off guard. Samantha almost burst into tears of frustration at being required to sit quietly in the courtroom. After Kimberly Hayward gently put her hand on Samantha's arm, Samantha managed with great effort to keep quiet, even though her face remained flushed.

"Did you observe any of the defendants and these Silicon Valley executives come into contact with each other at any *other* wine country event?"

"*Yes, indeed*. I saw *several* of them at the Sonoma Valley of the Moon Wine Auction," replied James. "On that occasion, Samantha kindly invited me to join her table."

"What did you observe at that auction?"

"When I *first* arrived at Samantha's table, Tom White and Tony Padilla were chatting merrily away with Samantha and Peter Smith—like they were old friends. However, I didn't catch what they were saying."

"Did you observe anyone else from Silicon Valley at this auction?"

"The venture capitalist chap, Marc Todd, was there. Joe and Janet Parks-Brown, who had just made a successful offer on a second home in Sonoma, were also sitting at Samantha's table. Since Samantha had helped seal the deal, we all congratulated them. At one point, Cecil Roberts came up and embarrassed me by wanting to talk shop. I thought that this was *not* the right occasion to talk business."

"Apart from Samantha Pond and Peter Smith, were any of the other defendants at this wine auction?"

"Oh, my dear chap! They were *all* there. The Sonoma Valley of the Moon Wine Auction is one of the *premier* events on the Sonoma Valley social calendar. Juan Rodriguez took part in a skit put on by the Keniworth Winery. Bob Goodwin sat at the next table with a group of rather flashy, overdressed celebrity types invited by my friend and former supermodel, Amanda Jones. Charlie Bartino was hosting another table farther away…but he spent most of the auction working the room and watching the bidding."

"That afternoon, did you observe any more contact between the defendants and the Silicon Valley executives?"

"During the actual auction itself, I noticed Samantha *avidly* listening to everything being said by Tom White, Tony Padilla, and Janet Parks-

Brown. One could almost see her mind clicking over." After a look of disapproval from the judge, Josh Kaplan persevered.

"Please follow Her Honor's instruction and refrain from making comments about your observations or giving us your thoughts and opinions. Now, when you saw Samantha Pond listening to Tom White, Tony Padilla and Janet Parks-Brown, could you hear what they were saying?"

James looked at the jury. "Unfortunately, I couldn't hear a word they were saying because they seemed to be *whispering*."

CHAPTER 32

The Defense Regroups

After court adjourned, the defense lawyers met at George's Pacific Heights mansion to discuss how best to confront James under cross examination.

Once they were all seated with drinks in George's magnificently furnished living room with its panoramic Bay view, they waited for George to begin the discussion.

"OK, so…let's begin with the obvious," he said. "The government has presented evidence that our clients all know each other and that, on more than one occasion, our clients came into contact with the guys who had the inside scoop." He rose and began to pace the room. "Today, Chistlehurst went out of his way to suggest to the jury that all these contacts were nefarious. He's even hinted that the insiders were involved in an insider trading conspiracy with our clients, an allegation that's not even in the indictment. Obviously, Chistlehurst's desperate to curry favor with the Feds. However, I can't see *where* we can catch the guy outright. It's the *insinuation* behind his testimony that's damaging, not the facts themselves, which may all be true.

"Obviously, our clients would love to see us verbally string the guy up by his thumbs," added George dubiously. "Trouble is, how can we show that the guy's *insinuations* are false?"

George paused to let his words sink in. He leaned on the back of his chair facing the group.

"And that raises *another* problem," he said in an exasperated tone. "After today, the Silicon Valley guys may refuse to testify. After today's performance, one's got to bet heavily that their lawyers will be beating up on them to keep their mouths shut and take the Fifth. That leaves the word of our clients against his."

After a long pause, Kimberly was the first to speak.

"George," she said slowly, "I'm not certain that we necessarily have to prove conclusively Chistlehurst is a bad guy. We just have to demonstrate enough *uncertainty* so that the jury does not send anyone to jail solely based on his *insinuations*, especially after the judge—and even Kaplan—admonished Chistlehurst not to make editorial comments about his testimony. It's in the bag that the judge will instruct the jury to ignore Chistlehurst's insinuations."

"Yes…but *that* jury instruction is only useful on appeal," replied George grimly. "We *all* know that asking any jury to disregard anything's like asking them to unplug their brains. It never works at trial."

"I agree with George," said Jack Murphy. "Asking any jury to *disregard* any testimony only makes them pay special attention to that testimony. They all know that they weren't supposed to hear it. It's only human nature."

"Here's one approach," Kimberly said thoughtfully. "When someone like James is questioned in greater detail, he will be forced to admit he cannot really remember the details, except for precise details that he has been asked to remember and that suit his own purpose. If we get James to say over and over again that he 'doesn't recall,' he may appear evasive—even fanciful—before the jury. This way, we might be able to suggest to the jury that his observations…shall we say it politely…are unreliable, without creating a slanging match between James and our clients?"

"Yeah, jurors don't like evasiveness," concurred Jack. "Let's also pursue the usual argument that he's desperate to please the Feds," suggested Jack. "Justice hasn't reached any agreement with the guy not to prosecute. They could still come after him. Maybe one of us plays Mr. Nice Guy to get him to describe how fearful he felt at being interrogated by the FBI."

"Go right ahead, pal—and lots of luck." said Deke in a voice reminiscent of a 1930s gangster movie. His scornful expression made the other lawyers laugh. "Jack…normally speaking, you'd be right," added Deke in a kinder tone of voice. "However, I seriously doubt whether *anyone* can make this witness be fearful of *anything*. Even a federal judge and prosecutor had a hard time keeping him in line."

Ann had been staring into space as she listened to her colleagues. "I wonder why?" she said suddenly.

"You wonder why *what*?" asked George.

"I wonder why Chistlehurst went out of his way to beat up on our clients like this? Now that he's reached a deal with the SEC, he's probably off the hook. Although I agree with Jack that Justice could still bring a criminal case, it sounds unlikely at this late stage. I don't see how blackening our clients before the jury benefits him. Where's the incentive?"

Kimberly shrugged. "Jack's right," she said. "Helping nail our clients was the *quid pro quo* for Chistlehurst to settle with the SEC and for Justice to keep the dogs leashed."

After everyone sighed, George turned to Deke.

"OK, wise guy," he said. "You've been holding back. How about you giving us your thoughts."

"He's gone quiet because his client is about to roll," joked Kimberly.

Deke leaned over in his chair and smiled at the group.

"You know, gang, I agree with Ann. Something's missing here." Deke paused to sip his drink. He nodded his head thoughtfully. "Having hit the law books over the last few months," he said in his nonchalant drawl, "I don't think the Feds had a damn thing on James Chistlehurst."

As the group listened attentively to the tough street-smart lawyer, he paused and then looked up. "All this guy *did* was trade on a tip broadcast publicly at a wine country event. In the absence of some special relationship of *trust and confidence* existing between him and the issuer of the stock or the guy who spilled the beans, it's highly questionable as to whether this behavior is even actionable by the SEC, let alone Justice.

"Remember, gang, Chistlehurst did *not* learn the information firsthand from Cecil Roberts himself, which might make an insider trading rap stick. Jason Lee blurted out the tip at a *public* gathering. Under those circumstances, the Feds' bitch, if any, lies with Cecil Roberts and Jason Lee for not keeping their traps shut. The case against Chistlehurst looks *flimsy* to me. I can't understand why Chistlehurst didn't hire a lawyer to tell the Feds to go hang."

After Deke paused to let the others think, he leaned over and spoke in a very deep voice.

"Kimberly's comment about "the Feds leashing the dogs" reminded me of the Sherlock Holmes story, *The Adventure of Silver Blaze*.

"How come?" asked Ann.

"Well, it's not just because the witness is British," replied Deke scornfully. "Do you remember the part where Sherlock Holmes famously refers to '*the curious incident of the dog in the night-time?*'"

"But, Mr. Holmes, the dog did nothing in the night-time," quoted Kimberly theatrically. Conan Doyle was also one of her favorite authors.

"Ah," Ann said pensively looking at the group, "…and Sherlock Holmes replies, 'That was the curious incident.'"

Unknown to Ann, her colleague at Horace & Fitzpatrick, Phil Taylor, returned to his home in Menlo Park that evening also feeling deeply perplexed about James' testimony.

Phil had decided to sit in and watch the trial that day so he could observe firsthand how his colleague, Ann Schiller, was doing. He also wanted to support his friend, James Chistlehurst, when James was called to the stand as a witness. Although Phil wasn't a trial lawyer, he knew that testifying in federal court was no walk in the park. Phil was concerned for his friend.

Phil worked in the corporate law department of their Palo Alto office. Since he was not on the trial team, Ann had not briefed him on the revelations concerning Chistlehurst, which had come to light shortly before the trial. Phil arrived at the courthouse assuming that James would be a reluctant witness for the prosecution.

Phil remembered attending the wine cellar tour and tasting at James' Yountville estate. He surmised that the prosecution wanted to use that event as evidence of contact between the Sonoma defendants and the people with the inside information.

James' testimony in the courtroom had shocked Phil. He'd been taken aback when James testified that he had shorted Cecil Roberts' company stock after overhearing a tip at the Newman fundraiser. To Phil, this tacky behavior didn't fit with James' image as a sophisticated connoisseur of fine vintage wine.

Phil was also disturbed that James had agreed to wear an FBI wire to entrap Phil's longtime friends, Samantha Pond, Marc Todd, Tom White and Tony Padilla.

After the case adjourned, Phil left the courthouse quickly so that he wouldn't run into James. Phil was feeling especially embarrassed and uncomfortable that he had introduced Tom White and Tony Padilla to James. *"What a mess!"* he thought.

As he drove home, Phil angrily puzzled over why his friend, James, had gone out of his way to implicate Phil's other friends in criminal wrongdoing. *"Tom and Tony are James' clients. They are also as honest as the day is long. What in God's name is going on here?"*

As he pondered James' courtroom testimony, Phil remembered a recent phone call he'd received from a Stanford alumni friend. This friend had told Phil that he'd tried on several occasions to contact James, but James never returned the calls. Phil had assured his friend that James was probably busy traveling, but that he, Phil, would contact James when they were both in wine country.

Phil's crazy work schedule had put the phone call completely out of his mind. *"Why had James proved so difficult to reach?"* he now wondered.

Phil decided that if he weren't too busy the following morning, he would speak to Tracy Sanchez. As a former federal prosecutor, Tracy might be able to offer him some insight before he contacted Ann with his suspicions. Phil Taylor didn't want to unduly bother Ann or his friend George when they were in trial. However…he was beginning to smell a rat.

CHAPTER 33

Phil Taylor Seeks Advice

"Tracy, do you have a moment?" Phil asked anxiously.

The petite middle-aged blond pivoted her chair towards him smiling at the seriously worried face of one of her partners.

Tracy was getting used to her new firm's white-shoe environment, where the firm's other lawyers who sought her advice were often scared out of their wits. She was beginning to appreciate how neither her new colleagues nor their clients had any prior experience with the Federal Criminal Justice System. Her first order of business was to simply calm everyone down.

"Sure. Take a seat," she said, moving to the small round guest table by the window in her office. In contrast to her busy law practice, the garden outside was a picture of tranquility.

"Phil, how can I help?"

"Have you been following the insider trading case involving some guys from Sonoma?" His voice was raspy.

"Ah, yes. Ann Schiller's case," she said with a short laugh. "What a fun case that must be!"

She looked at the strained eyes of the man sitting in front of her. "*He didn't get much sleep last night,*" she thought to herself. "Phil, you look quite pale. Do you know someone involved? If so, please excuse my flippancy."

Phil recounted bitterly how he'd taken time out of his busy work schedule to attend the trial to show support for one of the witnesses, only to see James implicate his other friends and place them in serious jeopardy. During his recital, he became so angry that he could hardly catch his breath between sentences.

Phil's story about James' cooperating witness testimony was so familiar to Tracy that she almost laughed out loud. However, she became less amused as she learned the impact of James Chistlehurst's testimony on Phil's Silicon Valley friends, who had not been charged with any wrongdoing.

As an assistant United States attorney in the U.S. Attorney's Office in Miami, Tracy Sanchez had witnessed firsthand the impact of law enforcement on the families of hard-core, violent criminals involved in drug smuggling. However, when she saw these families weep in court, she never felt any compunction about putting *those* bad guys away for life. Too many had destroyed other innocent lives, leaving other families destitute.

Now she listened to a sweet man describe how the prior day's testimony might seriously wreck the lives of decent people with no prior criminal record, who, in the absence of criminal charges, could not fight back. This was a new experience for her.

When Phil stopped speaking, Tracy left unsaid her cynical observation that cooperating witnesses in a federal criminal case *always* betray their nearest and dearest. Instead, she mentally put on her former prosecutor's hat.

"What do you know about this guy, James Chistlehurst?" she asked. Phil thought for a moment.

"He's an expert on fine French wines and owner of the famous wine blog ChistlehurstVintageWines. He's invited to give speeches all over the world. For several years, he's provided me and my Stanford alumni friends access to great deals on the finest vintage wines being produced in Burgundy and Bordeaux. One can make serious money from these wine futures investments. I know, because I have. After buying wine futures and then selling the wine through James' connections, my account with him now stands at well over a hundred thousand dollars in the black."

"Why does he live in Yountville if his expertise is mainly *French* wine?"

"God only knows! Maybe he just likes living in California?"

Tracy, whose multi-lingual skills and international crime background made her a natural for the international firm Horace & Fitzpatrick, only said, "Hmmmm." While working as an assistant U.S. attorney in Miami, Tracy became all too familiar with the con artist who moved in high society circles. This type of crook knew how to cater to the whims and egos of a wealthy elite. *"Fine wine and fine art rip-offs always top the list,"* she thought to herself.

Tracy spent the next half hour patiently putting her partner through an informal deposition to learn more about James Chistlehurst, his wine futures business, and his cooperation with the FBI. Some of the answers surprised her.

In Tracy's experience, someone moving in James' elite international circle would simply blow off a U.S. federal law enforcement investigation as beneath his contempt. James' eager desire to cooperate with the FBI struck Tracy as completely out of character. This cooperation seemed more suspicious to her than the all-too-familiar backstabbing of James' friends.

At Tracy's urging, Phil called his Stanford alumni friend who'd complained that James hadn't returned his calls. He followed up with calls to other Stanford alumni who he knew had purchased wine futures from James Chistlehurst. He also called the lawyers for Tom White and Tony Padilla, who had been present at the defense lawyers' conference in Lillian Johnson's office. After several phone calls, Tracy leaned back in her chair and looked hard at Phil.

"Let's call Ann during her lunch break to give her the scoop on what we've learned this morning."

CHAPTER 34

James Chistlehurst Returns to the Stand

Meanwhile, earlier that morning the defense lawyers and their clients arrived at the courthouse wanting to skin James Chistlehurst alive. However, their outer demeanor was cordial, giving no one in the courtroom an inkling of their sentiments. By consensus among the defense lawyers, Kimberly was first to rise and cross-examine James.

"Mr. Chistlehurst, I represent the defendant Samantha Pond in this case. Yesterday you testified that you attended a fundraiser at the Newman home and that my client Samantha Pond was also there. Can you remember what my client was wearing on that occasion?"

"No, but, gentle lady, knowing Samantha, I'm sure that it was something most fetching. It usually is."

"Nice one," thought Samantha. *"I could hardly call my golf shirt and khaki pants worn to the Newman fundraiser fetching."*

"Yesterday you also testified that you hosted a special wine tasting at your establishment in Yountville, and that my client Samantha Pond was one of your guests. Can you remember what my client was wearing on that occasion?"

"Not exactly, but I think she dressed rather formally, as a lady realtor might."

"And how might that be?"

"Well…I don't know, exactly. Like a lady professional is the best I can do."

"Yesterday you also testified that you attended the wine auction and sat at a table hosted by my client as her guest. Can you remember what my client was wearing on that occasion?"

"Sorry, I'm completely drawing a blank. I usually don't focus on what is known in high society circles as a female *wardrobe opportunity,*" replied James with a condescending smile.

"The wine auction lasted five hours, is that correct?"

"About that time period, yes."

"And you sat at my client's table for the entire event, is that correct?"

"Except when I went outside to speak with a friend, yes."

"What day of the week was the fundraiser at the Newman home?"

"Goodness, I don't recall. Can I look at my diary?"

"Not necessary," said Kimberly sharply. "Can you recall what time you arrived at the fundraiser at the Newman home?"

"Well, I was with Phil Taylor. Let me see…I think it must have been early afternoon."

"Did you drink anything at that event?"

"I think I may have had a couple of glasses of wine."

"You are an expert in wine, are you not?"

James now felt entirely on safe ground.

"Not quite to *James Bond's* standards, but tolerably so," he quipped.

"Can you recall the varietal of the wines that you drank at that event?"

"You know, it was *so* long ago that I simply don't recall."

For the next hour, at a rapid-fire pace, Kimberly questioned James in detail about the other two events and received similarly vague responses. As James repeatedly answered, "I don't recall," James' voice sounded tired and peevish. He dropped the "gentle lady" from his replies.

"Yesterday, you testified that you *observed* a conversation taking place at the Newman fundraiser among Samantha Pond, Tom White, Tony Padilla and Marc Todd. Did you *hear* any part of their conversation?"

"No."

"Where exactly were you standing when you *observed* this conversation?"

"Well, let me see, now. I must have been close by."

"I don't want you to speculate. Just answer the question. If you do not know or cannot recall, just say so."

"Frankly, I can't recall at this point."

"Was anyone else in the same area?"

"Not that I can recall."

"Yesterday, you mentioned that you hosted my client, Samantha Pond, and several Silicon Valley executives at your establishment in Yountville.

At any time that day, did you overhear Mr. Lee discussing his company or his company's business with either my client or anyone else?"

"No. He excused himself to take a work-related call. That's all I remember," James answered petulantly.

"What time of day did Mr. Lee excuse himself to make the call?"

"I don't recall," James replied contemptuously.

"Yesterday, you testified that at the wine auction, you *observed* my client listening to certain conversations taking place among Tom White, Tony Padilla and Janet Parks-Brown. How many conversations did you observe taking place among these individuals?"

"*I don't recall*," said James. He then sighed heavily.

"Did you *hear* any part of their conversation?"

"No."

"Approximately what time in the afternoon did you observe my client listening to these conversations?"

"*I don't recall*," shouted James with exasperation.

During the lunch break, George and Bob walked over to Kimberly and Samantha. Deke and Charlie also joined them.

"Do you think you managed to get the witness to say 'I don't recall?' enough times?" George spoke quietly.

"I think I counted at least 20," said Samantha proudly, smiling at her lawyer.

After their clients left, Deke leaned over and whispered to Kimberly in front of George. "Didn't you take a risk asking the witness about the *'fetching outfits'* that your client 'must have been wearing?'" Deke mimicked James' British accent as he repeated James' response.

"What if that British jerk had managed to describe each outfit in great detail to the jury?" asked George with one bushy eyebrow raised.

"Oh, guys!" Kimberly chided gently. "*Come on.* Most men are clueless when it comes to our outfits. You guys never remember what we wear."

After the lunch break, Jack Murphy rose to question the witness. In contrast to Kimberly's rapid-fire questions, Jack's tone of voice and manner were patient and sympathetic.

"Mr. Chistlehurst, I represent the defendant, Mr. Juan Rodriguez. Do you recall one Friday evening last year when the two FBI agents came to your door?"

"Gosh, I don't think I will *ever* forget it."

"That's because having two FBI agents come to your front door is quite an unnerving experience, is it not?"

"Yes, it certainly is."

"When they rang the doorbell and you opened the door, they immediately showed you their badges and said that they were from the Federal Bureau of Investigation, did they not?"

"Yes, I seem to recall that they did."

"Did they say something like, "We think you have information that will assist us in a *criminal* investigation?"

"I don't recall their exact words, but they said something like that."

Jack stopped for a moment to stroke his chin. He then looked up at the witness and smiled.

"Are you familiar with the federal agency known as the Securities and Exchange Commission, otherwise known as the SEC?"

"Yes, I am now."

"Are you aware of the fact that the SEC conducts *civil* investigations." And the FBI conducts *criminal* investigations?"

"I know that now…but I didn't when I was approached by the FBI."

"Turning to the two FBI agents who came to your door that Friday evening, they *didn't* tell you that they were conducting an investigation on behalf of the *SEC*, did they?"

"That's true," James conceded reluctantly. "I now recall they did mention a *criminal* investigation."

"When the agents came to your home, was it dark outside?"

"Yes, it was wintertime and very dark outside."

"Did you let the two agents come into your home?"

"Of course. It was the only courteous thing to so. I was also quite worried that they had mistaken me for a criminal. If so, I wanted to clear the whole thing up."

"Did they discuss with you the fact that you had made some stock trades?"

"Oh, my God, *yes*. They immediately zeroed in on the biotech stock trade that I made after the Newmans' party in December 2010. I was utterly terrified!"

"At that moment, did you fear that you might be facing *criminal* charges?"

"Yes, but I *quickly* explained to the agents that I didn't know I'd done anything wrong," replied James in an exasperated voice.

"When was it suggested that you wear a wire to assist the FBI in their *criminal* investigation?"

"Shortly after their second visit."

"When was the second visit?"

"About a week after the first visit"

"What happened during the agents' second visit?"

"They asked me to review scores of computer generated names. Really quite tiresome. As I testified earlier, I managed to pick out those I knew."

"What happened next?"

"They took my deposition. They also proposed that I wear a wire to assist them in their criminal investigation."

"So…your deposition was taken *shortly after* the FBI agents came to your home a second time, is that correct?"

"Yes."

"…And you agreed to wear the wire *shortly after* the FBI agents came to your home a second time, is that correct?"

"Yes."

"Did the deposition occur *before* or *after* you reached the settlement agreement with the SEC?"

"*Oh*, a long time before. I only reached a final settlement agreement with the SEC much later."

"Did you agree to wear the wire to assist the FBI in their criminal investigation *before or after* you reached the settlement agreement with the SEC?"

"Before."

"One final question. Other than what you have already testified to in this courtroom, did you see any of the *other* defendants, such as my client, speaking with anyone who works in Silicon Valley?"

"No."

"I have no further questions of this witness at this time."

After Jack sat down, George and Deke postponed their cross-examination of the witness. They did not want to disturb the fruitful testimony that had already been elicited from this trickiest of witnesses. Ann also reserved her right to cross-examine this witness. During a phone call with Phil Taylor and Tracy Sanchez during the lunch break, Ann learned that an intense investigation into James Chistlehurst's background and business activities was underway.

"Thank God for my colleagues, Phil and Tracy!" she thought to herself.

The prosecution finally called an expert witness, who, using stock trading charts, testified how news of a higher-than-expected increase in a company's quarterly earnings usually had a positive impact on a company's stock price, and that news of lower-than-expected quarterly earnings usually had a negative impact on a company's stock price. She also testified that news of a threatened lawsuit against a small start-up company, like Meediya, usually had a negative impact on a company's stock price. Conversely, positive news, such as the settlement of a patent lawsuit or the successful registration of a patent usually had a positive impact on a company's stock price.

After the prosecution rested its case, outside the presence of the jury, the defense lawyers all made motions to dismiss the case against their clients on the grounds of inadequate evidence of illegal insider trading. The judge denied each of these motions, ruling that the case could proceed before the jury.

Josh Kaplan returned to his office relieved. His opponents went home feeling resigned to the inevitable.

All five lawyers for the Sonoma defendants understood only too well that, *even* if they managed to shake James' credibility, the jury had to be highly suspicious of their clients' remarkably profitable trades.

CHAPTER 35

Jason Lee Testifies

Jason Lee slouched in the witness chair, checking his smartphone. The jury returned to the courtroom after a brief adjournment but the young man did not look up.

"All rise! The court is now in session!"

Everyone rose, except the young man still checking his smartphone messages. As Judge Camilla Baker took her seat, she briefly glanced at the witness stand and the lawyers, and then raised one eyebrow at the bailiff.

The bailiff went over to Jason Lee and yelled in the young man's ear so that everyone in the courtroom could hear.

"Show respect for this Court! Turn your phone off, put it away, and *pay attention!*"

As the courtroom erupted into laughter, Jason—clearly flustered—did as he was told. After putting his phone away, he blinked, as if waking from a hypnotic trance.

Kimberly Hayward re-introduced Jason Lee, the chief technology officer of H.I.T. Inc., who lived in Palo Alto.

"Other than your primary residence in Palo Alto, do you own a second home?" asked Kimberly.

"Yes."

"Where is that second home?"

"In Glen Ellen."

"…And for the members of the jury who may not be familiar with Glen Ellen, where is that town located?"

The young man shrugged. "It's in wine country," he mumbled. Kimberly persevered with patience.

"…And again for the benefit of the jury, where in wine country is Glen Ellen located?"

"About six miles north of Sonoma on Highway 12. Look it up on

Google maps," he added petulantly, as if her questions were wasting his time.

Kimberly smiled at the jury, concealing her fervent desire to give this young witness a verbal thrashing. His testimony was vital, but would the jury decide to disbelieve this arrogant, clueless young man?

"And, while visiting your home in Glen Ellen, have you ever attended any private wine tastings?"

"…May have done," Jason replied warily.

"And did you attend a private wine tasting event where you were, for example, given a presentation on investing in Bordeaux wine futures?"

"Anything wrong with that?" Jason replied defensively.

"Where did the event take place?"

"At some dude's place in Yountville."

"Can you remember the name of this person?"

"James Chistlehurst," said Jason, who was barely audible.

"At this event, did you discuss work-related matters with anyone present…such as your latest products, how your company is doing…that sort of thing?"

For the first time, Jason Lee stopped slouching in his seat and sat upright.

"Absolutely not." His reply was vehement.

"And…why was that?"

"I would *never* let anyone, not even my best friends, know what my team is working on," he replied indignantly. "None of us would let anyone get near our company's stuff. We encrypt everything—even internally."

"When you attended the wine tasting event in Yountville, were any of the defendants sitting at the defense table also present?"

"Yep…Samantha Pond was there. "

"During this event, did you have a private conversation with Ms. Pond outside the presence of everyone else?"

"Nope!" said Jason emphatically.

"Did you speak with anyone else privately at any time while you were attending the wine tasting event in Yountville that day?"

"Nope!" Jason was emphatic a second time. "Oh, wait. I had to take a call from work. However I moved away from the tasting room so that no one could hear."

"And why was that?"

"I was talking with our lawyers about something *really* confidential. We had to keep it highly confidential until it was announced to the public," he replied angrily.

"Please don't disclose your conversation with your lawyers. However, did the confidential subject matter involve information that was later made public?"

"Yes."

"And did that information concern a patent application pending before the United States Patent and Trademark Office?"

"Yes."

"Has that patent been successfully registered?"

"Yes."

"Did your company later disclose information about this patent registration to the public?"

"Yep. We had a big press release."

"And did that have an impact on H.I.T. Inc.'s stock price?"

"It sure did. Our stock price almost doubled overnight."

"Did you discuss the existence or registration of this patent application with my client, Ms. Pond, *at any time* before your employer released the news of the successful patent registration to the public?"

"Absolutely not! My company would have fired me."

"When you returned to Mr. Chistlehurst's tasting room after having the confidential conversation with your lawyers, did you have *any* conversation with my client, Ms. Pond?"

"Yes…I seem to remember that she asked me quietly how Cecil was doing."

"Is that Cecil Roberts?"

"Yep."

"Why did she talk to you about Cecil?"

"Cecil's a mutual friend of ours who was under a lot of pressure work-wise," Jason mumbled. "We were both really concerned about him."

"Do you recall Mr. Chistlehurst cracking a joke about your

conversation with Ms. Pond about Cecil?"

"We were talking quietly. He couldn't hear the conversation so he said something obnoxious about me being too young for her. He was just being a jerk. I didn't pay any attention to it."

"After you returned to the tasting room, did you discuss anything else besides Cecil with my client?"

"Nope."

"Did you make any investment decision that day regarding wine futures?"

"Yes, I felt happy about the patent so I signed up for some wine futures."

"Did my client, Samantha Pond, know this?"

"Sure. It wasn't a state secret or anything."

During their questioning, George, Deke and Ann successfully confirmed that Jason Lee only came into contact with their clients when in the company of many others. They also confirmed that he did not discuss his company's business with their clients. During their questioning, they tried to portray the young technology executive as honest and hardworking. However, from the judge's and jury's facial expressions, each lawyer could tell that Jason's surly demeanor was grating on their nerves.

When the judge finally adjourned the trial at 4:30 p.m., the defense lawyers inwardly sighed with relief. Jack Murphy hadn't had the opportunity to question this young witness. They had the weekend to try and straighten things out.

CHAPTER 36

The Venture Capitalists Intervene

On Saturday morning, Jason Lee, Janet Parks-Brown, Tom White, Tony Padilla and Tim Newman found themselves treated to a small surprise by their lawyers.

As they walked into Lillian Johnson's office, they were greeted by Marc Todd and Stan Becker, a world-renowned superstar in the world of start-ups and venture capital. Awed at meeting one of his superheroes, Stan Becker, Jason spilled his coffee on the conference room table.

Overnight, in desperation, the lawyers had sought the assistance of the "tribal elders" of the technology industry in the hope that they could make the techies "wise up."

After introductions, Stan Becker was the first to speak.

"Some of you are acknowledged to be brilliant in your space," he said slowly and patiently. "However, none of that will matter a damn if you end up serving 10 years for a crime you did *not* commit." As he paused to let his words sink in, the executives looked horrified.

"So far, the Feds have held off from filing any criminal charges against anyone from Silicon Valley," interjected Marc Todd, speaking in his famously understated style. "However, if the Sonoma guys go down, your necks are next on the Feds' chopping block." The group continued to look frightened.

"Many senior executives in this valley have gone through their fair share of legal proceedings," Stan Becker said, leaning back in his chair. "Unfortunately, it comes with the territory of running a successful technology company. *Everyone* gets to walk the plank in the courtroom at some point. But the courtroom is no one's idea of fun. It's more akin to being mauled by a grizzly." He paused and leaned forward. "The only way to survive is by *listening to your lawyers*," he said slowly, expressing the last four words as if they were a mantra. "Many of Marc's and my closest friends, who are still at the top of their game in this valley, only survived because they had the good sense to *listen to their lawyers.*"

Marc decided it was time to switch the conversation from the abstract to the personal. "Guys like you, Jason, know how to invent the next killer app," he said with a smile. "Stan and I know how to finance these brilliant ideas so they can be brought to market. The rest of you know to build a company from start-up to IPO and beyond. But, just because we may be acknowledged geniuses in our spheres, this doesn't mean we're brilliant at *everything*."

"Hopefully, none of you would try to take out your own appendix or wisdom teeth, right?" Stan Becker asked combatively.

Everyone agreed.

"Well, in much the same way as a surgeon knows how to perform surgery, *trial lawyers know the courtroom.* We tech guys don't know the courtroom."

After a pause Stan Becker continued. "Jason, we revere you, man, but you were *pitiful* in the courtroom yesterday," Stan looked straight at Jason, who blushed as the room erupted in nervous laughter. "If you guys go down, it will be a *huge* black mark against *our* community. Maybe you don't give a damn, but Marc and I have been around a few more years than some of you. We've seen firsthand how people have worked their butts off for *decade*s to make this valley what it is today. You have to understand you're not just individual silos. What happens to you impacts our *entire technology community*."

"Stan's right," Marc said quietly. "You all need to understand that this isn't just about *you* or *your* companies. The reputation of Silicon Valley may be at stake. Our firm has several companies in the pipeline waiting to go public. However, if the public gets the idea that people here in Silicon Valley are rigging the markets, these IPOs will never happen. For this reason, it's important to everyone here in the Valley that these insider trading allegations are *proven false*."

After the venture capitalists had finished, Lillian suggested that everyone take a short break.

After the break, Marc continued. "We think it might be useful if you all start to view the judge and jury as a VC panel reviewing your original business plan, without whose funding your company either won't get off the ground or won't survive. No one, except an idiot, fails to heed the advice of their deal lawyers when going through that process, right?"

The executives all nodded.

"You practiced your presentation with your deal lawyers before you went in front of the VCs like myself. Correct?"

Again, they nodded.

"This weekend, "continued Marc, "you're *all* going to have to spend serious time practicing your testimony before your lawyers, so that you learn how to tell the truth without alienating the heck out of the jury in the process."

"You guys seriously need practice," said Stan looking at each member of the group.

"The process will be exactly the same as if you were rehearsing the presentation for your first round of financing in front of my partners and me," added Marc. "You wouldn't want to bore or alienate potential investors like myself or my partners when presenting your company's business plan. Right?"

Everyone nodded in unison.

"To help you guys out, Stan and I have decided to give up part of our valuable weekend time with our families to return this Sunday afternoon and listen to your testimony. However, before we leave here today, get this into your heads. *Listen to your lawyers*. Because, if you don't, you're dead. *Got it?*"

All the executives nodded vigorously.

CHAPTER 37

Jason Lee Returns to the Stand

The following Monday morning, Jack Murphy called Jason Lee to the stand.

Miraculously, Jason Lee's tone of voice was modest, and the young executive responded respectfully and eagerly to Jack's laid back, casual questions. Many in the courtroom noticed the change in tone and concluded that the casual, red-haired lawyer knew how to interact better with the younger generation. *"Perhaps the other defense lawyer had been a little too overbearing with this young man,"* they thought.

Josh Kaplan rose to cross-examine the witness.

"Last week, you testified about speaking with the defendant, Ms. Pond, at a wine tasting event in Yountville. How did you first meet Ms. Pond?"

"Samantha—I mean Ms. Pond—is a realtor. She helped me buy my home in Glen Ellen."

"As your realtor in that transaction, did you expect Ms. Pond to keep your personal information confidential?"

"Absolutely!"

"Mr. Lee, do you recall attending an event at the home of Lucy and Tim Newman?"

"Yes, sir."

"Do you recall making a phone call during that event to your friend, Cecil Roberts?"

"Yes, sir…I do."

"Do you recall what you learned during in that phone conversation?"

"Cecil told me that the FDA hadn't approved his company's latest product and was demanding more clinical trials."

"Can you recall what you said in response?"

"I told him how disgusted I was with the FDA. I probably used some foul language."

"And your expression of disgust…was that in the presence of others?"

"I was looking out of a window at the time. A friend of mine overheard, so others probably did as well. I was upset that Cecil's job might be in jeopardy. I knew how hard he'd worked on this research."

"Did it occur to you that you were sharing confidential inside information with others at the fundraiser?"

"That never occurred to me because I only swore at the FDA. I didn't mention *anything* about Cecil's product, except to my friend Janet Parks-Brown. I knew she would keep something like that confidential."

Jack Murphy requested permission from the judge to reexamine the witness, which was granted.

"Do you know if your friend, Janet Parks-Brown, traded on the stock of Cecil Roberts' employer as a result of your conversation with Cecil Roberts at the Newmans' home?"

"I don't know, but I would be very surprised if she did."

"Do you know if any of the defendants traded on the stock of Cecil Robert's employer as a result of your conversation with Cecil Roberts at the Newman's home?"

"No, sir. Except for what we've recently learned about James Chistlehurst, to my knowledge, no one traded on Cecil's employer's stock."

"And what have you recently learned about Mr. Chistlehurst?"

"He's admitted at this trial that he traded on this stock."

"Mr. Lee, did *you* ever trade on Mr. Cecil Roberts' employer's stock?"

"No, sir, I have *never* traded on Mr. Cecil Roberts' employer's stock."

Kimberly Hayward called Janet Parks-Brown to the witness stand. Kimberly's auburn, shoulder-length hair and serious demeanor contrasted with Janet Parks-Brown's blond curly hair and pleasantly round face.

Kimberly introduced Janet as the chief financial officer of a telecommunications company and an adjunct professor at UC Santa Clara, who also owned a second home in Sonoma.

"When did you purchase your home in Sonoma?"

"During a weekend in July 2011."

"When did you begin looking at real estate in wine country?"

"We began casually looking in the fall of 2010, but we told our realtor that we weren't quite ready at that time."

"Who was your realtor?"

"Samantha Pond."

"Did you attend any fundraisers in the City of Sonoma before you purchased your second home?"

"Yes, my husband and I attended a lovely event at Tim and Lucy Newman's home."

"Apart from your host, Tim Newman, did you see anyone else at the event who works in Silicon Valley?"

"Yes, I saw several people we know from work. I saw Jason Lee, one of my former students, as well as Marc Todd, Tom White and Tony Padilla."

"Did you have a conversation with any of them?"

"Yes, I noticed that Jason was upset about something, so I went over to cheer him up."

"Where was Jason Lee at that time?"

"He was standing by the window of one of the reception rooms looking out the window."

"Do you recall the conversation you had with him on that occasion?"

"Jason did most of the talking. He said that he no longer wanted to stay because one of his friends had received bad news."

"Can you recall what the bad news was?"

"I recall that it had something to do with the FDA. But I do not recall the details. All I remember was that Jason was upset that his friend might lose his job."

"In the reception room itself, can you recall what Jason said about the FDA?"

"I apologize for using his language, but he said something like, "The FDA is so fucked…"

"Did Jason say why he thought that?"

"No, not in the reception room. He only said that he was leaving because he was no longer in the mood to stay. I walked him outside. While we were waiting for his car, he mentioned again that his friend might lose his job."

"Was my client or were any of the other defendants close by when he told you this?"

Janet looked over at the defense table.

"No. The only person nearby was the young man who was parking cars. However, he'd gone to retrieve Jason's car and hadn't arrived with it yet."

"When did you decide that you were ready to finally buy a second home in Sonoma?"

"When I knew that my company's stock price was about to recover from the economic downturn."

"Did you ever discuss your company's business or its stock price with my client?"

"Absolutely not. As a CFO, I have to keep all financial information very confidential. I merely told your client that we would let her know when we were ready to purchase. Having once worked in Silicon Valley, Samantha never pushed us or tried to pry into our financial circumstances…which is why we liked working with her. She understood the sensibilities ."

"Can you describe to the jury what those sensibilities are?"

"Those of us working in Silicon Valley know that the price of technology stocks can be extremely volatile. Just about anything can set them racing up or down. For that reason, none of us want to discuss our net worth, etc., with anyone, in case we accidently tip someone off about our company's financials."

"Did you ever trade on the stock of Mr. Cecil Roberts' biotechnology company?"

Janet laughed. "That's easy. We never invest in *any* stocks."

"And why is that?"

"My husband Joe and I both work in Silicon Valley. We are financially exposed to the technology industry's ups and downs on a daily basis. We never know if one of us will lose a job through downsizing or offshoring. That's enough risk for us. If we have any money saved, we invest it in real estate or municipal bond funds."

CHAPTER 38

A Sheepdog Arrives in San Francisco

Sidney looked out from the window of Lucy's SUV at the large hotel's massive facade. He felt scared for the first time since the helicopter rescued him from the Overlook Trail. His human parents got out of their car and gave their keys to a smartly dressed man in uniform. As Sidney walked into the imposing hotel on Nob Hill, he tried to look brave. However, the giant ceilings and massive walls of the elegant hotel made him feel very small. He was also missing Catherine, who was staying with her grandparents in San Carlos.

Sidney wondered why the hotel was called "pet-friendly" until one of the bellmen came over, knelt down, petted him, and gave him a treat. *"Thank you, mate, for making me feel welcome,"* Sidney signaled with a friendly lick. *"As a country sheepdog, I'm feeling a bit out of place in this huge city with massive tall buildings and giant hills. It's not dog-scale, like Palo Alto or Sonoma."*

After Tim and Lucy checked into their room, they left Sidney alone so they could attend a meeting with Lillian Johnson in preparation for their testimony the following morning. Unfortunately, Lillian Johnson's office landlord didn't allow pets, so Sidney had to wait for his Aunt Lillian to visit him later that evening.

Alone in the hotel room, Sidney was glad he'd had the good sense to reject a crazy idea from one of his pals at the dog park that he pretend to be a service dog to get into the courtroom. He calculated that an intelligent police dog would know instantly that he was a fake and might make mincemeat out of him if he were caught. However, Sidney was feeling unhappy that he'd be all alone in a hotel room while his human parents were testifying in court.

"Hey, Sidney…what's up, dog?"

Sidney looked up at the window and saw two large pigeons staring at him from the ledge. He went to the window, paws propped on the sill, to greet his new friends. He was excited that he'd been recognized in such a large, impersonal city.

"How do you know my name?" He asked the pigeons.

"Our country cousins told us you were coming into the City," replied the pigeon. *"I'm Archibald…and this is my wife, Loretta. We live up on top of Grace Cathedral. We told the family that we'd keep an eye out for you. Ah…here comes Basil from the courthouse and Sebastian from North Beach. What's up, guys?"*

Two more pigeons landed on the window ledge.

"We courthouse pigeons are really bored," replied Basil. *"No one's around to drop crumbs our way. The only serious criminal case that attracts a good-sized munching crowd is the insider trading case, and that adjourned early because a juror had to go to a medical appointment."*

Sidney wagged his tiny tail vigorously as the pigeon mentioned the criminal case involving his Sonoma friends.

"There's a really cool concert at the Jazz Center tonight. Hopefully we'll find more crumbs afterwards," Basil said nonchalantly.

"Yeah, I'm on my way over there right now," said Sebastian. *"Tonight's gig is supposed to be really hip."*

Thinking about the upcoming concert, Sebastian hopped from side to side on his webbed feet, pushing his head back and forth, making his green-blue neck glisten in the sun.

"You North Beach pigeons think you're such cool dudes, don't you," teased Basil.

"Hey, guys, stop being so pigeon-absorbed!" said Archibald. *"We've got to cheer Sidney up. He's in town because his humans have to testify in court tomorrow in that insider trading case. He's probably nervous at being in such a noisy, strange city and anxious about his humans."*

"Wow. Is this your first time in the City, Sidney?" asked Sebastian. *"You'll love San Francisco. I never want to leave the City. There's way too much fun stuff going on here."*

"Who's the lawyer for your humans?" Basil's puffed-up chest made him look judicial, and he asked the question seriously.

"Lillian Johnson," replied Sidney.

"Oh, she's one of the best," replied Basil confidently. *"They're in really*

CHAPTER 39

Tim Newman and Lucy Newman Testify

George DeRosa called Tim Newman to the witness stand.

"Mr. Newman, could you please state your full name for the record."

"Timothy Jeremy Newman."

"…And is your principal place of residence in Palo Alto, California?"

"Yes."

"Do you have any other homes or places of residence?"

"Yes, I own a home in the City of Sonoma."

"How long have you owned your Sonoma home?"

"A little over four years."

"Why are you are here to testify today?"

"Because my lawyer told me to."

Tim looked bashful as laughter broke out in the courtroom. George looked at the jury and smiled. He then continued soothingly.

"Please don't tell me or the court what your lawyer has said to you in private. By law, these communications are strictly confidential. None of us are allowed to know anything about them. However, with the court's and the people's permission, let me speed this up. Did you come here today because a legal document has been served on you?"

"Oh, yes. I received a subpoena."

"Do you know my client, Robert Goodwin?"

"Yes. He is my wife's caterer."

"Have you at any time discussed your company's affairs with my client?"

Tim stopped looking bashful. "Never!" he replied forcefully, looking serious and determined.

"Have you at any time discussed your company's business with *anyone* during an occasion where Mr. Goodwin was catering an event at your home?"

"Absolutely *not*. I am *very* careful *never* to discuss my company's business with anyone outside the company, except for maybe my wife."

"Do you recall holding a fundraiser at your Sonoma home in December 2010?"

"Yes…I remember it very well."

"Is there anything about the event that makes you recall it well?"

"Yes, it was a week or two after I learned that my company, Meediya, was about to settle a patent lawsuit brought against our company."

"Did you discuss this potential settlement with anyone?"

"Only my wife, Lucy."

"On what occasion did you discuss this potential lawsuit settlement with your wife, Lucy?"

"I immediately called Lucy after I got the good news that the lawsuit was about to be settled."

"Did you speak with her or leave a message?"

"She immediately picked up the phone after arriving in Sonoma."

"How did you know that she had arrived in Sonoma?"

"Well…she mentioned that she had just arrived and that our faithful gardener was also there."

" And what is the name of your gardener?"

"Juan Rodriguez."

"Why do you call him your 'faithful gardener?'"

"Because he and his family continued to take care of our pool and landscaping, even when we ran short of funds. Before I learned about the potential lawsuit settlement, things had been really tough."

"In what way had things been tough?"

"The company's stock was way down. Most of my stock options were under water. I wasn't drawing a salary."

"Why were you not drawing your salary?"

"Like many Silicon Valley CEOs whose companies are going through a rough patch, I chose not to. I wanted to conserve every last dime."

"If you were not drawing your salary, how were you able to afford to hold a fundraiser at your home?"

"It didn't cost us anything out-of-pocket. The organizers gave us some comp tickets to give to our friends, but most of the guests purchased tickets to attend the event. These tickets paid for the catering, wine and valet parking. We donated the space."

"Did the news of the potential patent lawsuit settlement in the fall of 2010 have any immediate impact on you or your wife financially?"

"Yes. We both felt a *huge* relief. We realized that I could now get back on salary and we wouldn't have to live off our savings. After I arrived in Sonoma later that evening Lucy excitedly told me how, after hearing the good news, she used the cash available in our bank accounts to pay several outstanding invoices, such as Juan's. She even gave Juan a personal bonus for being so patient."

Everyone in the courtroom laughed except Tim. He continued to look sad and embarrassed.

"Did the news of the potential lawsuit settlement cause your wife to make any other payments or purchases?"

"Oh…I remember now. Lucy purchased two gala tickets that afternoon. The following week, she also bought a new ball gown"

"Did you and your wife use a caterer for your fundraiser?"

"Yes, we used your client, Bob…excuse me, Your Honor, Robert Goodwin and his wife."

"Do you know the name of their catering service?"

"Yes, it's called Not Just Olives."

"Did you discuss your company's business prospects in front of my client, Mr. Goodwin, or his wife at any time during this fundraiser?"

"Absolutely not!"

"Did you discuss your company's business prospects in front of my client, Mr. Goodwin, or his wife at any time before or after this fundraiser?

"Absolutely not!"

"Your Honor, I do not have any further questions of this witness at this time. Mr. Newman, please stay where you are. Other counsel may have further questions."

Ann Schiller then rose to question the witness. After a few preliminaries, she followed George's example by asking Tim whether he recognized her client, Juan Rodriguez.

"Yes, he is my gardener."

"Is he the individual that you earlier described as your 'faithful gardener?'"

"Yes."

"Did you ever discuss your company's business affairs with my client?"

"Of course not!" Tim replied indignantly.

Jack Murphy then rose and asked if Tim recognized his client, Peter Smith.

"Peter works at Keniworth Winery. I often see him when I pick up our wine club shipments."

"On those occasions when you picked up your wine club shipments, did you ever discuss your company's business with my client, Peter Smith?"

"No. *Never.*"

"Did my client, Mr. Smith, attend the fundraiser at your home in the fall of 2010?"

"Yes…your client and Jeremy Keniworth poured wine at our fundraiser."

"Did you discuss your company's business with my client, Peter Smith, or with Mr. Keniworth before or during this fundraiser?"

Tim nearly burst out laughing. However, just in time, he remembered the weekend coaching on how to be respectful, regardless of how absurd some of the lawyers' questions might seem to him.

"No, sir. Except for Lucy, I never spoke with *anyone* in wine country about my company's business. Frankly, I try to avoid talking about work when we are up in Sonoma. Most people in Sonoma are not interested in technology. They're much more interested in food and wine. That's why we love it up there. It's such a welcome change to our daily lives."

During questioning by Kimberly Hayward, Tim acknowledged that Samantha Pond was the realtor who helped them buy their Sonoma home. However, he vehemently denied talking with her about the condition of his company's business at the fundraiser or at any other time during 2010.

After Kimberly Hayward sat down, Deke Little asked Tim if he knew his client, Charlie Bartino. Tim replied that Charlie had been a guest at his home, but denied ever discussing his company's business with Charlie.

Josh Kaplan rose to cross-examine Tim. This was the moment that Tim had been dreading.

"You have previously testified that the defendant, Mr. Rodriguez, provided landscaping services at your home in Sonoma, is that correct?"

"Yes."

"When Mr. Rodriguez worked at your home, did you expect him to keep any personal information he learned about you and your wife confidential?"

Tim glanced at Juan and replied reluctantly, "Well, I guess so…yes."

"You also previously testified that the defendants, Mr. Goodwin and Mr. Smith, also worked at your Sonoma home during a fundraiser, is that correct?"

"Yes."

"During that occasion when Mr. Goodwin and Mr. Smith worked at your home, did you expect them to keep any personal information they learned about you and your wife confidential?"

"Well, I suppose so…yes."

"Similarly, did you expect them to keep any personal information they learned about your guests confidential?"

"That's true."

"You mentioned earlier that before the fundraiser at your home in 2010, you had not paid Juan Rodriguez for tending your landscaping, is that correct?"

Tim looked down, embarrassed.

"That's also true."

"So you must have felt under some obligation to Mr. Rodriguez around that time."

"Of course. We owed him payment for his invoices."

"Did you feel that you owed him a special favor for tending your garden unpaid for several months?"

"No. We only *owed* payment for his *invoices*. We did not *owe* him anything else," replied Tim firmly.

"Why did your wife pay him a special bonus?"

"This was only to thank him for his patience. However, I never felt we *owed* him any bonus. We just *owed* him payment of his invoices."

Lucy was then called to support her husband's testimony. She testified that she never discussed her husband's company's business affairs with any of the Sonoma defendants.

During questioning by Ann, Lucy testified that she paid her gardener in full and gave him a bonus after she first learned the good news about the pending patent lawsuit settlement involving her husband's company.

"On the afternoon that you received a call from your husband, Tim, about the pending patent lawsuit settlement, did you make any other phone calls?"

Lucy thought long and hard. She could tell from Ann's expression that this was important.

"Ah, I remember now. I called my friend, Sally, to give her the good news."

"What good news?"

"That we could attend the de Young Patrons Gala."

"Did you discuss anything else with your friend, Sally, during that phone call?"

"Only typical girl talk."

"Such as?"

"We discussed going shopping at Saks," replied Lucy, looking bemused that the phone call had any importance in this grand courtroom.

"When you discussed going shopping in Saks, were you looking for anything in particular?"

"I wanted to try on a new gown that I'd spotted the prior week."

CHAPTER 40

Tom White Testifies

The following day, Tom White looked nervous as he took the witness stand for the first time. Under questioning by George DeRosa, Tom White confirmed that he was the chief operations officer for Software Telecom Solutions and that he also owned a second home in Sonoma.

"How frequently do you visit your second home?"

"As often as my wife and I can, which is usually two or three times a month on average."

"Is there any particular pattern to your visits? Are there occasions when you visit your second home more frequently than others?"

"We usually make it up to Sonoma on the weekends, even though I often have to arrive late, sometimes arriving after midnight. However, at the end of the quarter, it's tough for me to get up there."

"Why is that?"

"If we're struggling to make quarterly revenue target, it's all hands to the pump. Even the CEO works late nights to rally the troops."

"During the time you've have owned a second home in Sonoma, has your company had an unexpectedly good quarter?"

"Thankfully, yes"

"And on those occasions, did you have to forgo visiting Sonoma before the end of the quarter?"

"No. During a good quarter, my wife and I are usually able to drive up to Sonoma during normal hours, unless of course I encountered some last-minute glitch work-wise."

"And why did you not have to work late during those quarters?"

"Once the CFO confirms that we've made our revenue target, we can usually relax a bit and return to our normal work hours."

"Do you and your wife frequently attend local fundraisers in Sonoma?"

"Yes, we try to make an effort to help the local community, even though we don't live there full time."

"Did you ever attend a fundraiser at Tim Newman's home?"

"Yes."

"When was that occasion?"

"I think it was sometime in December of 2010."

"And did you discuss the frequency of your visits to Sonoma with anyone at the fundraiser?"

"I remember commenting to my friends, Tony Padilla, Mike Todd and Samantha Pond that things work-wise seemed to be getting better."

"Did you discuss with Mr. Padilla, Mr. Todd and Ms. Pond how your business was doing for the quarter?"

"No, I don't believe so. Oh…wait a minute. I did mention that, for once, I hoped to avoid working crazy hours at the end of the quarter. That's all."

"Based on your comment about not working crazy hours at the end of the quarter, would you have expected Mr. Padilla, Ms. Pond, Mr. Todd or anyone else, to trade on your company's stock?"

"Absolutely not! They would have been crazy to do so."

Following prompting by George, Tom explained. "Things change dramatically in our business from day to day. If I recall the date right, we were just beginning the third month of our quarter. Just about anything could have happened between then and the end of the quarter. No one in our business ever knows how things will pan out until right at the *end* of each quarter. No one could have traded on our stock based on my comment. It's ludicrous!"

George turned to the Judge: "Your Honor, I have no further questions of this witness."

Josh Kaplan stood to cross-examine the witness. After confirming that Tom White had access to his company's quarterly earnings results before these results were released to the public, he handed the witness three documents.

"You previously testified that you had a conversation with Mike Todd, Tony Padilla and the defendant Samantha Pond at a fundraiser. How did you first meet Ms. Pond?"

"She sold us our home in Sonoma."

"Do you know any of the other defendants?"

"Yes, I occasionally see Peter Smith working at the Keniworth Winery when I pick up our wine club shipments."

"Do you know Charlie Bartino?"

"Yes. We're both members of Wine Country Veterans."

"Looking at the exhibits I have just handed you, do you recognize these documents?"

"Yes. They are lists of names that our legal department asked me to review."

"And did you review those lists?"

"Sir, I'm sorry to say the answer is no. Unfortunately, I was under intense pressure at work each time one of these came across my desk. I put the lists on my PA's desk without carefully reviewing them."

"Did you know why you were asked to review these lists?"

"I do *now*. But at the time I didn't have a clue."

"Why you were asked by your company's legal department to review these lists?"

"Because they contain the names of people who had purchased our company stock just before our quarterly earnings were released.

"At the time you were asked to review these lists by your company's legal department, did you notice that the name of defendant, Charlie Bartino, appeared on each list?"

"No, I did not."

"At the time you were asked to review these lists, did you notice that the name of another defendant, Samantha Pond, appeared on each list?"

"No, I did not."

"Mr. White, do you always disregard requests for assistance from your company's legal department?"

Tom sighed. "I try my best but sometimes lawyers' requests seem really dumb when you're up to your ass…if you know what I mean."

CHAPTER 41

Tony Padilla Testifies

Kimberly Hayward called Tony Padilla to the witness stand. After Tony Padilla took the stand, he confirmed that he was marketing vice president of In-Grid, a Redwood City company that developed smart-grid technology. He also confirmed that he owned a second home in Kenwood, California, approximately 10 miles from Sonoma.

"Do you and your wife attend local fundraisers in Sonoma County?"

"Occasionally."

"Do you know Tim and Lucy Newman?"

"Yes, Tim and I are both Stanford alumni."

"Did you ever attend a fundraiser at Tim and Lucy Newman's home in Sonoma?"

"Yes."

"When was that occasion?"

"I think it was just after Thanksgiving two years ago."

"On that occasion, other than your host, Tim Newman, did you speak with anyone from Silicon Valley?"

"Yes, I remember having a conversation with Tom White and Mike Todd."

"How do you know these gentlemen?"

"They are both friends from the Menlo Circus Club."

"When you spoke with Mr. White and Mr. Todd, was anyone else part of the conversation?"

"Yes. Your client, Samantha Pond, was also there."

"How do you know Ms. Pond?"

"Samantha used to work in Silicon Valley. She first sold us our home in Atherton. After she moved to wine country, she sold my wife and me our second home in Kenwood."

"On that occasion, did you discuss your company prospects with Mr.

White, Mr. Todd or Ms. Pond?"

"Not that I recall. Well, wait a minute. I may have said that things seemed to be looking up work-wise…but nothing specific. I remember being excited about buying a new Tesla Roadster. I think that I mentioned that to them."

"And why were you excited about buying this Tesla Roadster?"

"They're really cool all-electric sports cars…beautiful lines. The chassis is made by Lotus but it's powered by electric motors. In 2010, they were very popular in the Valley." After prompting from Kimberly Hayward, Tony explained to the jury that "the Valley" was Silicon Valley.

"At the time you attended the fundraiser at Tim and Lucy Newman's home in Sonoma, had you taken delivery of this new Tesla Roadster?"

"No. The orders were backlogged. It was several months before Tesla could fill orders."

"And what was the purchase price of your Tesla Roadster?"

The jury gasped when Tony replied, "One hundred thirty-five thousand dollars."

"When did you decide to buy a Tesla Roadster"?

"Well…I had wanted to buy one for a couple of years, but I had to wait until I knew that our company was doing better. Like everyone else, our company had been hit by the downturn. By the end of 2010, our company was finally crawling out of the woods."

"At that time, did you tell anyone else that you had placed a deposit on a Tesla Roadster?"

"Some of our friends were still suffering from the downturn, so I kept it a secret from them."

"Did you attend any private wine tasting events around that time?"

"Early the following year, I attended a private tasting event at James Chistlehurst's place in Yountville."

"Did you see my client at this private wine tasting event?"

"Yes. I recall that Samantha arrived after James' tour of his wine cellars."

"Did you discuss your company's prospects with my client, Ms. Pond, on that occasion?"

"No…I didn't discuss my company's prospects with *anyone* on that occasion."

"Did you attend any wine auctions around that time?"

"I was a guest of Samantha Pond's at the Sonoma Valley of the Moon Wine Auction in 2011."

"Did you discuss your company's prospects with my client, Ms. Pond, on that occasion?"

"No…I didn't discuss my company's prospects with *anyone* on that occasion."

Deke Little rose to question the witness.

"You previously mentioned that you had attended the Sonoma Valley of the Moon Wine Auction in 2011 as Ms. Pond's guest. Did you attend this event before 2011?"

"After we bought our home in wine country, we always tried to attend if my company was doing well."

"Why did you always try to attend this event?"

"We wanted to be generous to the local community by bidding on the wine allotments donated by local wineries for charity."

"When the downturn happened in 2008, did you and your wife continue to attend this auction?"

"After the downturn in 2008, we just sent in donations," Tony said quietly.

"At any time, did you have a conversation with my client, Charlie Bartino, about your company's business affairs?"

"Absolutely not, sir."

"I have no further questions."

Josh Kaplan rose to cross-examine the witness.

"You previously testified that Ms. Pond had assisted you in buying two homes. As your realtor in those transactions, would you expect Ms. Pond to keep your and your wife's personal information confidential?"

"Of course, yes."

Meanwhile, Lucy and Tim were busy packing to leave San Francisco. Lillian Johnson told them that the defense lawyers were pleased with their testimony and they wouldn't need to "stick around" for the rest of the trial. Lucy and Tim were longing to get back to Sonoma. Since Sidney's disappearance and rescue, many neighbors had stopped by to offer their support for the young couple, dropping off pies, fresh fruit and vegetables. At the local farmers market, Amanda Jones and the other Sonoma residents had frequently complained to each other how "that nice young couple, Lucy and Tim, were under siege by innuendo."

Strangely, Sidney was reluctant to leave the big City. *"I need to know how it works out,"* he thought mournfully. *"I hope Charlie, Samantha and my other pals are OK."*

"Hey, Sidney…wanna hear the latest?" tweeted Sebastian. *"I just flew by the courthouse and Basil was holding forth in his usual pompous way. Looks like the Silicon Valley guys, like your Tim and Lucy, did OK. According to Basil, the lawyers on both sides seemed content. Who knows what the jury will make of this."*

"I'm being taken up to Sonoma," sighed Sidney. *"Lucy and Tim need a break. However I hate to leave before it's over. I need to know what happens at this trial. I want all my friends found innocent and Tim's name cleared completely, or he'll never be happy."*

"If they don't exonerate everyone, I'll get all my avian friends to poop on the courthouse steps," said Sebastian proudly.

Sidney was grateful for the young pigeon's support, but secretly wondered how this gesture would help clear Tim's name.

"And don't worry," continued Sebastian, *"since Sonoma and Palo Alto are next to our Bay waters and marshlands, we'll keep you informed about the latest developments via our avian network. Between the blue herons, egrets, seagulls and us courthouse pigeons, we've got the whole Bay wired,"* Sebastian added proudly. *"Besides, we birds all love a good, juicy piece of gossip."*

CHAPTER 42

Juan Rodriguez's Testimony

Dressed impeccably and looking as innocent as the choirboy he once was, Juan Rodriguez took the stand. Ann Schiller rose to question her client.

"Mr. Rodriguez, do you work for your family's landscaping and pool maintenance business?"

"Yes."

"When you worked as a landscape maintenance employee for your family, did you sometimes listen to the private conversations of some of your customers?"

Juan looked down at his feet with embarrassment. He finally murmured, "Yes." He paused, and then blurted out, "Honestly, I didn't know that this was wrong at the time. I was just trying to learn how to be an investor!"

Many in the courtroom laughed derisively. However, the women in the jury smiled at Juan sympathetically. Ann knew they liked him.

"What made you think this was 'learning how to be an investor?'"

"Well, Bob—Mr. Goodwin—the guy heading up our investment club, told me that I needed to research our target companies."

"Was one of your 'target' companies Tim Newman's company, Meediya?"

Juan replied meekly, "Yes."

"What type of 'research' were you conducting into Tim Newman's company, Meediya?"

Juan looked up. "For one thing, I *wasn't* listening for inside tips about their companies. Doing *that* would have made me very uncomfortable. Besides, Bob made it very clear that listening for *inside tips* about how a company was doing, and then trading on that information, was a *big* no-no."

"Did he tell you why?"

"Yes, he told all of us that if we traded on tips overheard from one of our clients, we might get nailed for insider trading and go to prison."

"So, Mr. Rodriguez, if you were not trying to listen in on any inside tips from your customers about their companies or businesses, how were you researching your target companies?"

"We were simply watching how their senior employees spent money, or didn't, as the case may be."

"Meaning…?"

"Well, we were all told to keep our ears to the ground…listen in on the business gossip going around Sonoma and Napa counties, and observe the spending habits of some of our customers."

After further prompting from Ann, Juan elaborated. "For example, we might find out that someone decided to spend big bucks on a new swimming pool. If we also found out during the same time period that other people from the same company were also spending big bucks, this might mean the company was doing really well. However, if a person later cancelled a big swimming pool project midway through, this might signal that his or her company wasn't doing so great. Stuff like that."

"Did you or the club ever discuss whether this information might be considered confidential inside information?"

"You must be joking! No one keeps that stuff confidential in Sonoma. It's a really small community. Everyone knows everyone else. Any big project, like a new swimming pool, becomes public knowledge once we get off work. You see…we don't have a lot to talk about in our small town."

Following more prompting from Ann, Juan went on. "The really *big* projects, involving important people, are discussed in our bars and cafes for months on end. Everyone gossips about who's been hired and how much he or she is spending on labor and raw materials. It gets kind of boring after a while."

Ann changed tack. "Mr. Rodriguez, how did you feel about Mr. and Mrs. Newman not paying your invoices for several weeks?"

"When the rich folks have money problems, the gardener or pool guy *always* gets stiffed. My Dad thinks that's because we are all invisible to their fancy friends."

"Did you feel 'stiffed' by the Newmans?"

"My Dad did." Juan remembered the well-cared-for baby and friendly, former shelter dog. "But I always felt that they were good people. I knew that we would get paid eventually. The Newmans are not like *some* rich people who think they're royalty—that we should all be grateful to work and work for *free*—like the rest of us don't have any bills to pay."

The judge instructed the jury to disregard Mr. Rodriguez's comments and instructed the witness to simply answer his counsel's questions.

"Other than spending habits, did you perform any other research for the investment club?"

Juan looked at his lawyer blankly.

"Let me rephrase this question. As a student of computer science, did the other members of the investment club rely on you to provide them with any information?"

Josh Kaplan rose to object that the question was leading and the judge sustained the objection. This allowed Juan time to think.

"Let me rephrase the question," said Ann with great poise. "Did the investment club ask you to perform any additional research of any sort?"

"Oh, *yes*," he replied. "I knew the tech stuff better than the others. They asked me to figure out and explain to the group what some of these tech companies were actually selling."

As some in the courtroom laughed, Ann continued. "Mr. Rodriguez, did you ever overhear that Mr. Newman's company might be about to settle a lawsuit?"

Juan looked sadly at his counsel. "I swear to God that I never overheard anything about Mr. Newman's company. I only overheard what Mrs. Newman said on her cell."

"And what was that?"

"She was thinking about buying a ball gown to wear to some fancy event. That's *all*."

"Did you observe anything else about Mr. and Mrs. Newman's spending habits that afternoon?"

"Only that we *finally* got paid. I also got a nice bonus. After that, I told the club that things seemed to be looking up for the Newmans, moneywise, so we bought Meediya shares. No one ever mentioned anything about any lawsuit…or *anything* like that!"

Amanda Jones had had enough.

She was very upset about how the trial was crucifying her darling Juan and his family, as well as her other Sonoma friends. She had repeatedly called the defense lawyers to tell them what the experts quoted in the press had advised about trial strategy. For some peculiar reason, none of the lawyers, including her niece, Ann, had returned her calls.

Amanda was determined to attend the trial with some of her celebrity friends in hopes that their presence might favor the jury towards her Sonoma friends. Amanda had warned Ann, George and the other lawyers of her planned arrival in the courtroom and they duly alerted the prosecution, the courtroom bailiff and the courtroom clerk. The defense lawyers all thought Amanda's enthusiastic effort to assist their clients was a mistake. However, Ann knew only too well that once her Aunt Amanda made up her mind, *nothing* would dissuade her.

As Amanda stepped from her stretch limousine parked on Golden Gate Avenue, cameras and smartphones flashed. The TV cameras, the paparazzi and press were there in full force.

One paunchy, red–faced British journalist, famous for his UK celebrity news columns, yelled out, "Amanda—you're looking gorgeous. Tell us your beauty secrets, my darling!"

Amanda smiled at him and replied in a deep sexy voice, "Only if you tell me yours, darling." The journalist laughed uproariously.

Another yelled, "Hey, Amanda! Did you ever sleep with Mick Jaeger?"

Amanda replied bashfully, "I am not going there, because I don't want to hear *any* of your bedroom secrets, darling!"

Everyone laughed. Amanda knew how to play a crowd. She elegantly climbed the steep steps to the Philip Burton Building as if she was modeling the latest fashion on a couture runway. Although most of the other courtroom attendees had chosen to enter the Federal Building discreetly through the Turk Street entrance, Amanda never liked to disappoint her fans.

As Amanda and her celebrity entourage reached the top of the steps, they were greeted by Lady Roberta. After hearing from Amanda how the trial was generating national publicity, Lady Roberta felt it her duty to stand by her friend. After an elaborate display of air kisses, Amanda and Lady Roberta posed red-carpet style for the cameras—much to the delight of the crowd below—before entering the courthouse. When they finally reached the courtroom, a hush of interest greeted their arrival. In the courtroom, the lawyers quietly watched Amanda and her friends enter. They inwardly groaned. It was amazing to them how celebrities could turn any courthouse into a zoo.

After the court resumed session, Josh Kaplan, during his cross examination of Juan, attempted to focus the jury's attention on whether Juan had overheard Lucy's conversation with her husband before she called her friend about the ball gown.

He also extensively probed the exact date and time when the investment club had bought shares in Meediya. However, by the end of the day, Josh was secretly concerned that the case against Juan was weakening. He knew the truth about Sonoma's gossip mill only too well. It was fine with him that everyone seemed both fascinated and distracted by the presence of celebrities in the courtroom. He noticed that even the judge couldn't resist glancing at them and comparing their faces to the numerous photographs she had seen in glossy magazines.

Peter Smith Testifies

As Jack Murphy called his client, Peter Smith, to the stand, Peter's nervousness and youthful good looks made him look like a deer caught in headlights.

After the preliminaries, in which Jack established that Peter worked in the Keniworth Winery tasting room, Jack also confirmed that Peter had joined the investment club.

"And who was in the investment club?"

Peter identified the names of the other Sonoma defendants sitting at the defendants' table with their lawyers.

"What was the purpose of the investment club?"

"To pool the scoop that we picked up at work to try to figure out who was spending the big bucks."

"Why was that important?"

"If a company or its employees start to splurge, it's usually a sign that the company is doing super well."

"Did you provide the club with any 'scoop' that you learned from work?"

"Only if a particular group of tech employees suddenly started splurging on our more expensive wines."

"How would you know where they work?"

"If someone's working for a high-flying company, it usually comes out."

"Comes out how?"

"In a wine country tasting room, we make small talk with the customers. We ask them where they're from…that sort of thing. If someone is with a super-hot company that's doing really well, they usually can't resist telling everyone about it."

"Anything else?"

"Hon…oh, I'm sorry, counselor, I'm no mental genius, but I did try to keep track of who signed up for our wine club and who dropped it."

"And why did you try to keep track of this information?"

"Again, it's a good barometer of who's in the money and who's not."

"How did you know where these people worked?"

"Someone over 21 years of age has to sign for the wine club shipments. The tech guys are never at home during the day, so they usually arrange to have their wine shipments delivered to their work addresses."

"When someone signs up to be a Keniworth Wine Club member, how much money are they required to spend on Keniworth wine?"

"We usually send three to four wine shipments a year, usually two shipments in the spring and two in the fall."

"How many bottles of wine are included in each shipment?"

"Three bottles."

"Do you have an idea of how much the wine shipment costs on average?"

"I always tell people that it averages out to around $150 per shipment."

"Did you ever overhear any gossip in the tasting room about any company mergers or stock splits or other similar gossip?"

"Oh, you better believe it! People shoot their mouths off in our tasting room *all the time.*"

"And did the investment club ever trade on that information?"

"No…more's the pity. We hear some really juicy stuff. However, Bob never let us trade on that stuff. I never saw why it was such a big deal. But Bob told us this might get us into *serious* trouble."

"Mr. Smith, that's all I have for now, but please stay seated in case some of the other counsel have questions."

Josh Kaplan rose to cross-examine the witness.

"When people sign up to join the Keniworth Wine Club, are they required to give the winery any credit card information?"

"Yes, sir. In Sonoma, *all* wine club members are asked to keep a credit card on file to pay for their wine club shipments."

"Do you know any of the people who work in Silicon Valley who testified earlier in this trial?"

"Yes. I've gotten to know Lucy and Tim Newman because they are wine club members. We poured wine at a fundraiser in their home. I also know a few of the others because they're also wine club members, and I see them around town quite a bit."

"Of the other people who have previously testified at this trial, who else are Keniworth Wine Club members?"

"Tom White and his wife, Leslie, and Janet Parks-Brown and her husband, Joe. They're all nice people."

"Have you had any opportunity to speak with Tom White about his work?"

"*God, no,*" exclaimed Peter vehemently. "I'm sorry, Your Honor. I apologize for getting overly excited, but, except for finding out where people work, I *never* discuss business with *any* of our wine club members. They all come to wine country to try to relax and have a really good time. They want to *escape* from work. The *last* thing they want is to talk shop."

"Did you have any opportunity to speak with Janet Parks-Brown about her work?"

"No, *absolutely not.*"

"Mr. Smith, you previously testified that you poured wine at a fundraiser at the home of Lucy and Tim Newman, is that correct?"

"Yes, sir."

"How many times did you visit their home before the fundraiser?"

"Just once…to check out the lay of the land for our wine stations."

"Were you with anyone from the winery during that visit?"

"Yes, my boss, Jeremy Keniworth, met me there."

"How long did Mr. Keniworth stay at the Newmans' home on that occasion?"

"Oh, he was there just 10 minutes and then he had to leave."

"After Mr. Keniworth left, when did you leave?"

"About an hour later."

"Why did you stay an hour longer?"

"Well…Lucy and I started shooting the breeze about the

renovation of her home. Somehow the time ran away from us.

"Why were you so interested in the renovation?"

"I used to work as an interior designer, so *naturally* I was really curious."

"While you were at the home of Mr. and Mrs. Newman on that occasion, did you learn from either Mr. or Mrs. Newman that Mr. Newman's company might be about to settle a patent lawsuit?"

Peter looked indignantly at the lawyer.

"*Never!* All Lucy and I ever discussed was the renovation."

"Did you have any discussion with Mr. Newman on that occasion?"

"Tim came out and briefly said, 'hello,' when Jeremy and I first arrived. He was holed up in his home office with the door closed the rest of the time."

"At the fundraiser, did you see Mr. Tom White?"

"At one point, he and a couple of other guys I didn't know were shooting the breeze with Samantha in front of my wine station. I was too busy pouring wine to pay much attention. You'll have to ask Samantha."

"Right now, I'm asking *you* the questions. Did you overhear their conversation?"

"No, sir. I did not," replied Peter firmly.

CHAPTER 44

Samantha Pond Testifies

After Peter Smith stepped down from the stand, Kimberly Hayward called her client, Samantha Pond, to the stand. However, as soon as Kimberly asked her client to state her full name and address, the tension that had been building inside Samantha throughout the trial came to the surface. Her large brown eyes filled with tears. As she blinked her eyes, these tears began to trickle down her cheeks causing havoc with her carefully applied eyeliner and mascara.

Fortunately for Samantha Pond, Her Honor Camilla Baker understood how defendants who take the stand could become overwhelmed and lose their self-dignity. She called a brief 15-minute adjournment. As the judge left the courtroom, many in the courtroom felt sympathy for the petite brunette who had previously seemed so self-assured in the courtroom.

Samantha's lawyer was silently relieved. Kimberly had been secretly worried that her realtor client might come across as prickly and arrogant, causing the jury to dislike her. "A few tears will humanize my client," she thought to herself.

After the break had restored her client's composure, Kimberly took her client through the preliminaries, in which Samantha confirmed that she had worked as a realtor, first in Silicon Valley and then in Sonoma and Napa. She also confirmed that she was a member of an investment club with the other four defendants.

"You previously heard Juan Rodriguez and Peter Smith speak of providing information from work to the investment club. Did you provide any information to the club?"

"Since I once worked in Silicon Valley, I would often hear if someone from Silicon Valley was looking for property in wine country. Don't get me wrong. I *never* revealed my client's intentions if they wanted their interest kept private…as most of them do. However, if my client wanted people to *know* that they were in the market to buy a piece of wine country real estate, I would inform the group."

"When you gave the group that information, did you think that you might be divulging *confidential* information?"

"*Not at all*," replied Samantha indignantly. "My clients no longer wanted it kept private. In my mind, it was no longer confidential information."

"Can you give me an example?"

"Yes. Joe and Janet Parks-Brown were happy for people to know that they were finally realizing a dream in buying a cottage in wine country. At the wine auction, we all congratulated them. I remember that I passed on that information to the group just after the auction."

"Did you reveal any other real estate information to the club?"

"Yes. I kept everyone informed of most of the real estate deals that had *closed*."

"When you informed the club of these closed real estate deals, did you think that you might be divulging *confidential* information?"

Samantha struggled to keep a straight face. "Real estate deals are not closed until the transaction has been filed with the County Recorder's office," she replied with a smile. "Once the transaction is recorded, it becomes a matter of *public* record within a few hours. *Of course* I didn't think I was divulging *confidential* information," she added with exasperation as her head shook vehemently. "I was only giving the group public information."

"Earlier in the trial, Mr. Smith and Mr. Rodriguez testified that they had informed the club about people's spending habits. Aside from what you learned as a realtor, did you ever pass along to the club about what you observed about people's spending habits?"

"Hmmm…I did let the group know who was purchasing super expensive items, like cars or wine futures. However, I never disclosed the person's identity—only the company where they worked. I didn't want to embarrass anyone. I also trusted the investment group to keep the information under their hat."

"Did you ever overhear and pass on any gossip about companies getting acquired or other similar information?"

"Absolutely *not*. I worked in Silicon Valley selling real estate for many years. I know that *any* information about a merger or buyout is *highly confidential*. No one is allowed to breath a word to anyone about something like that."

"Did you ever hear any news about quarterly earnings before they were released?"

"No…hardly ever. My clients are much too smart to talk to me about their quarterly earnings. If someone lets something slip, I would never tell a soul about it."

"Ms. Pond, that's all the questions I have for now. Please remain where you are. The other counsel might want to ask you some questions."

Josh Kaplan rose to cross-examine the witness.

"You previously testified that, after the wine auction, you informed the investment club of Joe and Janet Parks-Brown's offer. Did the investment club purchase shares of the company where Janet Parks-Brown worked immediately after this wine auction?"

"Yes, we thought it might be a good investment."

"Do you know any of the people who work in Silicon Valley who testified earlier in this trial?"

"Yes. I know almost all of them. I've sold houses to most."

"Did you gossip with the investment club about any of their *spending* habits?"

Samantha looked embarrassed. "I *do* recall telling the group about someone from Tony Padilla's company putting down a deposit on a Tesla Roadster," she replied quietly.

"When was that?"

"Just after the fundraiser at Lucy and Tim's home."

"Did the investment club make an investment in Mr. Padilla's company around that time?"

"I can't exactly remember, but I think we did."

"Did you gossip with the investment club about anyone else's spending habits?"

"Around the time of the fundraiser, I think we *all* gossiped about the *amazing* renovation that Tim and Lucy had done to their home."

"Did the investment club invest in Meediya around that time?"

"Yes, I think we did but I don't exactly recall why. Some of us had known about the expensive renovation for quite sometime, so it had nothing to do with that."

"Did you gossip with the investment club about anyone *else's* spending habits?"

"I remember sharing with the group that someone working at H.I.T. was shelling out some big bucks to buy expensive wine futures. That was Jason Lee. However, I didn't tell the group his identity."

"When did you learn about this purchase?"

"At a private wine tasting at James Chistlehurst's home in Yountville."

"At that private wine tasting event, did you also learn that H.I.T. Inc. had just successfully registered a patent?"

"No, but we could tell that Jason Lee was pleased about something. He never told us what."

"Did the investment club make an investment in Mr. Lee's company around that time?"

"Yes, we did."

"Did you *later* learn that this company had successfully registered a patent?"

"Yes."

"And did you learn this information *before* or *after* your investment club invested in Mr. Lee's company, H.I.T. Inc.?"

"*After*," Samantha replied vehemently.

CHAPTER 45

Charlie Bartino Testifies

The grower walked slowly to the witness box and carefully took the stand. His face looked calm as his lawyer, Deke Little, rose to question him. They went through the preliminaries; he confirmed that he worked as a grower on his family's estates in Napa and Sonoma and was a member of an investment club with the other four defendants.

"Why did you decide to join this investment club?"

"Hey, I thought it might be interesting to get to know some people in Sonoma who don't grow grapes. Growers like us only talk about one thing: the current price our grapes are getting in the market. I also thought I might learn more about other types of investments."

"You heard Peter Smith testifying that the investment club members would pool information to try figure out who was spending the big bucks. Did *you* provide the investment club with any information?"

"I attend all the charity auctions and fundraisers that we have in our area. We like to support local charities. "

"Did you provide any information to the investment club from those auctions and fundraisers?"

Charlie smiled mischievously. Leaning over to address the jury, he replied in a loud voice.

"Like everybody else, they always wanted to know who was splashing the money around and who was not."

The courtroom erupted in laughter.

"When you say 'splashing the money around,' what do you mean, exactly?"

"The guys who were bidding the big bucks on the wine lots to impress everyone. Some of those wine lots have very valuable wine, and they go for the big bucks, *especially* in the Napa Valley Wine Auction. We don't do so badly in our Sonoma Valley wine auctions either, come to think of it."

"On the occasion of the 2011 Valley of the Moon Wine Auction, did you observe any bids that you passed along to the group?"

"Sure. I noticed that Janet Parks-Brown's boss, who's a bit of a show-off, was bidding very generously. Tom White's boss was also splashing around some big bucks. I passed that along to the group."

"By splashing around the big bucks, did you mean spending a lot of money?"

"Sure do. That guy was bidding on almost everything. I figured his business must be doing OK."

"Mr. Bartino…when you told the investment club that Janet Parks-Brown's boss was bidding very generously, and that Tom White's boss was also making many bids, did you think that you might be divulging *confidential* information?"

"No! That's just plain stupid," replied the grower. "That stuff's not confidential. The bidding at these wine auctions takes place in broad daylight in front of *hundreds* of people. Everyone in wine country gossips about who bid what for weeks after. What's confidential about that?"

"Did you give any other information to the club?"

"I usually only kept track of the high rollers. I noted whether they turned up again the following year, and so on. If they didn't show up, it sometimes meant that they moved out of the area. In these hard times, they might simply be pulling back. Heck… what's so confidential about that?" Charlie was edgy and indignant.

After the judge instructed the jury to disregard the argumentative testimony of the witness, Deke Little said he had no further questions.

Josh Kaplan rose to cross-examine the witness.

"When people sign up to attend the Sonoma Valley of the Moon Wine Auction, they are required to give the organizers their credit card information, are they not?"

"I think so…yes."

"The guests are given a bidding paddle with a number on it that's linked to their credit card, are they not?"

"True!"

"And this allows the organizers to match the successful bid to the bidder's credit card, isn't that correct?"

"Yes, sir…that's correct."

"You previously testified that you recognized the boss of Mr. Tom White and the boss of Mrs. Janet Parks-Brown. How did you learn these people's identities?"

"Well…I usually make a point of getting to know the folks who turn up to support our wine auctions. I feel it's the friendly thing to do, since they're supporting our local charities. That's not a crime, is it?"

"When you attended the Sonoma Valley of the Moon Wine Auction in 2011, did you know ahead of time who was on the guest list?"

"I might have known…if my wife, Diana was one of the organizers."

"Was your wife, Diana, one of the organizers of the *2011 Sonoma Valley of the Moon Wine Auction?*"

"Yes sir…I believe she was."

"Did you discover ahead of time that the boss of Mrs. Janet Parks-Brown was attending this wine auction?"

"Yes, sir, I think I did. No harm in that, is there?"

"Your Honor, I have no further questions."

CHAPTER 46

Bob Goodwin Testifies

The following Monday, Bob was called to the stand. After the preliminaries, George asked Bob about his employment background and established that, at one time, Bob had worked as a lawyer and trader on Wall Street.

"When did you stop working on Wall Street?"

"When my wife complained that she never saw me."

The jury laughed.

"When did you move to Sonoma?"

"In early 2000."

"Why did you move to Sonoma?"

"To get a life."

"After you moved to Sonoma, did you work?"

"Yes. I started our Not Just Olives catering business with my wife. She's a great chef."

"Did you also start an investment club?"

"Yes."

"Did the investment club have any particular strategy?"

"Well, we'd pool what we observed from work about the spending habits of some of the wealthier people working in Silicon Valley. We would then decide whether to invest in their company stocks."

"Did it ever occur to you that you might be illegally trading on inside information?"

"Absolutely *not*. Traders in New York trade on this type of gossip all the time. It's their job."

Following prompting from George, Bob continued. "Our investment group traded on spending splurges that we learned about in public places, like the tasting rooms, auction rooms or wine country receptions. We never thought of this as trading on inside information. These spending habits are *often* the subject of gossip here."

After a short break, Josh Kaplan rose to question the witness.

"Mr. Goodwin, you previously testified that you worked as a lawyer and trader on Wall Street. As a former Wall Street lawyer, you are familiar with law concerning insider trading, are you not?"

"I certainly am—but *none* of us were insiders. I also made sure that our group *didn't* trade on inside information."

"You previously testified that you started an investment club. When did you start this investment club?"

"When the economy tanked in 2008, I figured that this might provide a opportunity for buying stocks. However, I don't think we started making any trades until 2010."

"Who provided the capital for the investment club to trade stocks?"

"Mr. Charlie Bartino provided most of it. However, my broker allowed the bulk of the trading to be done on margin."

"You testified that your investment group traded on spending splurges. Did the investment club make any trades based on information *other* than spending patterns?"

"Sometimes I performed some independent research, based on what I had learned while working as a trader on Wall Street."

"What do you mean by *independent research*? Can you give me an example?"

"I might check on whether some of the Silicon Valley guys who had second homes were working late at the end of their quarter. If they weren't working late, I figured that their companies had already made their numbers for the quarter."

"Did you perform this type of research in connection with any of the trades that were mentioned at this trial?"

"Yes, I made a point of going by Tom White's home at the end of each quarter to see what time he arrived in town."

The courtroom went suddenly very quiet. Had a pin dropped, it would have been heard by everyone.

"And you didn't consider this obtaining *inside* information?"

"No! Again, I figured that a car parked in a driveway and lights switched on at night were information publicly available to anyone driving by."

Bob looked around the courtroom and added sadly, "I never expected to end up here!"

CHAPTER 47

Josh Kaplan's Closing Argument

Josh Kaplan rose to address the jury.

During the prior day, the lawyers had argued before the judge over the nature of her final instructions to the jury regarding the law of insider trading. All the lawyers were able to agree on one thing: this wasn't the standard insider trading case. Not by a long shot.

Josh Kaplan argued that, since the evidence was clear that defendants had illegally stolen and traded on inside information, the judge should instruct the jury to return a guilty verdict. The defense argued that the judge should throw out the case against the defendants. The judge ruled that, while she would take both sides' legal arguments under advisement, the jury must weigh the unusual facts before deciding whether the defendants had illegally traded on inside information.

The battle lines were drawn.

Since the government had the burden to prove its case beyond a reasonable doubt, Josh Kaplan was the first to stand and address the jury.

"Members of the jury, the strength of the United States' stock markets lies in the government's ability to keep the markets fair for the average investor.

"You've heard testimony during this trial that our publicly listed companies regularly release information that is important to investors. This release of information helps the average investor decide whether the stock is a wise investment. You have also heard testimony during this trial that the release of certain types of information to the public often has a predictable impact on the price of a company's stock.

"For example, higher-than-expected quarterly earnings usually raise the price of a company's stock. Similarly, lower-than-expected quarterly earnings usually depress the price of a company's stock. News that a company has been sued can depress the stock price. Similarly, news that a lawsuit has been settled can increase the price of a company's stock.

"Members of the jury, until this information is released to the public, it is *inside information*. Her Honor will instruct you that the legal definition of inside information is *non-public information that a reasonable investor would consider important, significant or useful.*

"Inside every publicly listed company, there are people who, as part of their job, have access to inside information before this information is released to the rest of us.

"Members of the jury, for our stock markets to remain fair, the average investor must have confidence that our stock markets are not rigged in favor of these insiders. No one wants to roll the dice with anyone using loaded dice. Similarly, the average investor does not want to invest in a rigged stock market.

"You will be instructed by Her Honor that, under our U.S. Securities Laws, these *insiders* are not allowed to trade on inside information unless and until this information is released to the public. Similarly, these insiders are not allowed to give inside information to others—such as friends or family members—so that *they* trade on this information for the benefit of the insiders.

After pausing to take a sip of water, Josh Kaplan proceeded. "Her Honor will instruct you that a person can *also* be guilty of violating the U.S. Securities Laws if they knowingly *steal* inside information in a situation where they are under a legal duty to keep the information confidential.

Her Honor will cite examples where, by law, certain people—such as professionals and family members—are under a legal duty to keep inside information confidential. However, she will also instruct you that these examples are *not* exhaustive. Instead, you must decide *in this particular case* whether the defendants stole inside information and, if so, whether they had a duty to keep the information confidential.

"You will recall how an insider, Tim Newman, testified that he had called his wife, Lucy to give her the good news that a patent lawsuit that had previously depressed his company's stock price was about to be settled. You will recall that Lucy Newman testified that, immediately after this phone call, she called a friend and said that the Newmans were in a position to attend a gala event and Mrs. Newman might buy a new ball gown from Saks Fifth Avenue. That same afternoon, Lucy Newman testified that she paid defendant Juan Rodriguez several past-due invoices and gave him a bonus for his patience. The defendant Juan Rodriguez testified that he took the information about the Newmans' improved finances to the investment club, and the investment club then traded Mr. Newman's employer's stock.

"Members of the jury, Mr. Rodriguez only learned the information about the Newmans' obviously improved personal finances by working at the Newmans' private residence. Had he not been working at the Newman private residence that afternoon, he might never have learned of the Newmans improved personal finances in such a timely manner.

"Mr. Tim Newman testified that he had assumed that Mr. Rodriguez and other defendants working at his home would keep all personal information learned about them and their guests confidential.

"Members of the jury, this is a reasonable expectation. Don't we all expect that anyone working inside our home—such as a plumber and other tradespeople—will keep confidential any information learned about us while they are working in our homes?

"However, instead of keeping information learned about the Newmans while working at their home confidential, Mr. Rodriguez knowingly stole this information so that the investment club could trade and make a handsome profit. By stealing this information, and sharing this information to trade stocks, Mr. Rodriguez breached the duty of confidentiality *he* owed Lucy and Tim Newman.

"Members of the jury, you will recall how the defendant, Mr. Goodwin, testified that he overheard another insider, Tom White, describe his end-of-quarter travel schedule to his friends. Tom White testified that, if his company had made its projected earnings at the end of a quarter, he would leave work at the usual time and drive to his second home in Sonoma. In contrast, if his company was struggling to meet its numbers at the end of a quarter, it was 'nose to the grindstone,' making it difficult for him to leave work. You will also recall how, after overhearing this information, Mr. Goodwin checked Tom White's arrival in Sonoma at the end of each quarter, so that the investment club could trade on that information.

"Members of the jury, just as the Newmans reasonably expected Mr. Rodriguez to keep information learned about them while he was working on their home confidential, similarly, they also had a reasonable expectation that Mr. Goodwin would also keep personal information about *their guests* confidential. By knowingly stealing information about Mr. White's end-of-quarter travel schedule, and sharing this information to trade stocks, Mr. Goodwin breached the duty of confidentiality *he* owed the Newmans and their guests while working at the Newmans' home.

"Members of the jury, you will also recall that the defendant, Samantha Pond, testified that, at an event at the Newmans' home, she learned that insider Tony Padilla had placed a deposit on an expensive Tesla Roadster. You will recall that Ms. Pond informed the group of this deposit and the group had immediately purchased Mr. Padilla's employer's stock.

"Ms. Pond also testified that, at a private wine-tasting event in Yountville, she saw another insider, Jason Lee, purchasing expensive wine futures following a work-related phone call. You will recall that Ms. Pond informed the group of this purchase, and the group immediately purchased Mr. Lee's employer's stock.

"Mr. Padilla and Mr. Lee had been real estate clients of Ms. Pond. As such, she had been in a professional relationship with both men. Mr. Padilla and Mr. Lee had a reasonable expectation that Ms. Pond would keep their private purchases confidential and not use this information to trade stocks. By knowingly stealing information about the men's purchases, and sharing this information to trade stocks, Ms. Pond breached the duty of confidentiality that she owed Mr. Padilla and Mr. Lee, her former real estate clients.

"Similarly, as real estate clients of Ms. Pond, Joe and Janet Parks-Brown had a reasonable expectation that their realtor, Ms. Pond, would keep their offer to buy a Sonoma home confidential until the transaction closed and not use this information to trade stocks. By stealing this information, and sharing this information to trade stocks, the People submit that Ms. Pond breached the duty of confidentiality that *she* owed Joe and Janet Parks-Brown.

"Members of the jury, you will also recall how the defendant, Peter Smith, monitored the purchasing behavior of wine club members and others visiting the Keniworth tasting room so that he could share this information with the investment club. You will also recall that members of the Keniworth Wine Club are required to keep a credit card on file with the winery to pay for their wine club shipments.

"Members of the jury, wine club members and other visitors to the Keniworth Winery had a reasonable expectation that their wine club shipments and other purchases would be kept confidential by the winery *and* its employees. By stealing this information and sharing that information to trade stocks, Mr. Smith breached a duty of confidentiality that *he* owed both his employer and customers of the Keniworth Winery.

"You will also recall how Mr. Bartino carefully monitored the bidding by attendees at the Sonoma Valley of the Moon Wine Auction. You have heard that these attendees are all required to give a credit card so that this card can be matched to the successful bids at the auction. Members of the jury, all these attendees had a reasonable expectation that their bidding behavior would be kept confidential by the organizers of the wine auction and their volunteers. By stealing this information and sharing that information to trade stocks, Mr. Bartino breached the duty of confidentiality that *he* owed every attendee at the Sonoma Valley of the Moon Wine Auction."

Josh Kaplan then looked the jury squarely in the eye. "None of the insiders, Tim Newman, Tom White, Tony Padilla, Jason Lee, and Janet Parks-Brown, would have been allowed to trade on the information that was used by the defendants until it was released to the public.

"For example, Mr. Newman would not have been allowed to trade on information that the settlement of a patent lawsuit would improve his company's financial prospects. However, once one of the defendants learned that the Newmans' finances were improving, the defendants traded Mr. Newman's employer's stock and made a profit in excess of $310,000."

"Similarly, Mr. Tom White would not have been allowed to trade on the inside knowledge that his company had already reached its forecasted quarterly earnings. However, once one of the defendants learned from

Mr. White's travel schedule that his company had reached its forecasted quarterly earnings, the defendants traded Mr. White's employer's stock three quarters in a row making a profit in excess of $456,000.

"Mr. Tony Padilla would not have been allowed to trade on information that his company sales were improving, making it possible for him to put down a deposit on an expensive Tesla Roadster. However, once one of the defendants learned that Mr. Padilla had placed a deposit on an expensive Tesla Roadster, the defendants traded Mr. Padilla's employer's stock and made a profit in excess of $245,000.

"Mr. Lee would not have been allowed to trade on information that his company had successfully registered a U.S. patent until this information was released to the public. However, after one of the defendants observed Mr. Lee purchasing expensive wine futures after he had apparently received good news from work, the defendants traded Mr. Lee's employer's stock and made a profit in excess of $166,000.

"Finally, Ms. Parks–Brown would not have been allowed to trade on the information that her company's business had improved to a point that she and her husband could afford to buy a second home in Sonoma. Similarly, her boss would not have been allowed to trade on this information. However, once the defendants learned that Mr. and Ms. Parks–Brown had made a successful offer on a wine country property and her boss had generously bid at the local wine auction, the defendants traded Ms. Parks–Brown's employer's stock and made a profit in excess of $124,000.

"Members of the jury, the entire purpose of the investment club was to learn and trade on *inside information* about Silicon Valley companies ahead of the market by learning and pooling information that they learned from insiders working at these companies.

"At the beginning of this trial, evidence was introduced showing how the defendants profited from their trades in excess of $1,300,000. These trades were not lucky flukes. Instead, they were the result of the defendants acting willfully to break the U.S. Securities Laws by knowingly conspiring with each other to actively search for, share, and trade on confidential, material, non-public inside information in violation of their duty to the insiders to keep this information confidential.

"I urge you to return verdicts of *'guilty'* against each one of these defendants!"

It was 5:30 in the evening when Josh Kaplan finally sat down and the judge recessed the trial.

227

CHAPTER 48

Ann Schiller's Closing Argument

The next morning, Ann Schiller rose to address the jury.

"Members of the jury, I represent Juan Rodriguez, one of the defendants in this case. As you heard yesterday, Mr. Rodriguez is accused by the prosecution of violating the U.S. Securities Laws by trading on inside information.

"Members of the jury, my client is a gardener. He is not a chief executive officer, a chief financial officer, or even an employee of any Silicon Valley or other publicly traded company."

Ann paused. "As he testified in this courtroom during this trial, Mr. Rodriguez works for his family's gardening and landscaping business in Sonoma while attending college courses part-time.

"Yesterday, counsel for the prosecution reminded you that Mr. Newman's company was attempting to settle a patent lawsuit that had previously depressed this company's stock price. You have heard testimony that Mr. Newman informed his wife about these negotiations. I think that we can all agree that, had *Tom or Lucy Newman* traded on this information, they would have been guilty of insider trading.

"Members of the jury, there is absolutely no evidence before you that anyone told my client about the patent lawsuit settlement discussions involving Mr. Newman's company, Meediya. To the contrary, both Mr. Newman and his wife, Lucy Newman, vehemently *denied* that they had told anyone else about these negotiations.

"So…let us focus on what exactly Mr. Rodriguez learned that afternoon. Firstly, Mr. Rodriguez learned that Mrs. Newman was considering buying a ball gown at Saks Fifth Avenue to attend a gala event. Secondly, Mrs. Newman paid him some past-due invoices and a bonus.

"Her Honor will instruct you that, for the defendants' trades to be illegal insider trading under our U.S. Securities Laws, the prosecution must prove *beyond a reasonable doubt* that the information used by any of the defendants to trade stocks was both *material and non-public information.*

"As mentioned by the prosecution, Her Honor will also instruct you that the legal definition of *material* information for the purpose of these criminal proceedings means information that a reasonable stock market investor would consider *useful* or *significant* in making a decision as to whether to buy or sell a company's stock.

"Counsel for the prosecution reviewed with you yesterday how certain types of information frequently move the stock markets, which is why the insiders are required to keep such information secret before it is released to the public. However, members of the jury, counsel for the prosecution did *not* say that employees of a publicly traded company are required to keep secret the fact that they or their spouses have purchased a personal item, like a ball gown, in the same manner that they are required to keep their company's quarterly earnings secret.

"Similarly, you were not told by counsel for the prosecution that employees of a publicly traded company are required to keep secret whether they are attending a gala event at a museum or have paid their gardener in the same manner that they are required to keep their company's quarterly earnings secret.

"Why is that? Why the discrepancy? The simple answer is that buying ball gowns and gala tickets and paying the gardener is *not* the type of 'material, non-public information' that will move the stock market. It is *not* the type of information that any investor would find useful or significant.

"Her Honor will also instruct you that, before a person can be found guilty of insider trading, the prosecution must prove *beyond a reasonable doubt* that the defendant learned and traded on information while *under a duty of trust and confidence* to keep the information secret.

"You have heard testimony that business folks in Sonoma frequently gossip about landscaping, construction and other similar work projects after they leave work. They sometimes gossip about who is and who is not paying their bills. You have also heard testimony in this courtroom that gossip of this type is a fact of life in a small town like Sonoma.

"Members of the jury, no one should be jailed for engaging in this type of gossip. None of this gossip is the type of information a reasonable person would expect to remain strictly confidential for the purpose of protecting the nation's stock markets. No reasonable person would expect that Mr. Rodriguez would be jailed under the insider trading laws for failing to keep this information confidential.

"Finally, Her Honor will also instruct you that in a case of this nature, where a person's personal liberty is at stake, even if the prosecution convinces you that the information was 'material, non-public information' that would move the stock market, *you must still acquit Mr. Rodriguez if he didn't know* that he was violating the U.S. Securities Laws when he participated in these stock trades.

"There has been *no* testimony at this trial that Mr. Rodriguez knew that any of his activities and those of his investment club might be illegal. To the contrary, Mr. Rodriguez never worked in the securities industry and had no personal knowledge that he might be trading on any inside information.

"Mr. Rodriguez and the other defendants have testified that they thought their trades were legal because these trades were based on information gleaned from many different publicly available sources. Mr. Rodriguez and the other defendants also testified how the group painstakingly avoided trading on any overheard 'tip' that might be considered inside information.

"Why this restraint? The answer is that Mr. Rodriguez and the other investment club members wished to *avoid* doing anything illegal. By refraining from trading on insider tips, Mr. Rodriguez testified that he believed that his activities and those of the other defendants were all perfectly legal.

"Members of the jury, I urge you to find my client, Mr. Rodriguez *not guilty* of any of the charges of illegal insider trading because firstly, the information he learned was not inside information; secondly, the information was not the type of information that the average stock market investor would find useful or significant; and finally, my client had no idea whatsoever that any of his or the other investment club members' activities were illegal."

CHAPTER 49

Jack Murphy's Closing Argument

After a lunch break, Jack rose to address the jury. He spoke slowly and calmly. Following the intense, forceful closing arguments of Josh Kaplan and Ann Schiller, Jack's laid back, low-key, charming style was a welcome respite to everyone in the courtroom.

"Members of the jury, I represent defendant, Peter Smith, who lives in Sonoma, California.

"The other lawyers in this courtroom have helped me out by telling you what the prosecution must prove beyond a reasonable doubt before *my* client can be found guilty of illegal insider trading.

"We have heard that the prosecution must prove beyond a reasonable doubt that the information used to trade stocks was both non-public and material. In other words, the information must be both confidential *and* the type of information that a reasonable investor would consider significant and useful.

"The prosecution must also prove that my client was under a *duty of confidentiality* to keep the information secret."

Jack paused and continued in his quiet deliberative manner, "…And the prosecution must prove beyond a reasonable doubt that my client knew that he was doing something illegal."

He paused to look at the floor. He finally looked up at the jury and smiled. "All of this is a little head-spinning, don't you think?"

The jury smiled back. One or two in the courtroom laughed outright. Even Josh Kaplan allowed himself to smile.

"Members of the jury, my client is not an *insider* of the type that we are all familiar with…such as an executive or employee working *inside* a publicly traded company.

"My client in not working in an occupation that would normally place him in a strict duty of confidentiality—like a lawyer, doctor or accountant.

"My client, Peter Smith, is not the type of person who knows the ins and outs of U.S. Securities Laws. No, sir, he is not a stockbroker, stock analyst, securities lawyer, or someone similar."

Jack continued in almost a whisper. "*My client works in a tasting room.*"

After the courtroom laughter subsided, Jack resumed. "Now, I think we can all imagine a situation where someone working in a tasting room might overhear tips…snippets of information…that might be considered inside information, can't we? We can all imagine a situation where, after a couple of glasses of wine, someone might spill the beans to their friends about an upcoming merger or other juicy piece of news likely to impact a particular stock price.

"Members of the jury, can you imagine the temptation to run out and trade stocks in that situation? How many of us might be tempted to do just that?

"However, members of the jury, is *that* what we have here?

"Well, guess what? According to the evidence before you today, we *don't* have that situation here. My client and the other defendants have testified that they were specifically warned against trading on that type of stock market tip—*and they didn't.*

"You heard the prosecution speak about my client having access to credit card information. Members of the jury…I think that we can all agree that stealing credit card information is *seriously bad news.* Who among us wouldn't be scared of a guy who steals credit card information?

"However, members of the jury, is that what we have here? Did my client or the other defendants steal and misuse credit card information?

"Well, guess what? During this trial, *no one* has testified anything of the sort. No one took the stand to tell you that my client—or any of the other defendants—stole and misused credit card information. Members of the jury…all this talk about access to credit card information is a complete red herring.

"So what are we left with?

"My client testified that he shared general information about the purchasing behavior of Silicon Valley company employees. He kept track of who was signing up to receive quarterly wine club shipments and who was buying the more expensive wines. He also testified that the wine club shipments average around $150 per shipment. He also testified that these wine shipments are shipped from the winery at most four times a year, usually in the spring and fall.

"Members of the jury, you will recall that my colleague, Ms. Schiller, argued that the average stock market investor would not be interested in learning about ball gown purchases. Common sense tells us that the average investor would not be interested in wine club shipments that cost around $150 or whether an individual Silicon Valley company employee was splurging on the Keniworth Winery's more expensive wines. That's *not* the type of material information that is likely to move the stock markets."

Jack then threw his hands in the air and exclaimed, "Well—that's it! That is the *only* information that my client shared with the investment club."

After another pause, he continued: "In order for you to find my client guilty of insider trading, the prosecution must also prove beyond a reasonable doubt that my client knew that he was breaking the law. However, my client testified that he had no idea that he or any of the other defendants might be breaking the law. Members of the jury, there is nothing about my client's background that would make any of us think that he might be lying about that.

"If my client was a stockbroker, stock analyst—or someone similar— it might make us all wonder whether he was telling the truth when he testified that he did not know anything about the U.S. Securities Laws. Why? Because those folk have to know something about the U.S. Securities Laws in order to do their jobs. However as I stated earlier, my client was never a stockbroker, stock analyst…or anyone similar.

"For my client to do his job competently as a tasting room salesman, my client needs to know how *wine* is made and the different varietals of *wine* on offer in his tasting room. However, no knowledge of the Securities Laws of the United States of America is required to work in a tasting room.

"Members of the jury, I urge you to find my client is *not guilty* of insider trading for the following reasons. Firstly, the information my client learned in the tasting room that he shared with his friends was *not* confidential inside information. Secondly the information he shared with his friends is *not* the type of material, non-public information that moves the stocks market. Thirdly, my client testified that he had no idea that he or the other defendants were doing anything wrong."

CHAPTER 50

The Closing Arguments Continue

The following morning, George DeRosa rose to address the jury in his famously deep, sonorous voice.

"Members of the jury, I represent Bob Goodwin. My colleagues, the other lawyers in this courtroom, have explained at great length the various elements required to prove a person guilty of insider trading. Her Honor will remind you of these required elements far more eloquently than I. However, I would like to revisit some earlier points as they relate to my client.

"Members of the jury, there are two legal theories under which a person can be found guilty of illegally trading on inside information. The first theory is known as the '*classical* theory,' whereby an *insider* illegally trades on inside information."

George went slowly over to a flip chart placed in front of the jury and wrote: "Classical theory = <u>insider</u> trades on information."

"Members of the jury, the second theory is known as the '*misappropriation* theory' of insider trading, whereby someone misappropriates or steals and trades on inside information while under a duty to keep the information confidential."

George returned to the flip chart and wrote: "Misappropriation theory = someone <u>steals</u> and trades on inside information while under a duty to keep the information confidential."

"The prosecution has presented absolutely *no evidence* in this case that *any insider* traded on inside information. As agent Nelson testified before you earlier in the trial, *none* of the defendants sitting in this courtroom today were insiders under the classical theory because *none of the defendants worked at the companies whose stocks they traded.* Therefore, for the purposes of your deliberations, you can rule out the classical theory as applying to the defendants."

George walked up to the blackboard and erased "Classical theory = insider trades on information" before returning to the podium.

"Members of the jury, for my client to be found guilty of insider trading, the prosecution must prove beyond a reasonable doubt that my client and the other defendants misappropriated—in other words, *stole*—and traded on inside information while under a duty to keep the information confidential. However, before the defendants can be found guilty of stealing inside information, the prosecution must prove to you beyond a reasonable doubt one very important fact—that *the defendants had access to inside information, which they used to trade stocks.*

"The prosecution is right on one point. We can all agree that if the *insiders* had traded on inside information about their companies, *they* would be guilty of insider trading. However this is *not* what we have here.

"According to the testimony in this trial, none of the defendants were aware that Meediya was in settlement negotiations because *no one told them* about these negotiations.

"According to the testimony in this trial, none of the defendants were aware that Jason Lee's company had successfully filed a patent because *no one told them.*

"According to the testimony in this trial, none of the defendants were aware that Tom White's company had reached its forecasted earnings three quarters in a row because *no one told them.*

"Similarly, according to the testimony in this trial, none of the defendants were aware that Tony Padilla's company's forecasted sales improved because *no one told them.*

"Finally, according to the testimony in this trial, none of the defendants were aware that Janet Parks-Brown's company's financials had improved because *no one told them.*

"Members of the jury, the prosecution wants you to believe that the defendants traded on *inside information.* However, the defendants could not have possibly have traded on any inside information because they were never given *any* inside information to begin with. It's a logical impossibility to trade on information *you don't have.*

"The prosecution is *also* required to prove *beyond a reasonable doubt* that the information used by the investment club was material, non-public information. As other counsel has informed you, this means that the information must be both non-public and the type of information that a reasonable investor would think significant.

"As my esteemed colleagues have already pointed out, the information pooled by the investment club was extremely trivial…pieces of information, which in isolation, no reasonable investor would think significant.

"This information included such items as a decision to purchase a ball gown, that a gardener was finally being paid his past-due invoices and given a bonus, and that certain Silicon Valley employees received quarterly shipments of wine from the Keniworth Winery worth on average $150 a shipment. It was only by cleverly pooling and analyzing this information that the investment club was able to make any successful trades.

"Members of the jury, the defendants did nothing wrong. By pooling and carefully analyzing this trivial information, the investment club simply did what every stock analyst on Wall Street is paid to do every day for clients. In other words, they analyzed insignificant pieces of information that alone would not be significant, but taken together, might reveal the current financial status of certain technology companies. This is how analysts make their living. This type of market analysis and trading is *not* illegal.

"My client and others have testified that they had plenty of opportunity to trade on inside information in the form of overheard tips. However, you have also heard testimony that the investment club *refrained* from trading on overheard tips. Why? They decided not to trade on these tips because of *my client Mr. Goodwin's* concerns that this activity might be considered illegal insider trading.

"Members of the jury, the testimony heard in this courtroom supports the verdict that my client neither traded on inside information or had any idea that he was breaking the law. In fact, according to the testimony at this trial, my client made great efforts to steer the investment club away from any activity that he thought might be judged as being illegal insider trading. Furthermore, none of the defendants tried to *conceal* their trading activity in manner that might indicate that they knew they were doing something wrong. To the contrary, as FBI agent Nelson testified earlier in this trial, my clients name and the names of the other defendants were on *every single trade.*

"I urge you to return a verdict that my client is *not guilty* of any of the charges of illegal insider trading."

After George finished his closing argument, the lawyers for Samantha Pond and Charlie Bartino made similar arguments on behalf of their clients.

After arguing that information about car and wine futures purchases was not the type of confidential inside information that the securities laws were designed to cover, Kimberly Hayward added, "Members of the jury, Joe and Janet Parks-Brown were congratulated by many at the wine auction after making a successful offer for a second home in Sonoma. This information was neither confidential nor the type of inside information that anyone should be jailed for sharing with friends."

At the end of his closing argument, Deke Little said, "Members of the jury, there are few activities more public in wine country than successful bidding at wine auctions. The local press frequently trumpets this bidding at these auctions because these generous bids help organizations that assist the needy in the area. How can information about this bidding, which was shared by my client with the other defendants, be *confidential* or *inside information* after this bidding took place in front of hundreds of people at a public wine auction?"

In his rebuttal argument, Josh Kaplan focused on a reasonable person's expectation that the information used by the investment club would be kept confidential and the unusually lucrative nature of the defendants' trades.

By the time Judge Baker had finished her instructions to the jury, everyone in the courtroom felt that the misappropriation theory of insider trading had been thoroughly hammered to death.

That evening, the bailiff joked to the court clerk that he would be dreaming about the classical and misappropriation theories of insider trading in his sleep.

The case was now in the hands of the jury.

CHAPTER 51

Jane Phelps Receives a Visitor

While final closing arguments were being presented in court, Tracy Sanchez sat across the table from Jane Phelps on another floor in the Federal Building in San Francisco.

The two women had known each other since Tracy had worked for the Department of Justice. Everyone on the defense team felt that Tracy's background and seniority made her the right person to share with the DOJ results of the defense counsels' investigation into one of the prosecution's chief witnesses, James Chistlehurst.

"We know that the affidavits will look unconvincing to your office, given that at least two of the affidavits are signed by individuals suspected by your office of being the source of the inside information in the current trial in Judge Baker's courtroom," acknowledged Tracy. "However, according to our forensic accountants, the *exhibits* attached to these affidavits alone warrant law enforcement investigation, *even if* you disregard the affidavits."

"I'm not ready to concede that the sworn testimony of one of our witnesses has problems quite yet," replied Jane stiffly. "However, I have to agree with you that these affidavits and exhibits warrant some attention." She looked at her former colleague and smiled.

"I'm sorry, Tracy. I don't mean to be abrupt, but this insider trading case has consumed quite a lot of this office's time, effort and resources. I'm sure you'll understand that our agents will have to conduct a thorough, independent investigation before we decide whether your report has any impact on this insider trading case. I can also tell you that, based on my personal understanding of this case, this office and the FBI have absolutely no information about this guy's allegedly dubious activities that might have required earlier disclosure by my office of exculpatory facts under 'Brady.' All this will be fresh news as far as this office is concerned," she added firmly.

"I believe you, Jane," replied Tracy quickly. "We all understand that your agents will need time to get their heads around the implications of our investigative findings. This obviously can't happen until after the jury reaches its verdict."

Tracy stood up. "It's going to be very interesting to learn what the jury thinks of it all."

"I certainly appreciate you coming in today to bring us this information," Jane said, smiling graciously as she stood by her desk. "As we both know, nothing is worse than a case falling apart on appeal simply because some damn witness is engaged in wholly unrelated, but questionable, activity that wasn't properly investigated and disclosed."

"Whatever happens, I hope Kaplan does OK," said Tracy as they waited at the elevator. "From what I've heard from Ann Schiller, he's one heck of a trial lawyer. The Government is lucky to have him."

Jane smiled at her longtime friend. "You keep your thieving hands off my prosecutor," she joked. "You big law firms keep stealing the government's best legal talent."

After Tracy left in the elevator, Jane immediately returned to her office and picked up the phone.

"Herb, you'll never freaking believe what I have on my desk," she said gloomily, thinking about the suspiciously identical exhibits attached to affidavits signed by several Stanford University alumni members. "I need you over here right away."

The Verdict

An anchorman turned to the cameras. Simultaneously, a continuous stream of onscreen and online banners proclaiming "*Breaking News*" appeared at the bottom of screens.

"We are now getting some breaking news that there's been an important development in the Sonoma insider trading case. We again go *live* to our reporter at the U.S. District Courthouse in San Francisco. Jennifer, what can you tell us?"

A slim, attractive woman holding a TV microphone appeared on the screen. "Yes, Jerry; we've just been informed that the jury *has* reached a verdict in this case. After nearly a full week of deliberations, they have finally reached a verdict on all counts facing the five defendants from Sonoma."

The anchorman asked, "Weren't some of the lawyers afraid that the long week of deliberations might produce a hung jury, so that this case would have to be tried all over again?"

"Yes indeed, Jerry. However, it appears that the jury *has* reached a verdict regarding all of the defendants. My colleague will be sending us text messages of the jurors' verdict as soon as court protocol allows. I will be bringing these verdicts to our viewers *live* in the next few minutes."

While they waited for the results to appear, Jennifer engaged in small talk with the anchorman about the testimony at the trial and the insider trading laws involved in the case. Finally, Jennifer saw news appear on her smartphone.

"Jerry, four of the defendants have been found '*not guilty*'—and I repeat—'*not guilty*' of any of the charges. However one defendant, Bob Goodwin, was found '*guilty,*' I repeat, '*guilty*' of one charge of committing securities fraud.

"Only *one* violation?"

"Yes! According to my colleague inside the courtroom right now bringing us the jurors' verdicts, this count involves Robert Goodwin tracking Tom White's end-of-quarter travel schedule."

The anchorman came back onscreen. "My goodness! Let's now go live to one of our experts helping us cover this case. Attorney Bill Reed, what do you think of these verdicts?"

A handsome lawyer appeared onscreen.

"Well, Jerry, I have to say that this is a *big* loss for the government. They must now be hoping that the *only* defendant found guilty of one count of securities fraud will now roll over and help them prove a case against at least one or more of the Silicon Valley insiders. However, from what I observed in the courtroom during the trial, I'm not sure the government correct with that theory." The camera jumped back to the anchorman.

"Let's now get some reaction to this news from the North Bay. Jake, what's the reaction to this news in downtown Sonoma?"

Another reporter appeared onscreen. "Jerry, I am here in downtown Sonoma at the Tuesday night farmers market and the overall reaction is of *jubilation* at the acquittals. However everyone's bemused by the guilty verdict against the caterer, Bob Goodwin. The people here tonight at the Tuesday farmer's market tell me that they don't believe anyone from Sonoma could be guilty of insider trading. It's just not Sonoma."

The anchorman flashed back onscreen.

"Well, for at least for four of the five defendants, this must be good news. They and their families are going to be happy with this outcome. Wait a minute, folks, there's breaking news at the courthouse. Jennifer, tell us what's happening over there."

Jennifer reappeared onscreen holding a large black umbrella shielding her from snow-like white drops falling either side of her.

"Jerry…the courthouse steps are beginning to resemble Seal Rocks over by Ocean Beach. Everyone's running for cover."

"Is that *snow?*

"No—it's bird shit."

CHAPTER 53

Dmitri Romakoff Wants His Wine

On a mega yacht anchored in the Bay, Lady Roberta was mulling over what action to take.

She had just overheard her husband, Dmitri Romakoff, giving instructions to his henchmen to dispatch the couple's helicopter to pick up his French Bordeaux vintage wine from James Chistlehurst's wine cellar and bring it to the yacht…forcefully if necessary.

Although Roberta's knowledge of Russian was not perfect, she could tell that the mission would be far from friendly. Speaking to his employees, Dmitri sounded angry and threatening. He wanted not only the wine, but also James Chistlehurst brought to his private yacht to explain why several bottles of vintage wine had not been delivered in time as promised for the prior evening's reception at which he and his wife had entertained local San Francisco and Silicon Valley dignitaries. Dmitri was as angry as a Cossack that he had been unable to wow these local dignitaries with his fine collection of vintage French wine.

In recent months, Lady Roberta had grown tired of Dmitri, her third and wealthiest husband. The man had turned into a brute who did not suit Lady Roberta's blue blood background. Dmitri and his friends had relieved themselves in her antique vases just once too often for her high society taste.

Roberta's marriage settlement agreement had handsomely compensated her for the indignity of putting up with Dmitri. The millions that had landed like clockwork in her personal bank account made up for her smart friends' feline taunts wrapped in saccharine words of heartfelt sympathy and concern. Roberta had been brought up by New England society hostesses to acquire a savvy expertise in negotiating lucrative marriage settlements. If Dmitri tangled with U.S. law enforcement while visiting the West Coast, she would be given ample excuse to part company with her husband without her best friends whispering behind her back that she had been unceremoniously "dumped." Coming on top of her prior marriage settlements, a divorce at this juncture would leave Lady Roberta in the happy position of being independently wealthy with sufficient funds to enjoy her luxurious lifestyle.

Lady Roberta was familiar with some of the shady business dealings involving her husband's business. Friends of her husband had often joked with her about how Dmitri had built his international business in part to accommodate the discreet needs of his friends in high places who wished to "diversify" ill-gotten wealth into more respectable investments.

Roberta remembered seeing a TV advertisement featuring Michael Douglas urging people to contact U.S. federal law enforcement if they suspected anyone of wrongdoing. After Dmitri retired to his office to return some pressing business phone calls, she locked her office door and sat down at her computer. After putting on her earphones, she conducted a Google search. She picked up her cell phone when the world famous logo of the FBI appeared on her computer screen at the end of the Douglas advertisement.

After making the phone call, Roberta started thinking about life post-Dmitri. She remembered that a friend from her Junior League days had recently set up a headhunting business for Silicon Valley talent in hopes of meeting and marrying a man who fit the same profile as the heads she hunted for her corporate clients. Her friend also informed her that once she'd bagged a husband, the headhunting operation would cease. Roberta pleasantly mused over the fact that *she* would not have to work that hard to find a new husband. Instead, Roberta happily pictured herself as an angel investor helping finance startups run by cute entrepreneurs from Silicon Valley, similar to those who had eagerly visited the yacht the last week, business plans in hand.

"*There are worse dating strategies*," she thought to herself. Yes…this time she would finally marry for lust.

CHAPTER 54

The Post-Trial Conference in the Judge's Chambers

A week after the jury verdict, at the request of Judge Camilla Baker, Josh Kaplan and George DeRosa returned to her courtroom after the day's court session had ended.

As they sat in the courtroom waiting for the judge's clerk to call them into chambers, both lawyers still experienced difficulty absorbing the jury verdict.

As reported in the press, the jury had acquitted Juan, Peter, Samantha, and Charlie of all counts of insider trading and Securities Law violations. However, they'd found Bob Goodwin guilty of one count of securities fraud by listening and trading on Tom White's end-of-quarter travel schedule.

Post-trial juror interviews had revealed that, during deliberations, the jury had agreed with defense arguments that the information used to trade stocks was either too trivial or public to be inside information. One female juror was quoted in the press as saying that she didn't want anyone to go to jail over hearing and repeating the fact she was about to buy a ball gown. One of the male jurors said that *he* did not want to anyone to go to jail over hearing that he'd purchased a case of wine. However, the jurors all agreed that Bob's action in tracking Tom White's end-of-quarter travel schedule was illegal insider trading. The other defendants were found not guilty because they had relied on Bob's advice that they weren't doing anything illegal.

After the clerk announced that the judge was ready to see both counselors, the lawyers left the courtroom and entered the judge's chambers. She greeted them politely, first by asking them to take a seat and then thanking them for the hard work they had put into the case.

After the lawyers sat down, the judge surprised them both by saying that she had called this post-trial conference because she was uncomfortable with the jurors' guilty verdict against Bob Goodwin.

George was stunned speechless. He had never had *any* judge in his corner before. He kept very quiet, as the judge gently began to put pressure on his opponent.

"Counsel, I am concerned at the unsettled case law pertaining to *this* guilty verdict," said the judge pointedly looking at Josh Kaplan. "Before closing arguments began, this court issued a ruling that the jury should decide on the facts whether Mr. Goodwin owed Mr. White a duty of confidentiality. At that time, I took under advisement defense arguments that none of the defendants were under any fiduciary duty or similar relationship of trust and confidence. However, after reviewing the current case law in light of this guilty verdict, the jury's decision that a caterer owes a legal duty of confidentiality towards *everyone attending a public fundraiser* seems quite a stretch.

"I appreciate that other District Courts have ruled that this duty of trust and confidence extends to situations where there's a reasonable expectation of confidentiality—such as members attending AA meetings. However, in those cases *the parties had a need to disclose information in confidence.* In this case, there is no evidence before the court that Mr. White had to disclose his end-of quarter travel habits to his friends.

"Another legal point…even if we receive appellate guidance tomorrow that Mr. Goodwin owed a legal duty of confidentiality to Mr. White, Mr. Goodwin might still argue that he didn't know he was violating the law *at the time he traded* because the law was then unsettled."

George nodded vigorously when the judge invited the defense to file a motion to address these issues. However the judge warned that her ruling alone might not resolve the matter. Either side might have grounds for an appeal—regardless of which way she ruled.

Josh informed the judge that the FBI was conducting a new investigation into the activities of one of the prosecution's chief witnesses as a result of new information learned from the defense. After listening intently, she turned to George.

"What's the defense's current position concerning this new investigation?" she asked.

"Your Honor, after this investigation is complete, the defense reserves its right to bring a motion to dismiss the entire indictment on the grounds that one of its prosecution witnesses may have committed perjury."

"I see…" the judge replied.

"However," George added, "the defense also believes that it should not, at this stage, interfere with the government's own investigation in any way. In fact, the defense stands ready, willing, and able to assist the prosecution in the conduct of this investigation."

The judge looked at both lawyers in turn. "Since the prosecution and defense are co-operating with this new investigation, you should let the court know if it can be of assistance in helping the two sides reach a compromise resolution regarding Mr. Goodwin," she said before ending the chambers conference.

As both lawyers stood by the elevators, Josh said to George that he'd have to consult his office about the judge's concerns. He added that, whatever the final outcome, he had been honored to try the case against such a distinguished trial lawyer as George.

George suddenly looked up and then said, "Sorry, counselor…I didn't hear a word you said. I was distracted by my phone!" He gave Josh a big wink. As they entered the elevator, they both laughed as they remembered Jason Lee's clueless behavior in the courtroom earlier in the trial.

As they walked from the building, Josh saw a car driven by Ann Schiller stop to allow George to get in the back. Jack Murphy was in the front passenger seat. Josh smiled and waved at Ann, and she waved back. As Josh walked through the drifting fog towards his bus stop, he felt sad. Ann had been such a great colleague!

As they drove away, George briefed Ann and Jack about the conference.

"You would have been so proud of me, Ann. I may be verbose at times…but I know to keep my mouth shut when I have the judge in my corner!"

CHAPTER 55

James Chistlehurst's Establishment, Yountville

James Chistlehurst was packing his last suitcase in preparation for his international flight aboard a private Learjet to France when he heard a knock on the door.

"In only a few hours, I will be entering a civilized country with the good manners to lack an extradition treaty with the United States," he thought happily to himself.

Anticipating that his helicopter taxi had arrived early, he danced a little jig as he cheerfully opened the front door. He nearly fainted when a gun was thrust in his face and another poked in his stomach.

"Oh, hello there. Gosh! What's up? Has Dmitri sent you?" he croaked.

"The boss wants to know why his wine was not delivered yesterday for the fancy party on his yacht," replied a man with a heavy beard, dark eyes and a thick Eastern European accent.

"I'm sure there must be some misunderstanding," replied James. "I can get you chaps some cases of excellent wine if you like," he gushed obsequiously, looking hopefully at both men at the door.

"Put your hands up and show us where you keep the boss' wine," said the second man with a beard. "Any funny business and you get a bullet in the head. Got it?"

James then went inside and pointed to several large cases of wine that were marked "Par Avian – Paris."

"You can take these cases if you like," he suggested hopefully.

"How do we know that's the boss' wine?" one of James' bearded visitors asked skeptically, as he walked over to the cases. "…And why are these cases labeled for Paris?" he asked suspiciously.

"Your boss' wine is located all the way in the back of my cellar. I just thought it might be easier for you to take these cases. I can get more out later. However, I am just leaving on a trip overseas." He smiled bravely. "I'm expecting my helicopter taxi at any minute to take me to the airport."

"You're leaving on a trip, all right," said one of the bearded guys menacingly. "You and the boss' wine are coming in *our* helicopter."

"Oh, I say. That's awfully bad news. It'll mean I will miss my flight," protested James.

"That's the least of your problems, friend!"

From their stakeout location, FBI agents Herb Nelson and Frank Potter had seen the helicopter arrive. After capturing a video of the helicopter's arrival, they forwarded the video to their HQ for analysis.

At first, they surmised that James was making his getaway using a helicopter and that it was time to move in and make an arrest. However, they stopped walking towards the house and dropped behind some nearby bushes when two bearded men jumped out of the helicopter with AK-47 rifles and walked to James' front door. After seeing James held up at gunpoint, they quickly realized that their quarry hadn't ordered the helicopter. Taking careful note of the high-powered rifles held by the two bearded men, the agents decided to text HQ for reinforcements.

As James Chistlehurst, carrying a case of wine, was being escorted from his home by the bearded men, the three men suddenly stopped walking and stood still. The FBI agents peering from the nearby bushes watched carefully to see what had grabbed the attention of their quarry. They, too, raised their eyebrows and stared in disbelief at what they saw.

"*Our reinforcements couldn't have made it here that quickly,*" thought Agent Nelson to himself. "*In God's name, who the hell are these guys?*"

Everyone stared as a military convoy, consisting of two tanks and three military jeeps slowly and majestically made its way up the long driveway to the Yountville mansion.

"Boss or no boss, I'm not taking on them tanks," one captor said quietly to the other.

At gunpoint, they shoved James ahead of them.

"Put down the wine and go tell them we don't want trouble. We're just here to pick up the boss' wine."

As the three men continued to stare at the approaching convoy, the FBI agents made their move. Coming up from behind, Frank Potter cocked and aimed his gun.

"FBI…drop your weapons and put up your hands."

Assuming that the FBI and the military convoy were acting together, the bearded men instantly complied with the FBI agent's instructions. By the time the military convoy finally arrived at the end of the long driveway, James Chistlehurst and his two assailants had been handcuffed. The FBI agents looked at each other and nodded with satisfaction. Not a single shot had been fired. No reinforcements had been required, and they had their suspect plus a couple of highly suspicious characters under arrest.

The driver and two passengers climbed out of the first jeep.

"Tom White of the Wine Country Veterans paying a courtesy call to raise donations for our upcoming wine country event to help our severely injured troops," yelled the driver of the military jeep, as if giving orders to one of his platoon. "These are my buddies, Tony Padilla and Charlie Bartino," he said with a smile pointing to his companions.

As Tom White approached the FBI agents, he noticed weapons that might be loaded with live ammunition, and the three other men in handcuffs. He swallowed hard.

"Hey, guys…anyone need any help?"

"FBI conducting a criminal investigation," replied Agent Nelson, "and we're sure glad to see you veterans!" He and his colleague gratefully shook the hand of each veteran in turn.

CHAPTER 56

News Conference at the Phillip Burton Federal Building

The reporters again camped outside the Phillip Burton Federal Building in San Francisco. They were all waiting for an announcement from the U.S. Attorney's Office.

This time, they knew that the announcement didn't involve the insider trading case against the Sonoma defendants. The caterer, Bob Goodwin, and the other defendants had reached agreement with the SEC to disgorge all profits made from tracking Tom White's end-of-quarter travel schedule in return for the prosecution dismissing the remaining criminal charges.

Josh Kaplan stepped in front of the cameras.

"Members of the press. Today, several people have been arrested and charged with operating a sophisticated international money laundering scheme involving buying and trading valuable international wine futures.

"One of the defendants, James Chistlehurst of Yountville, in Napa County, was arrested before he was able to board a private Learjet parked at the Napa Airport chartered to fly him to France. In addition to laundering proceeds from criminal activity, this gentleman also faces charges of operating a local Ponzi scheme involving Bordeaux wine futures."

Following questions by the journalists, Josh Kaplan revealed that the suspects allegedly sold the same Bordeaux wine futures to different clients. The government also believed that Mr. Chistlehurst was able to perpetrate this scheme over many years because his clients paid him to store their valuable wine in his Yountville cellar.

Following more questions from the journalists, Josh also revealed that the federal authorities had first become aware of these illegal activities during the FBI's investigation into the insider trading case involving the Sonoma defendants.

Josh Kaplan finished the news conference with a summary statement. "The government is pleased to announce that many of the Silicon Valley executives who were anonymously referred to in the Sonoma Insider Trading Case indictment have come forward and expressed a willingness to assist us in our investigation of money laundering and the Ponzi scheme. The government now believes that Mr. Chistlehurst victimized these individuals by first selling them the same wine futures. To undermine their credibility in any future government investigation of his Ponzi scheme, Mr. Chistlehurst victimized these individuals a second time by wrongly suggesting that they were complicit in an insider trading conspiracy. We urge that if anyone else has had wine futures dealings with Mr. James Chistlehurst, they come forward and contact us. "

After Josh Kaplan returned to his office, he found a voicemail message from George DeRosa. Josh sighed deeply before picking up the phone.

"After we had settled your client, Robert Goodwin's, case, I thought that I wouldn't hear the sound of your voice for a while. What's up?"

George DeRosa's deep voice rumbled over the telephone. "Deke and I want you to know that *we are on the government's side* on this Ponzi scheme. Let us know what we can do to help."

"Yeah, *right*," said Josh. "And I have some ocean front property in Nevada to sell to you, too. George, I'm tired and this is not the time to play April Fools."

"Josh, just listen, man," said George excitedly. "You just asked in your press conference that people contact you if they had wine futures dealings with Mr. James Chistlehurst. Deke and I *also* invested in Chistlehurst's wine futures. It looks like that jerk has also ripped *us* off."

Josh grinned broadly into the phone. "George, I am so sorry to hear that."

Amanda Jones' Vineyard, Sonoma

"Now I know why James was always so keen that I never sell my wine futures," said Phil gloomily. "According to the FBI, he sold the same wine futures to me and at least *50 different people*. If you add the payment for wine futures to the storage fees he charged all of us, he must have made a fortune!"

"Don't let that sod stop you from enjoying our celebratory dinner, darling," said Amanda. "I'm so sorry that you got burned. I'm relieved that I never allowed James to sell *my* wine as futures," she said. "He could have ruined me."

Phil Taylor sat at a long table with George DeRosa at a private dinner hosted by Amanda Jones. The five Sonoma defendants and their lawyers were present. Sidney lay on the floor beside Tim and Lucy Newman and their tiny daughter, Catherine. Amanda had also invited the witnesses and their lawyers whose testimony had helped bring about the favorable result for her "Sonoma Five."

Jason Lee came up to congratulate the defendants.

"Everyone in social media has fallen in love with you people, especially Juan. I can't believe the number of followers Juan's got on Twitter. Juan did a much better job testifying at the trial than some of us Silicon Valley guys…but that's not saying much," Jason added with a chuckle.

"Know of any job openings at your company or somewhere else?" Juan asked hopefully. "I'll be graduating this summer. Can't wait to work in Silicon Valley."

"I'm sure we can find something for someone as smart as you, my friend," replied Jason smiling. "Send me an e-mail and we'll get together." Juan grinned broadly as he took Jason's card.

After Jason left, Amanda leaned over to speak with Bob.

"Bob, darling, now that your case is resolved, please do us all a favor.

Stop trying to be such a clever dick. Stay away from the stock market!"

Everyone laughed, including Bob.

"I've promised my wife that I will never buy any stocks without talking it over with her first," he replied. "Trying to beat the market has proved too dangerous. Fortunately the people of Sonoma have rallied to support us and the case hasn't hurt our catering business."

"So how's everyone's else's business since the verdict came in?" George asked.

"The people of Sonoma have been great, and I'm still getting good referrals," said Samantha. "However—like Bob—I think I'll stay away from the stock market."

"Hey, my grapes don't know anything about insider trading, so they're doing fine," Charlie joked.

"Our Keniworth Winery is seeing lots of visitors," Peter said enthusiastically. "Maybe they're all hoping to pick up some hot stock tips," he joked. "Talking of tough times, does anyone know how Cecil Roberts is doing these days?" asked Peter.

"Cecil's doing *great*," replied Phil. "Marc Todd and some of his VC buddies have recently formed a not-for-profit corporation to fund the type of medical research that's difficult to fund through normal channels because the clinical trials take too long. They plan to take Cecil's company private and hire Cecil to lead the non-profit research team. Cecil will be able to focus his attention more on research and less on pleasing investors."

"Cecil's also selling me some of his grapes, darlings," said Amanda gleefully. "When I found out from Samantha that poor Cecil was in danger of losing his job and his vineyard, I hoofed it over there with my winemaker to check out his grapes. The quality is exceptional. Buying Cecil's grapes saved his vineyard and the extra fruit helped me expand my winery business."

"I always said that you supermodels are the smartest business people on the planet," said George.

The wild animals of the Sonoma Wildlife Council waited in anticipation. They had received word via the avian network that they might be lucky enough to receive a visit from the president of the National Wildlife Council. They had all gathered on one of the highest peaks in the mountains bordering Sonoma Valley, hoping that the president would stop by on his way to visit family members nesting in a quiet area of Lake Sonoma.

Eventually they saw an elegant bald eagle with his impressive wingspan descend, landing at the top of a tall tree.

"He looks quite Lincolnesque, don't you think?" The deer lowered her head to speak to the duck.

"Members of the Sonoma Wildlife Council," said the bald eagle from his perch, *"I am delighted to be able to join you this evening. I have been asked to give you a message from the courthouse pigeons in San Francisco that the U.S. Government did the right thing regarding Sidney's dad. Everyone implicated in the recent insider trading case is now in the clear. To paraphrase Sir Winston Churchill, whose mother was American, 'one can always count on the U.S. Government to do the right thing after it has exhausted all the other possibilities.'"*

The wild animals then explained that that they had bought him some dead rodents from the vineyards of Sonoma Valley as a treat.

"You should start with the white wine grape vineyard rodents first, then move on to the red wine grape vineyard rodents," explained the turkey buzzard, who fancied himself a local foodie.

"My…these are delicious," replied the bald eagle. *"However, I mustn't eat too much. I have to fly safely."*

The following Monday Tim walked through the entrance of the Meediya offices. The evening before, the Meediya board of directors had voted to end his leave of absence. They understood that his leave had been more theoretical than real. Like the other Silicon Valley executives placed on leave, Tim had worked many hours to help his team carry on the business in his absence. Tim was relieved that he could now officially return to work.

Accompanying Tim, Sidney was jumping up and down with excitement. He, too, wanted to return to work.

As they entered the Meediya offices, Tim saw a large "Welcome Back" sign. The office was full of festive balloons. Many employees left their desks to sing a chorus of "Oh, he's a jolly good fellow!" Tim shook hands and hugged his employees. They all applauded as he finally made his way to his private office.

Several yaps could also be heard. All Sidney's canine friends had rushed out to greet him.

After the applause, handshakes, and hugs were over, the humans returned to their desks. Sidney rushed back to Tim's office and strategically placed himself between Tim and anyone walking into the office. He lay down with a deep sigh, keeping one eye focused on Tim working at his computer.

"My human dad and his friends all brag that they work 24/7. But it's us Silicon Valley dogs—who protect them at work, herd them home to those who love them, and watch over them and their families at night—who really work 24/7."

EPILOGUE

The following letter marked Exhibit A lies in a FBI file marked United States v. James Chistlehurst.

"To whom it may concern:

I am leaving this letter in my Yountville tasting room so that, once I am safely in France, everyone will understand my sad predicament—none of which is my fault.

After the dotcom boom, my business suffered a terrible decline. I started to sell the same wine futures to different clients in the hope that, once my business improved, I would have sufficient cash flow to make amends. Unfortunately, that never happened. No one seemed to mind. All my clients seemed happy to have me store their wine in my cellar as a hedge against inflation.

In 2010, I had a lucky break when I overheard a tip at a Sonoma fundraiser that Cecil Roberts' biotech company had failed to win FDA approval for its latest product. I knew that this meant the stock price was about to go south, so I moved fast to short the stock before this information became public. Sure enough— in a matter of days, the shares began to tumble and I made a handsome profit.

I was utterly terrified when the FBI agents came to my door one Friday evening. I thought that they were investigating the creative accounting methods used to hide my cash flow problems. Much to my surprise, the FBI agents were more interested in the handsome profit I'd made from shorting the biotech company stock. Obviously, I had to do my best to win them over, didn't I?

During the FBI agents' next visit, my heart almost stopped when I saw several clients on a list of names and addresses. At first, I thought that the FBI might be playing games with me. I was relieved when it became clear that they were investigating some dodgy insider trading racket, in which I had no involvement.

However, it suddenly dawned on me that my wine futures clients whose names were on the lists might soon be in need of some cash. That meant that I would receive redemption requests that I couldn't meet. Obviously, I had to do my best to help the FBI nail these clients from the Silicon Valley—and seriously undermine their credibility—before they nailed me. Survival of the fittest and all that.

An upset client, Jon Welsh, called me last week and accused me of being a crook. Apparently, he'd found out that his wine futures invoice was identical to several others. I learned that the defense lawyers in the recent insider trading case were snooping into my business affairs after they'd became suspicious of my assisting the FBI. This puzzled me. Why should my cooperation with the FBI be in the slightest way suspicious?

After the FBI first contacted me, I called my English lawyer for advice. I didn't go into any detail, but I told him that I'd overheard a hot stock tip about a biotech company at a fundraiser in London and was scared that I might be in some sort of trouble for trading on this tip. My solicitor did not sound very hopeful. He told me that the UK authorities could prosecute me if, at the time I traded the stock, I knew—or should have known—that I was in possession of inside information.

After Jon Welsh's phone call, I telephoned a U.S. lawyer who amazed me by saying that I probably had a pretty decent defense to a similar insider trading charge under U.S. law. That's because, at the time I traded Cecil Roberts' biotech company, I wasn't in any fiduciary relationship or similar relationship of trust and confidence with Jason Lee, Cecil or Cecil's biotech company. He politely explained that the definition of illegal inside trading under U.S. law is much narrower than under UK law.

It's all George III's fault for losing the colonies. Time to move to France!

Yours sincerely,
James Chistlehurst,
Proprietor and Editor
ChistlehurstVintageWines

About the Author

Admitted to practice as a barrister in England and an attorney in California, Elizabeth Monnet practiced law in San Francisco and Palo Alto, most recently at the Palo Alto office of Squire Sanders & Dempsey (now Squire Patton Boggs). She began her career in litigation and eventually moved into international corporate law representing companies from around the world setting up business in California.

To help overseas companies set up in California, she wrote two publications for the U.K. Department of Trade & Industry: *Establishing a Business Presence In The USA* and *Selling Through US Agents and Distributors*.

While at Squire, Sanders & Dempsey, she co-authored with Nicholas Unkovic: EXPECTATION GAME: *How To Manage The Rock Star CEO* published August 13, 2008 in the Corporate Counsel supplement to the Los Angeles and San Francisco Daily Journal.

After retiring from practicing law, she lives with her husband, Bill Monnet and bossy Australian sheepdog, Jim.

Elizabeth is working on her second novel featuring the fictional Australian shepherd, Sidney.

For more information visit www:elizabethrmonnet.com.

Acknowledgments

While writing this novel, I received invaluable advice and encouragement from my editor, Deb Carlen, my book cover designer Patti Britton, and my book layout artist Todd Towner.

I wish to thank my friend Debra Guerin Beresini for her insights on the venture capital industry, Buck Sangiacomo for his insights on the wine industry and my husband Bill Monnet for his insights on working life in Silicon Valley.

I am also grateful for the excellent input received from my readers Jim Schock, Elizabeth Unkovic, George Bereschik, Jane Downing, Ian Sidey, Carol Kerr and Doug Kerr.

The following friends provided useful advice about publishing in today's world: Suzanne Sangiacomo, Katherine Forsythe and Helen Sedwick.

Finally, I'd like to thank my family and friends who have patiently inquired during the past five years: "When will we get the opportunity to read your d----- novel? "

The wait is over.